Peach Fuzz

by

Lindsay Cibos
and
Jared Hodges

HAMBURG // LONDON // LOS ANGELES // TOKYO

Peach Fuzz Vol. 1
created by Lindsay Cibos and Jared Hodges

Production Artist - James Dashiell
Cover Design - Raymond Makowski

Editor - Carol Fox
Digital Imaging Manager - Chris Buford
Production Managers - Jennifer Miller and Mutsumi Miyazaki
Managing Editor - Lindsey Johnston
VP of Production - Ron Klamert
Publisher and E.I.C. - Mike Kiley
President and C.O.O. - John Parker
C.E.O. - Stuart Levy

A  Manga

TOKYOPOP Inc.
5900 Wilshire Blvd. Suite 2000
Los Angeles, CA 90036

E-mail: info@TOKYOPOP.com
Come visit us online at www.TOKYOPOP.com

ISBN: 1-59816-486-4

First TOKYOPOP printing: December 2005
10 9 8 7
Printed in the USA

Table of Contents

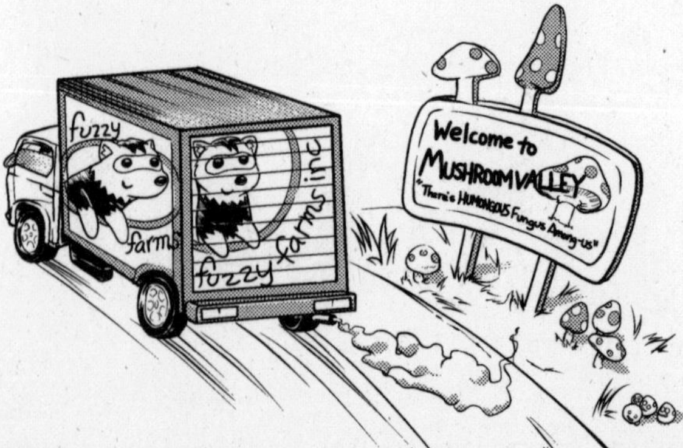
fuzzy
farms
fuzzy farms inc
Welcome to
MUSHROOM VALLEY
"There's HUMONGOUS Fungus Among-us"

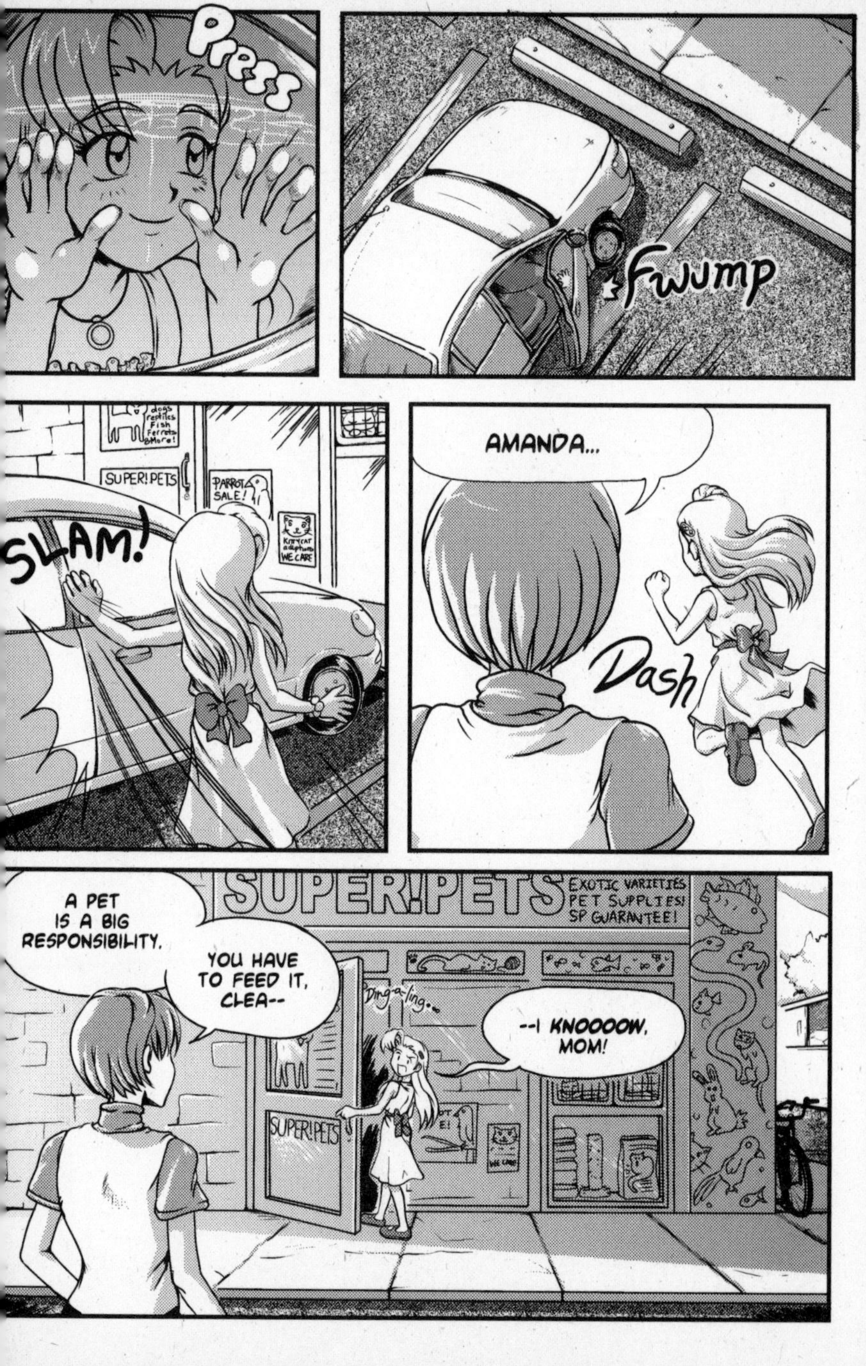
Press
Fwump
dogs reptiles Fish Ferrets &More!
SUPER!PETS
PARROT SALE!
WE CARE
SLAM!
AMANDA...
Dash
SUPER!PETS
EXOTIC VARIETIES
PET SUPPLIES!
SP GUARANTEE!
A PET IS A BIG RESPONSIBILITY.
YOU HAVE TO FEED IT, CLEA--
Ding-a-ling...
--I KNOOOOW, MOM!
SUPER!PETS

Chapter 1
First encounter

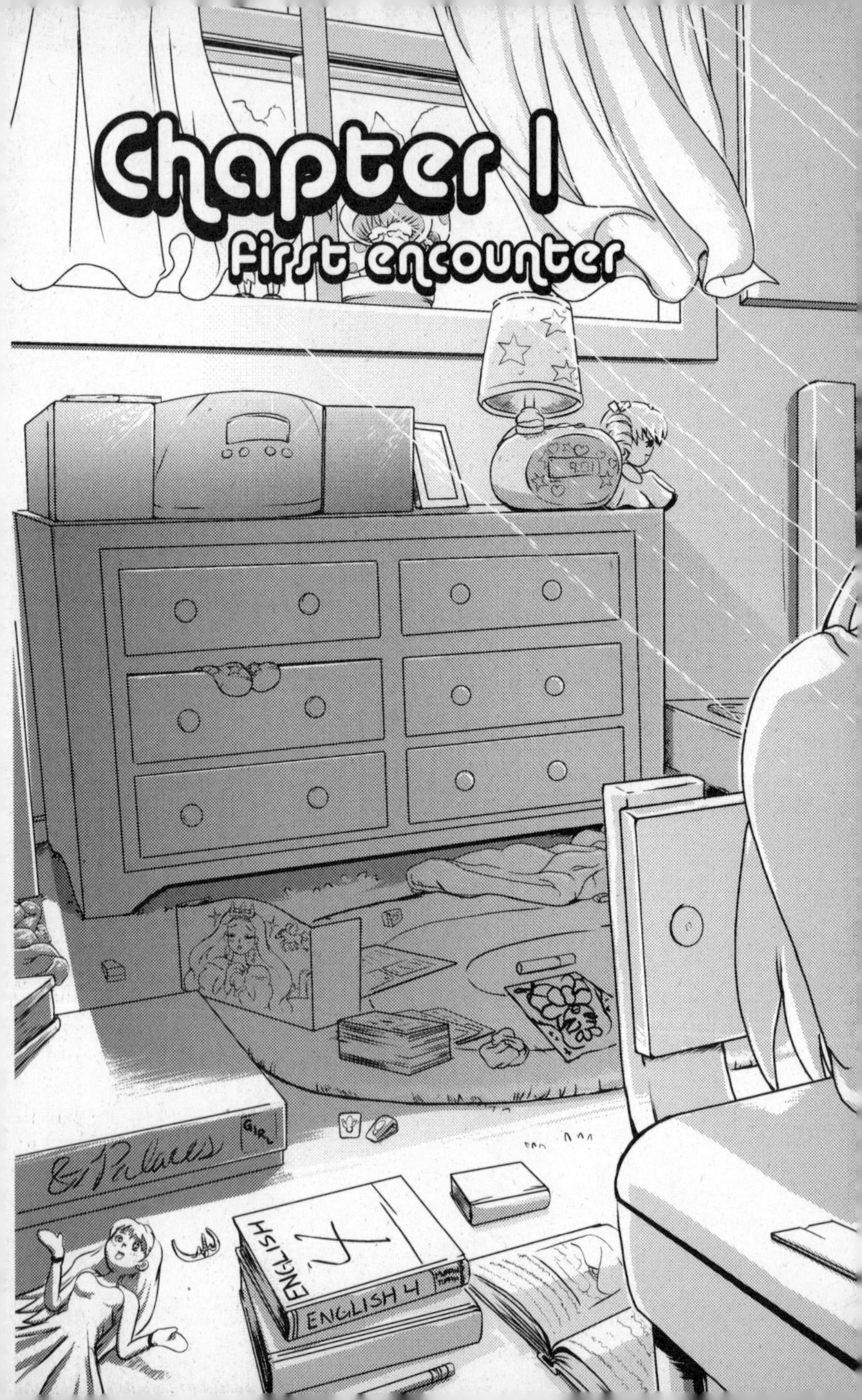
ENGLISH
ENGLISH 4

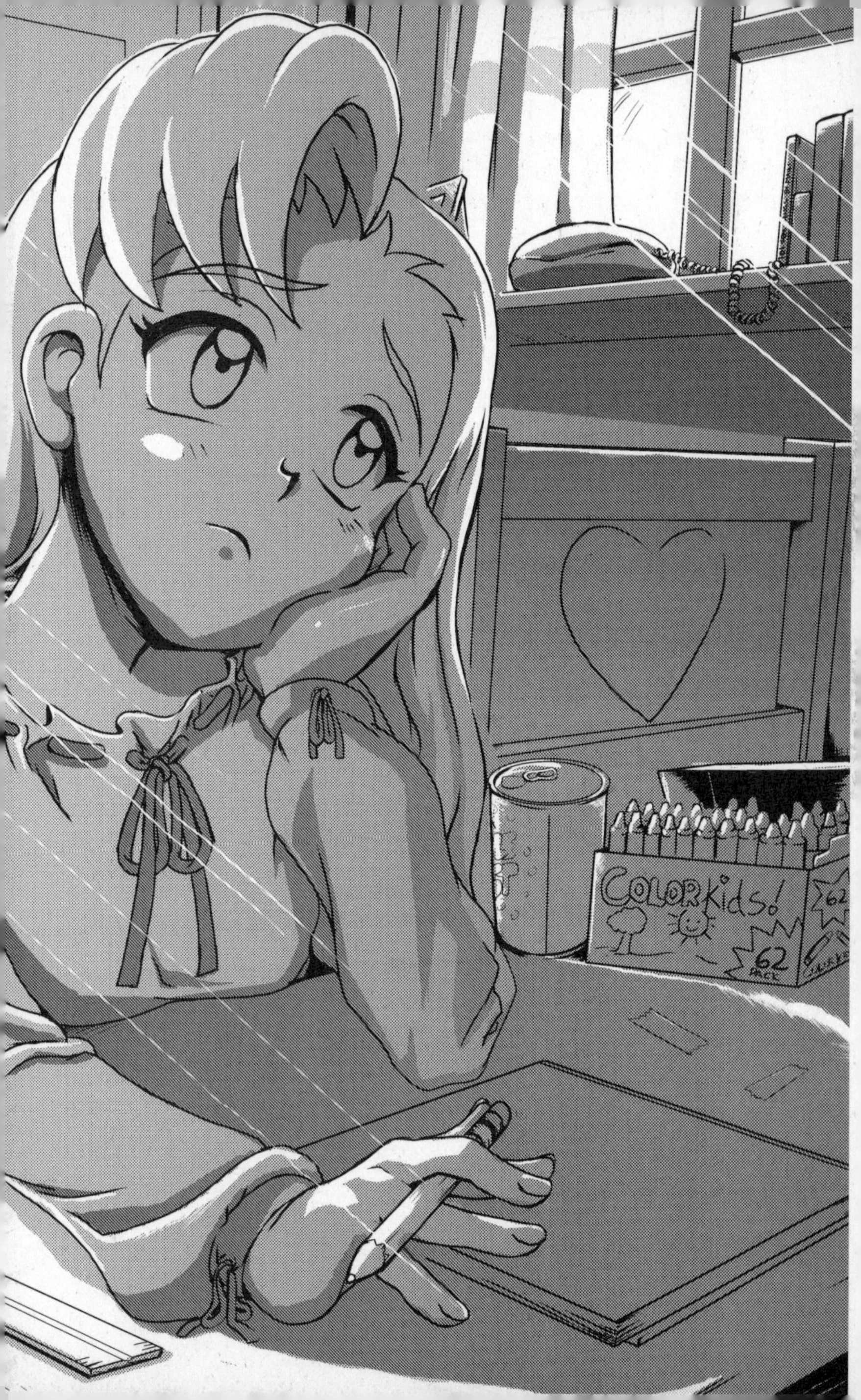
COLOR Kids!
62
PACK

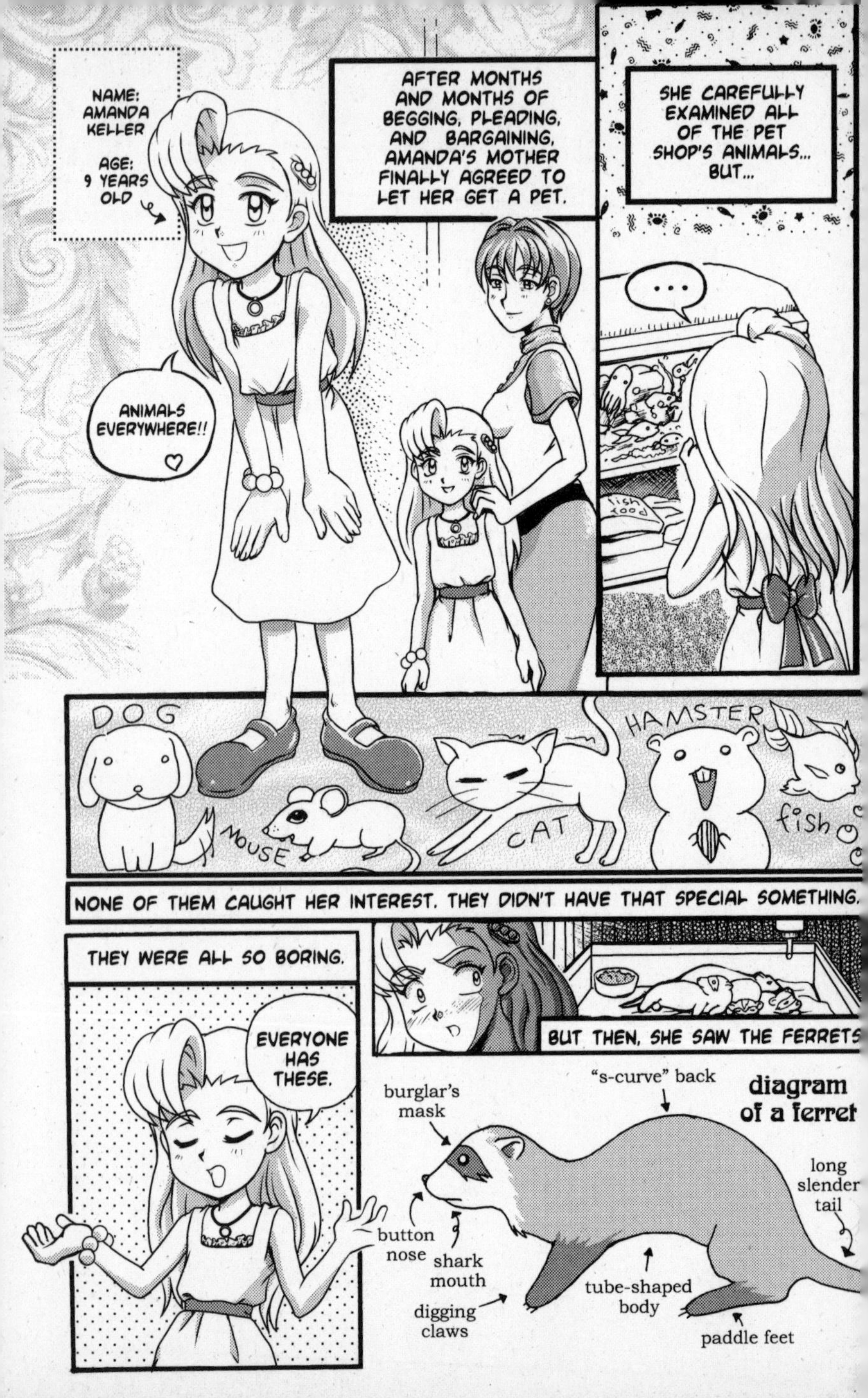
NAME: AMANDA KELLER
AGE: 9 YEARS OLD
AFTER MONTHS AND MONTHS OF BEGGING, PLEADING, AND BARGAINING, AMANDA'S MOTHER FINALLY AGREED TO LET HER GET A PET.
ANIMALS EVERYWHERE!! ♡
SHE CAREFULLY EXAMINED ALL OF THE PET SHOP'S ANIMALS... BUT...
...
fish food
DOG
MOUSE
CAT
HAMSTER
fish
NONE OF THEM CAUGHT HER INTEREST. THEY DIDN'T HAVE THAT SPECIAL SOMETHING.
THEY WERE ALL SO BORING.
EVERYONE HAS THESE.
BUT THEN, SHE SAW THE FERRETS
diagram of a ferret
"s-curve" back
burglar's mask
long slender tail
button nose
shark mouth
tube-shaped body
digging claws
paddle feet

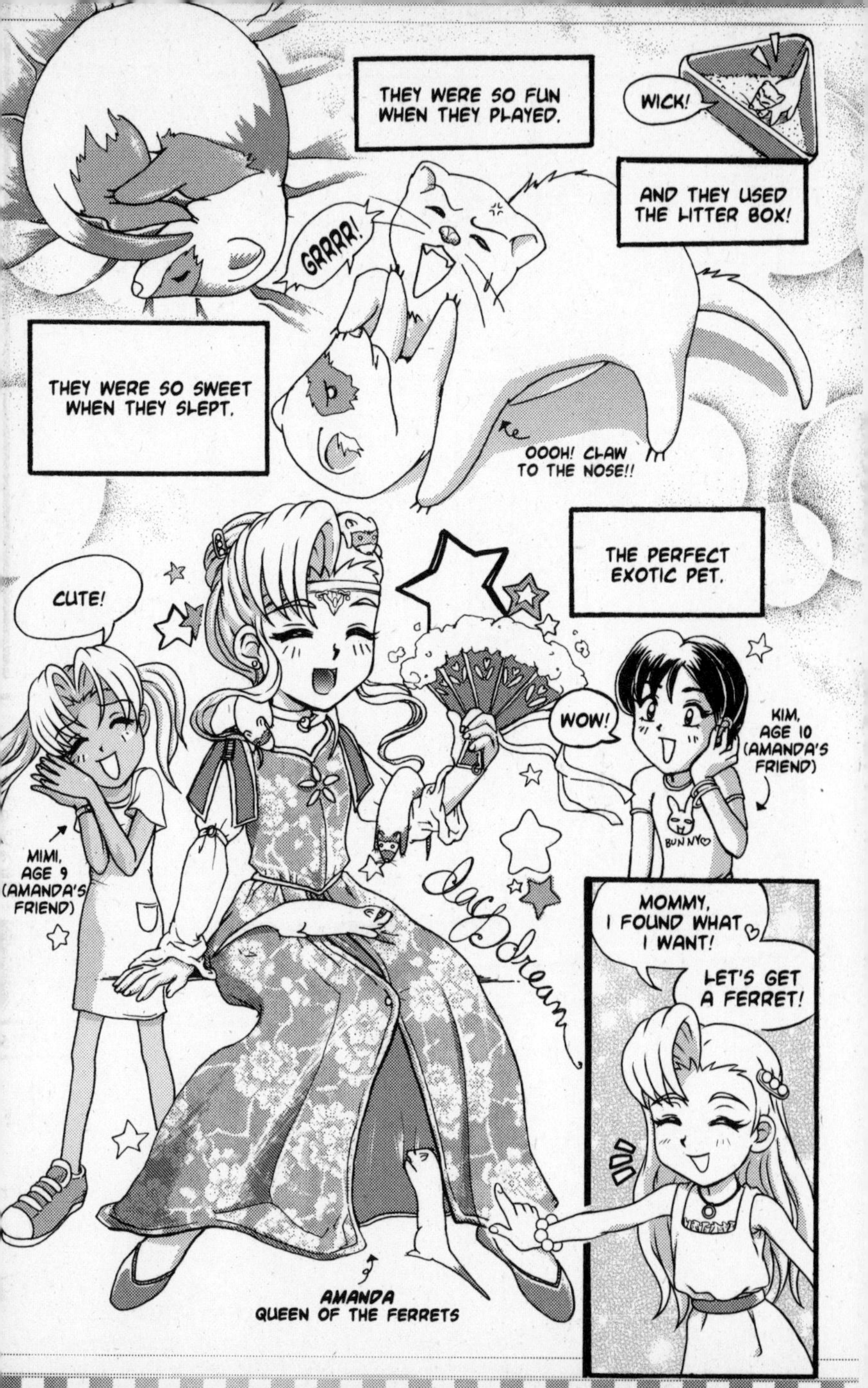
THEY WERE SO FUN WHEN THEY PLAYED.
WICK!
AND THEY USED THE LITTER BOX!
GRRRR!
THEY WERE SO SWEET WHEN THEY SLEPT.
OOOH! CLAW TO THE NOSE!!
THE PERFECT EXOTIC PET.
CUTE!
WOW!
KIM, AGE 10 (AMANDA'S FRIEND)
BUNNY
MIMI, AGE 9 (AMANDA'S FRIEND)
Daydream
AMANDA
QUEEN OF THE FERRETS
MOMMY, I FOUND WHAT I WANT!
LET'S GET A FERRET!

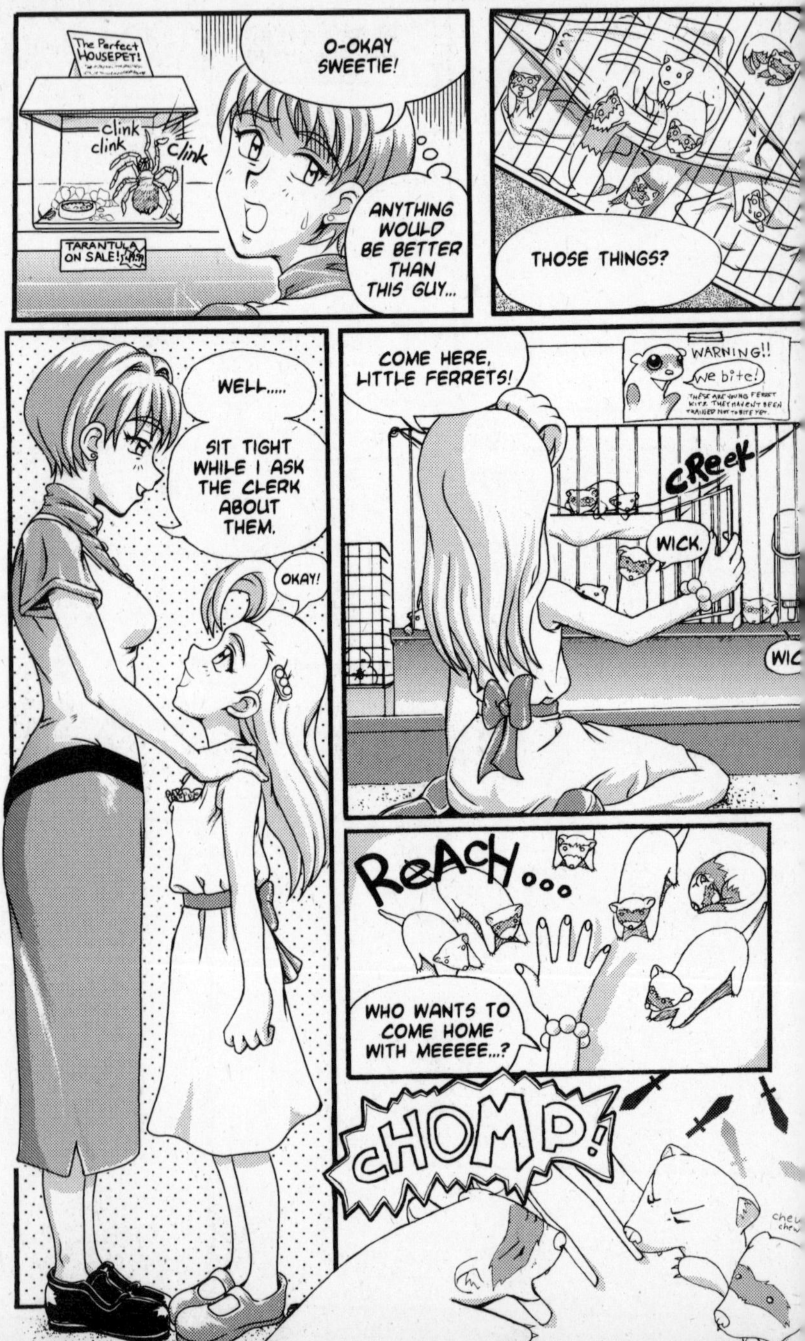
The Perfect HOUSEPET!
clink
clink
clink
TARANTULA ON SALE!
O-OKAY SWEETIE!
ANYTHING WOULD BE BETTER THAN THIS GUY...
THOSE THINGS?
WELL.....
SIT TIGHT WHILE I ASK THE CLERK ABOUT THEM.
OKAY!
COME HERE, LITTLE FERRETS!
WARNING!!
we bite!
THESE ARE YOUNG FERRET KITS. THEY HAVEN'T BEEN TRAINED NOT TO BITE YET.
CReek
WICK.
ReACH...
WHO WANTS TO COME HOME WITH MEEEEE...?
cHOMP!

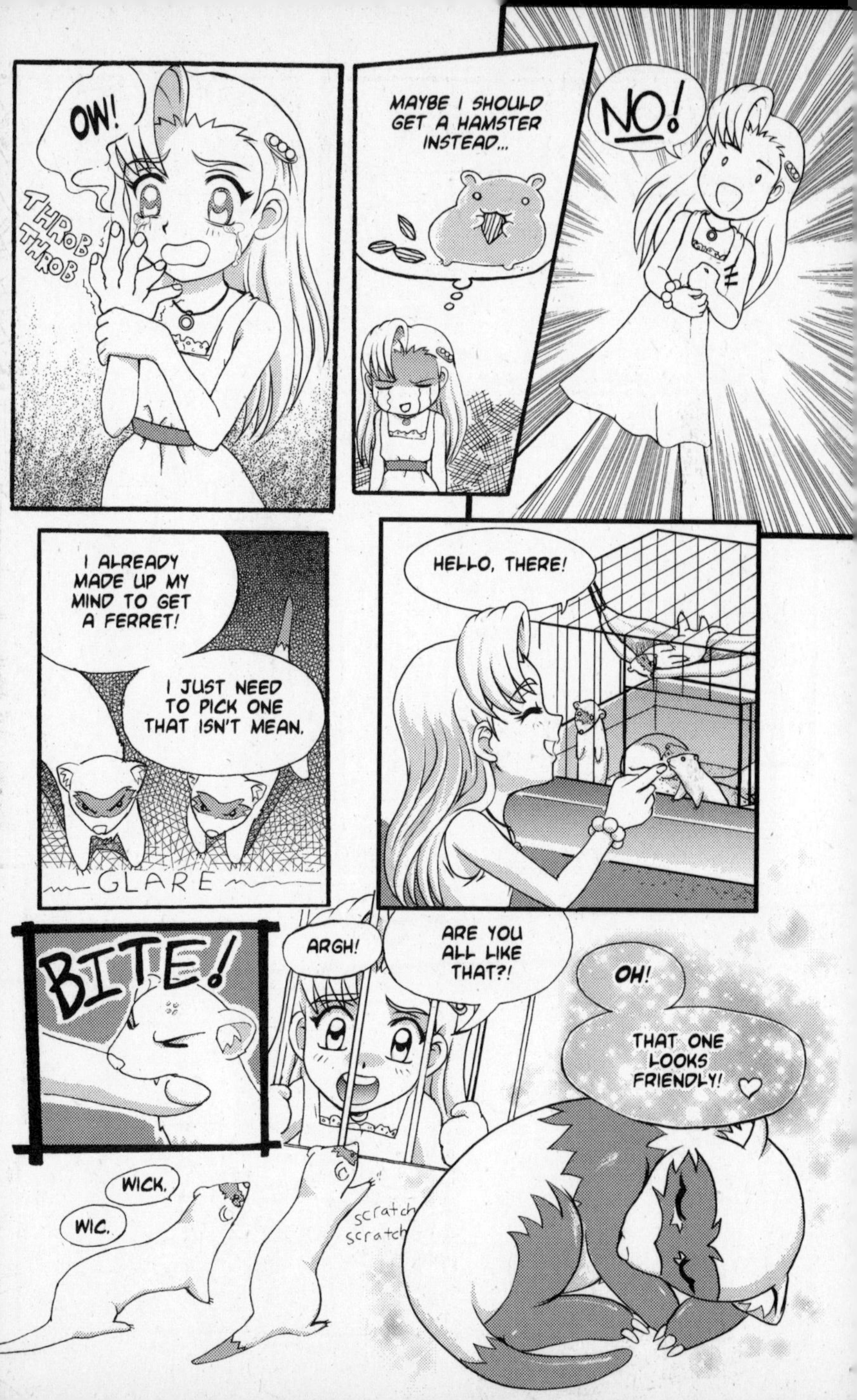
OW!
THROB THROB
MAYBE I SHOULD GET A HAMSTER INSTEAD...
NO!
I ALREADY MADE UP MY MIND TO GET A FERRET!
I JUST NEED TO PICK ONE THAT ISN'T MEAN.
GLARE
HELLO, THERE!
BITE!
ARGH!
ARE YOU ALL LIKE THAT?!
WICK.
WIC.
scratch scratch
OH!
THAT ONE LOOKS FRIENDLY!

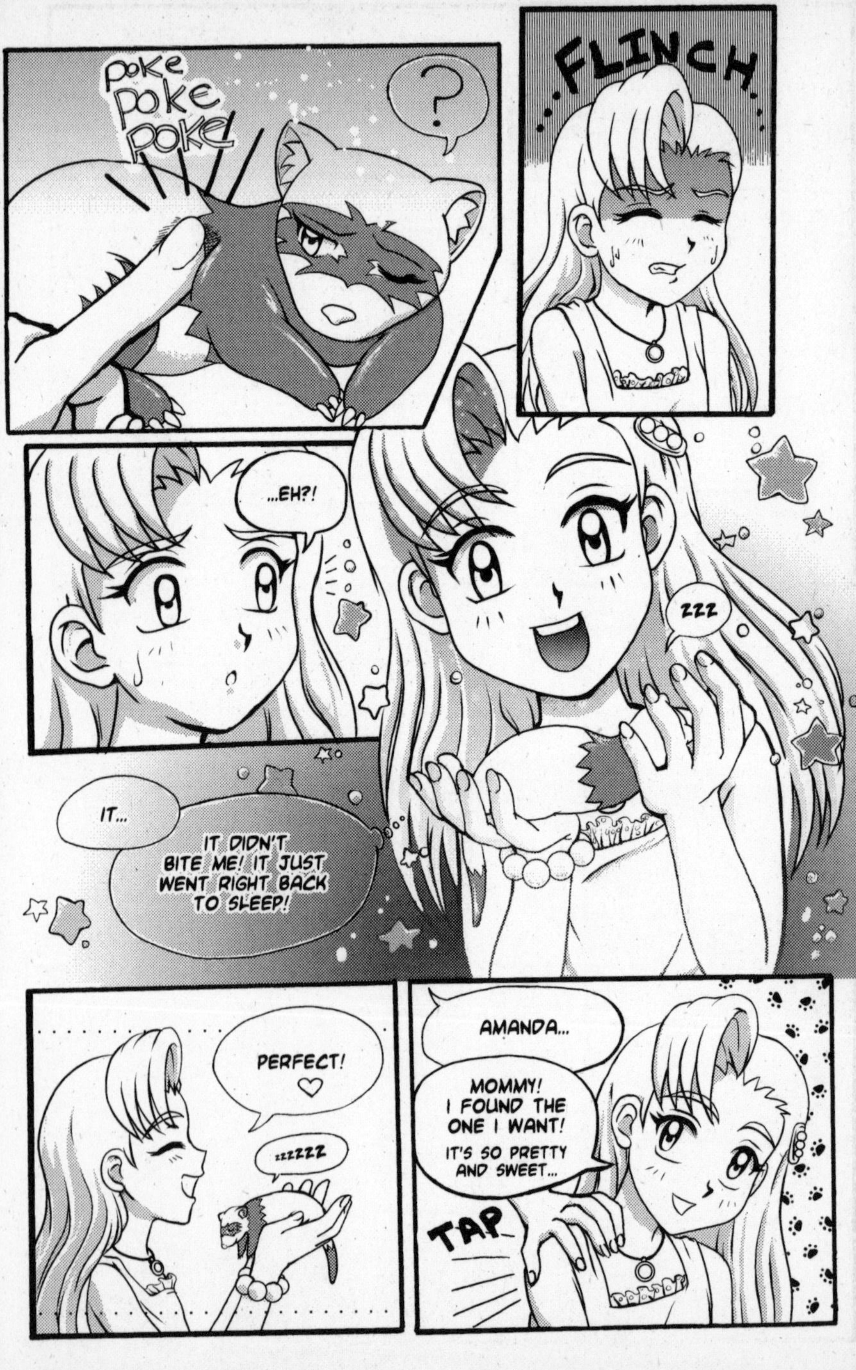
POKE POKE POKE
?
FLINCH
...EH?!
ZZZ
IT...
IT DIDN'T BITE ME! IT JUST WENT RIGHT BACK TO SLEEP!
PERFECT! ♡
ZZZZZZ
AMANDA...
MOMMY! I FOUND THE ONE I WANT!
IT'S SO PRETTY AND SWEET...
TAP

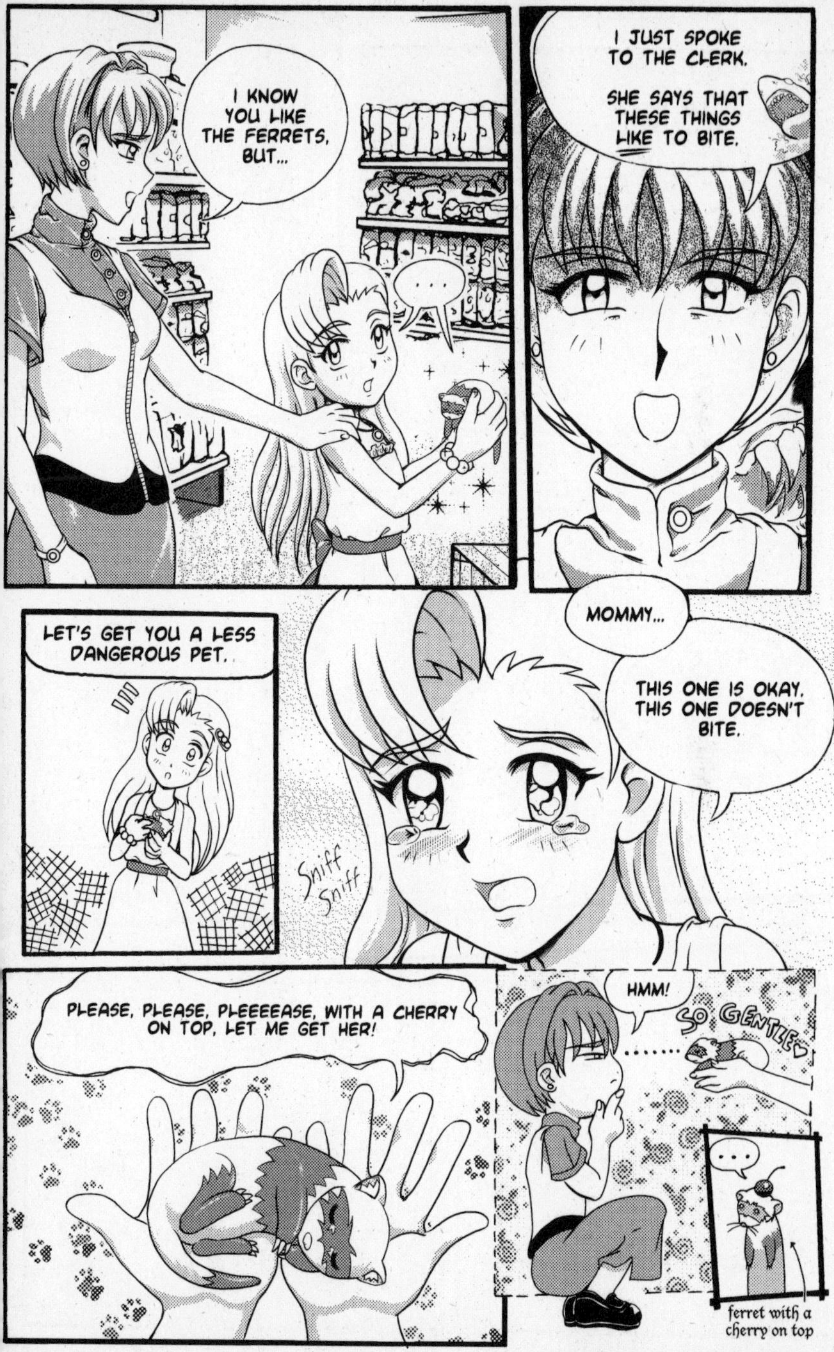
I KNOW YOU LIKE THE FERRETS, BUT...
. . .
I JUST SPOKE TO THE CLERK.
SHE SAYS THAT THESE THINGS LIKE TO BITE.
LET'S GET YOU A LESS DANGEROUS PET.
MOMMY...
THIS ONE IS OKAY. THIS ONE DOESN'T BITE.
Sniff Sniff
PLEASE, PLEASE, PLEEEEASE, WITH A CHERRY ON TOP, LET ME GET HER!
HMM!
SO GENTLE♡
. . .
ferret with a cherry on top

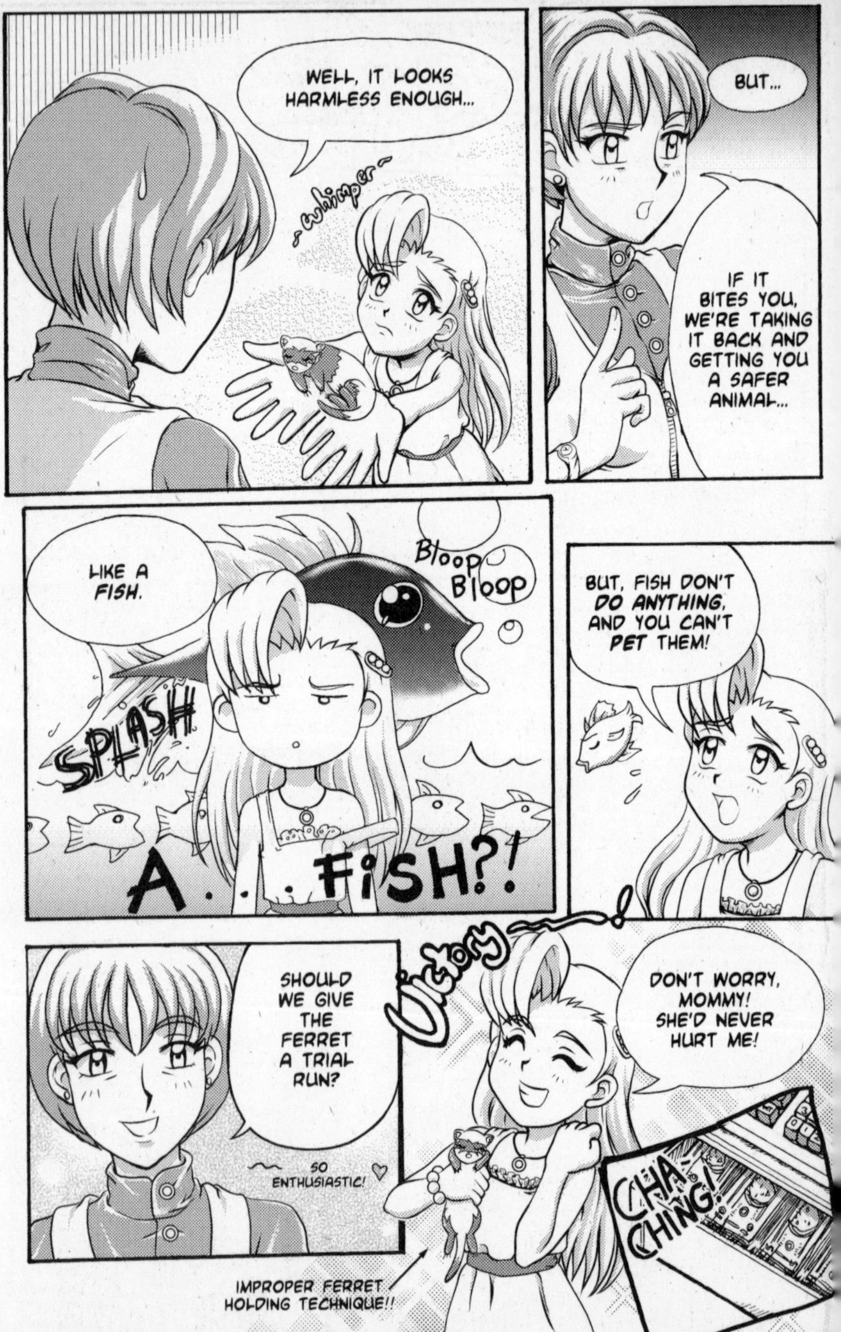
WELL, IT LOOKS HARMLESS ENOUGH...
~whimper~
BUT...
IF IT BITES YOU, WE'RE TAKING IT BACK AND GETTING YOU A SAFER ANIMAL...
LIKE A FISH.
Bloop Bloop
SPLASH
A...FISH?!
BUT, FISH DON'T DO ANYTHING, AND YOU CAN'T PET THEM!
SHOULD WE GIVE THE FERRET A TRIAL RUN?
~ SO ENTHUSIASTIC! ♡
Victory
DON'T WORRY, MOMMY! SHE'D NEVER HURT ME!
CHA-CHING!
IMPROPER FERRET HOLDING TECHNIQUE!!

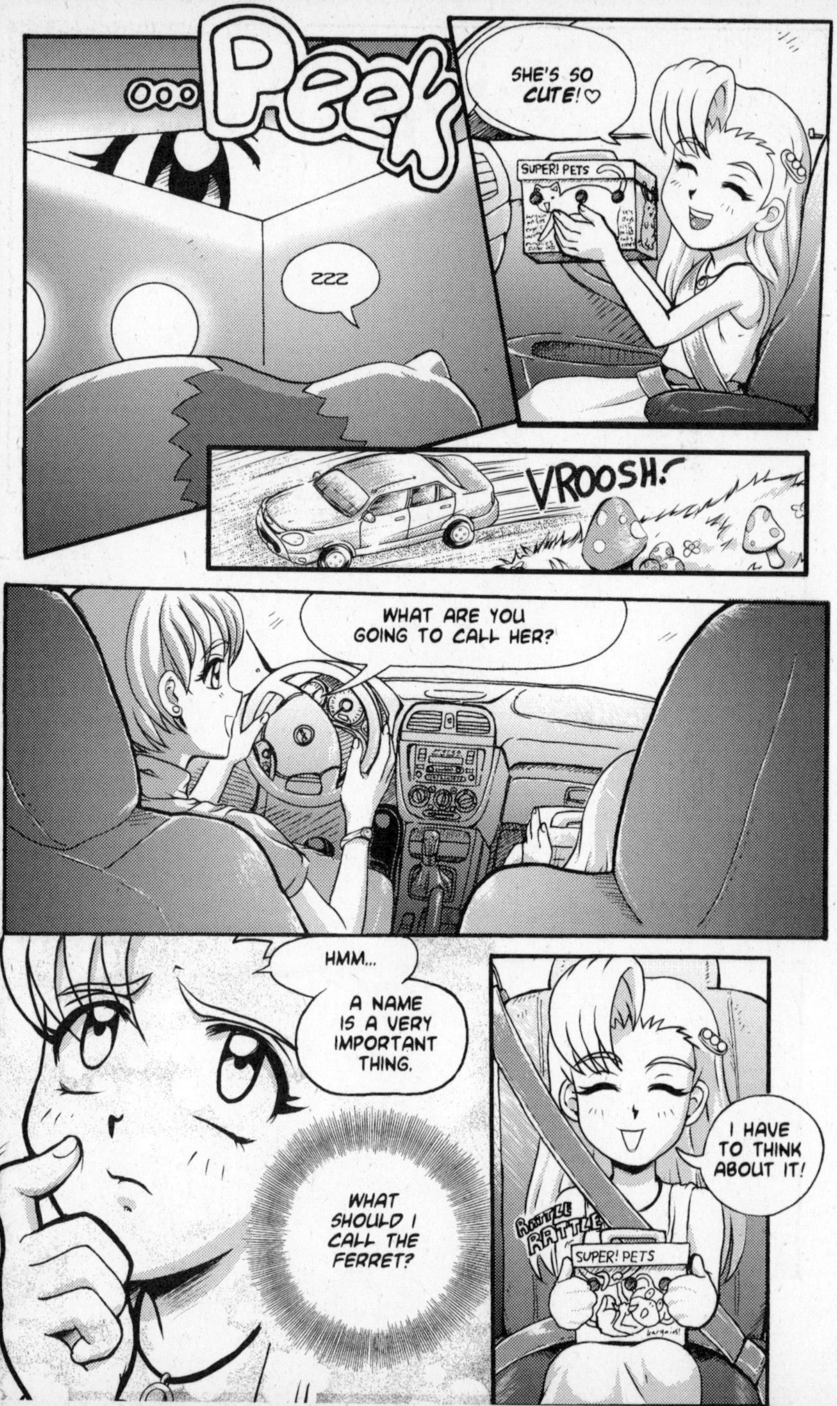
...Peek
zzz
SHE'S SO CUTE! ♡
SUPER! PETS
VROOSH!
WHAT ARE YOU GOING TO CALL HER?
HMM...
A NAME IS A VERY IMPORTANT THING.
WHAT SHOULD I CALL THE FERRET?
I HAVE TO THINK ABOUT IT!
RATTLE RATTLE
SUPER! PETS

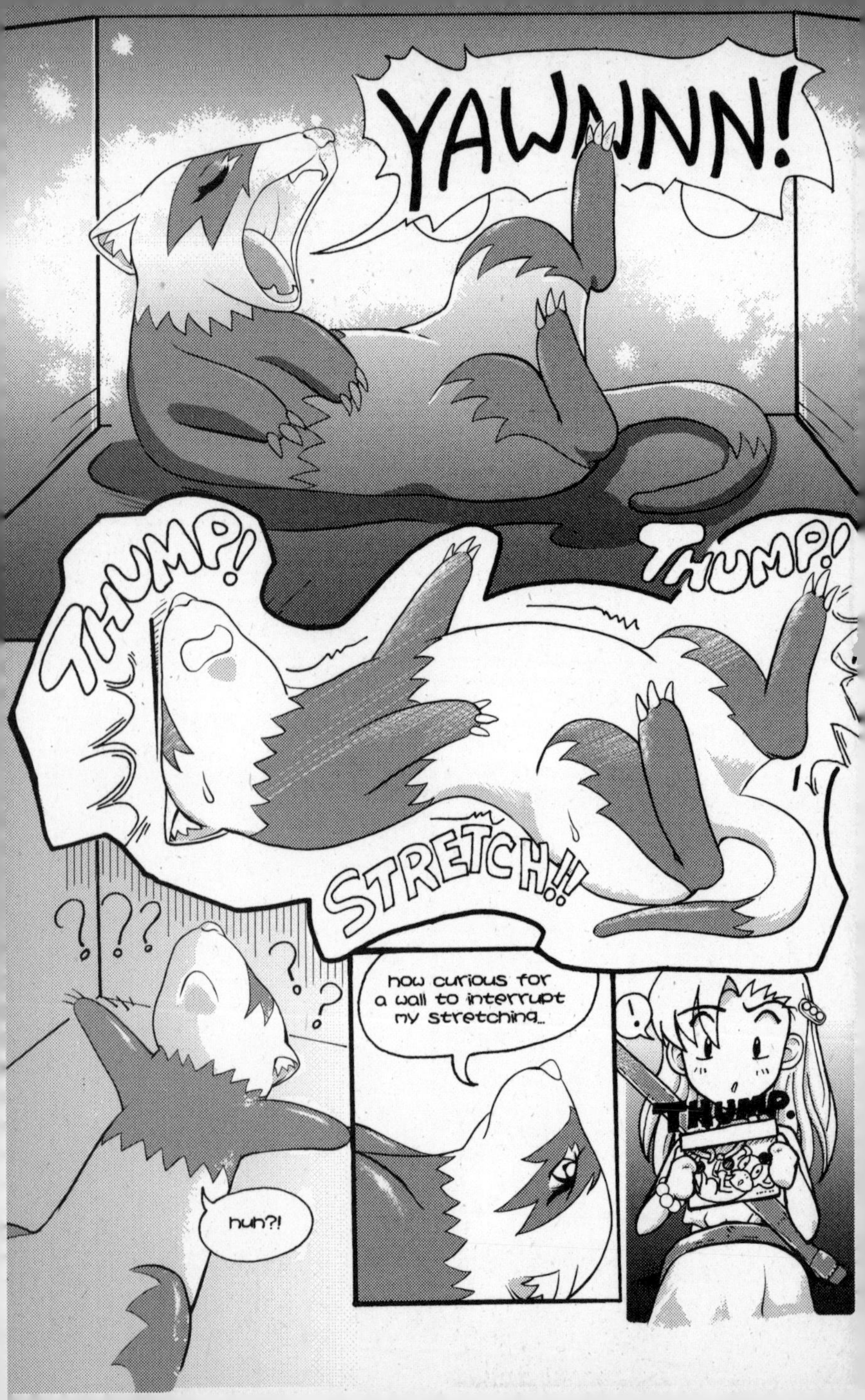
YAWNNN!
THUMP!
THUMP!
STRETCH!!
huh?!
how curious for a wall to interrupt my stretching...
THUMP.

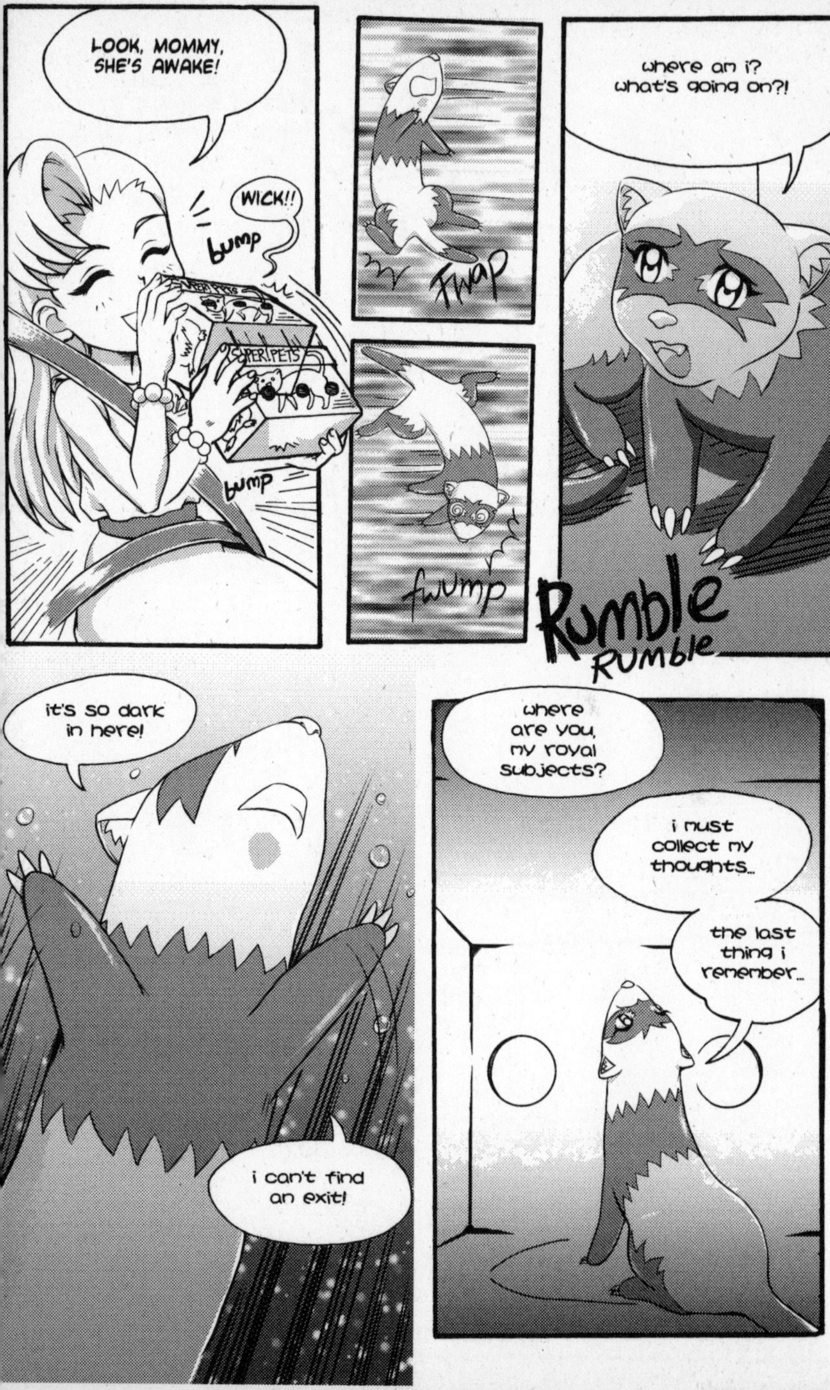
LOOK, MOMMY, SHE'S AWAKE!
WICK!!
bump
SUPER!PETS
bump
FWap
fwump
where am i? what's going on?!
Rumble
Rumble
it's so dark in here!
i can't find an exit!
where are you, my royal subjects?
i must collect my thoughts...
the last thing i remember...

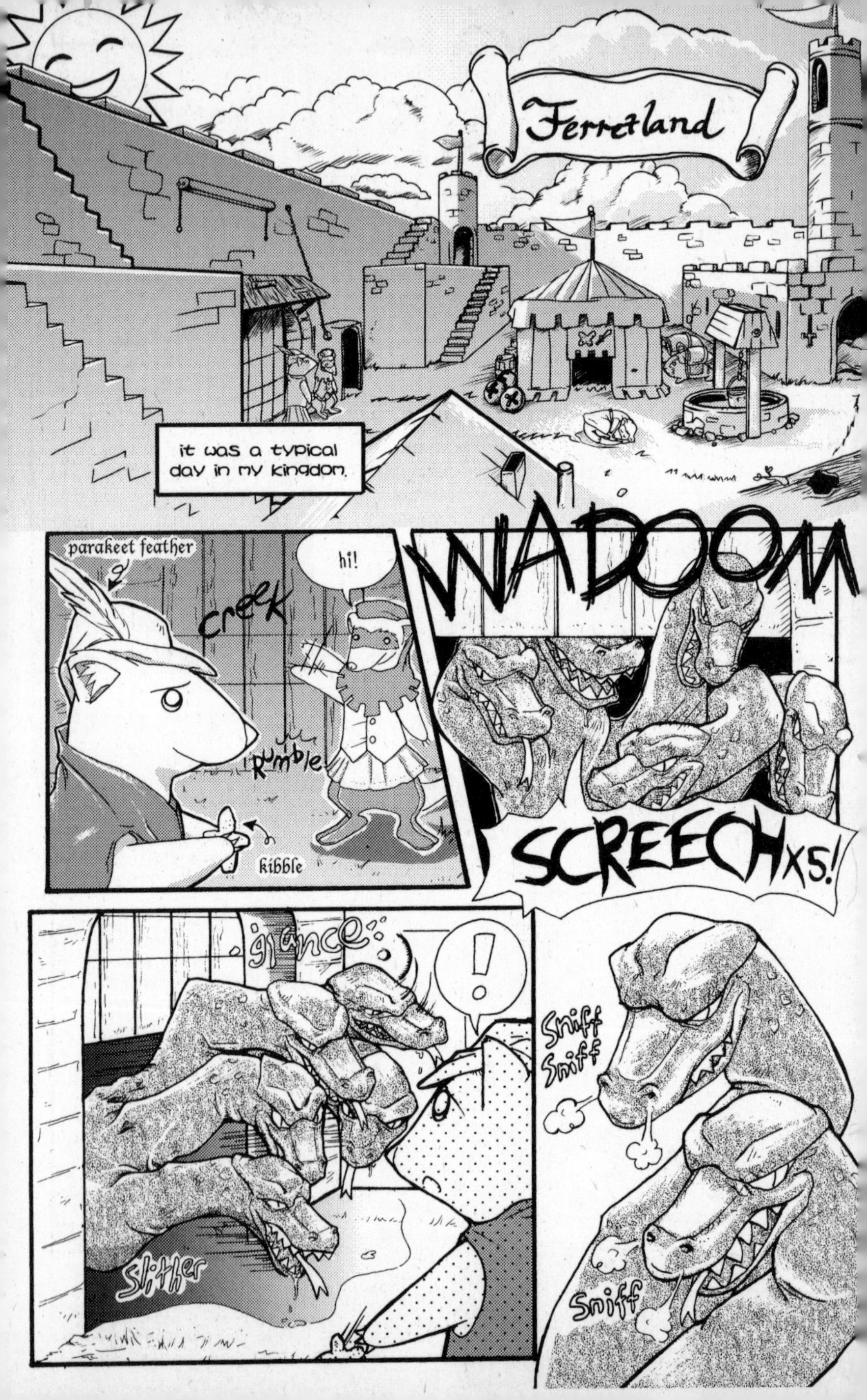
Ferretland
it was a typical day in my kingdom.
parakeet feather
hi!
creek
rumble
kibble
WADOOM
SCREECH x5!
glance
!
slither
Sniff Sniff
Sniff

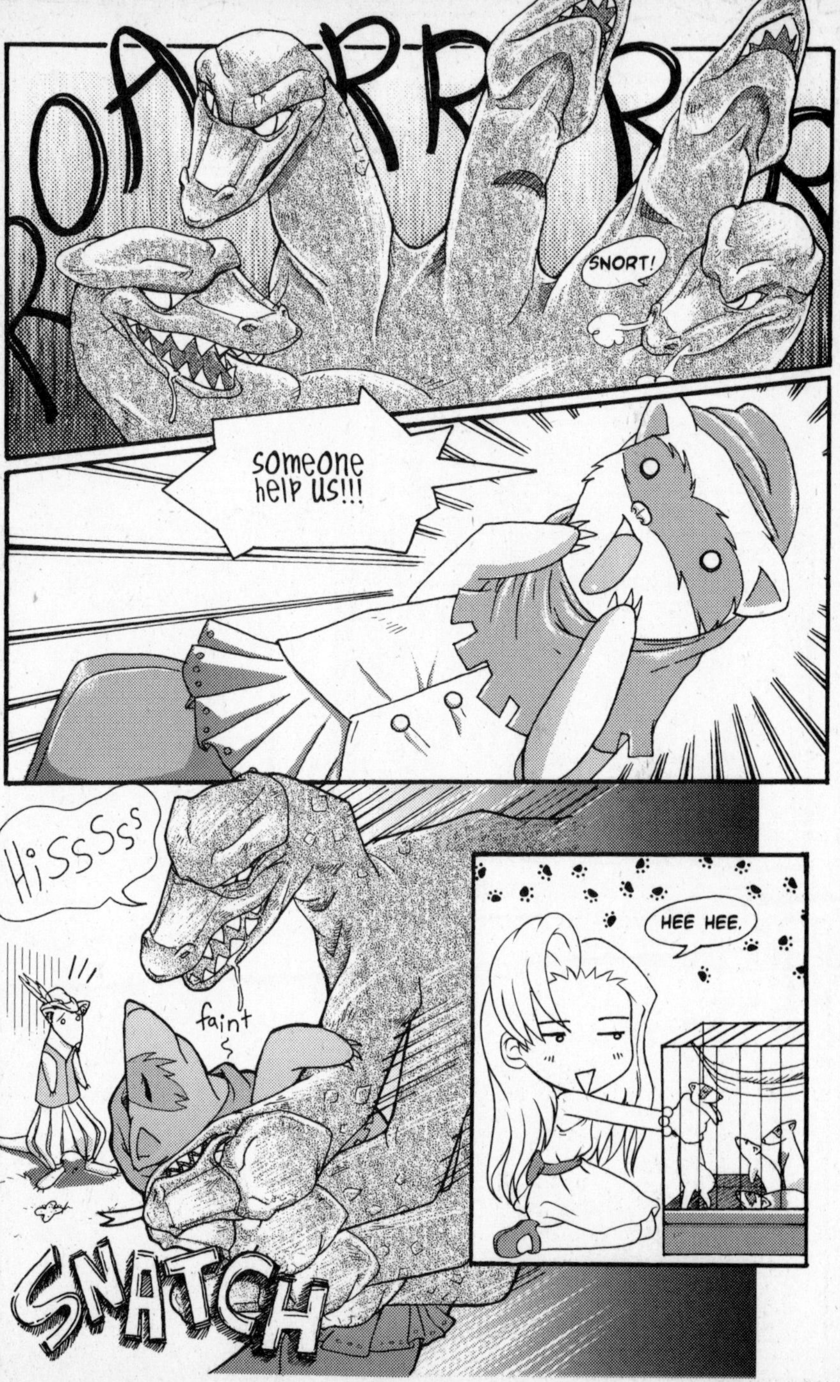
ROARRRRR
SNORT!
someone help us!!!
HiSsSsS
faint
SNATCH
HEE HEE.

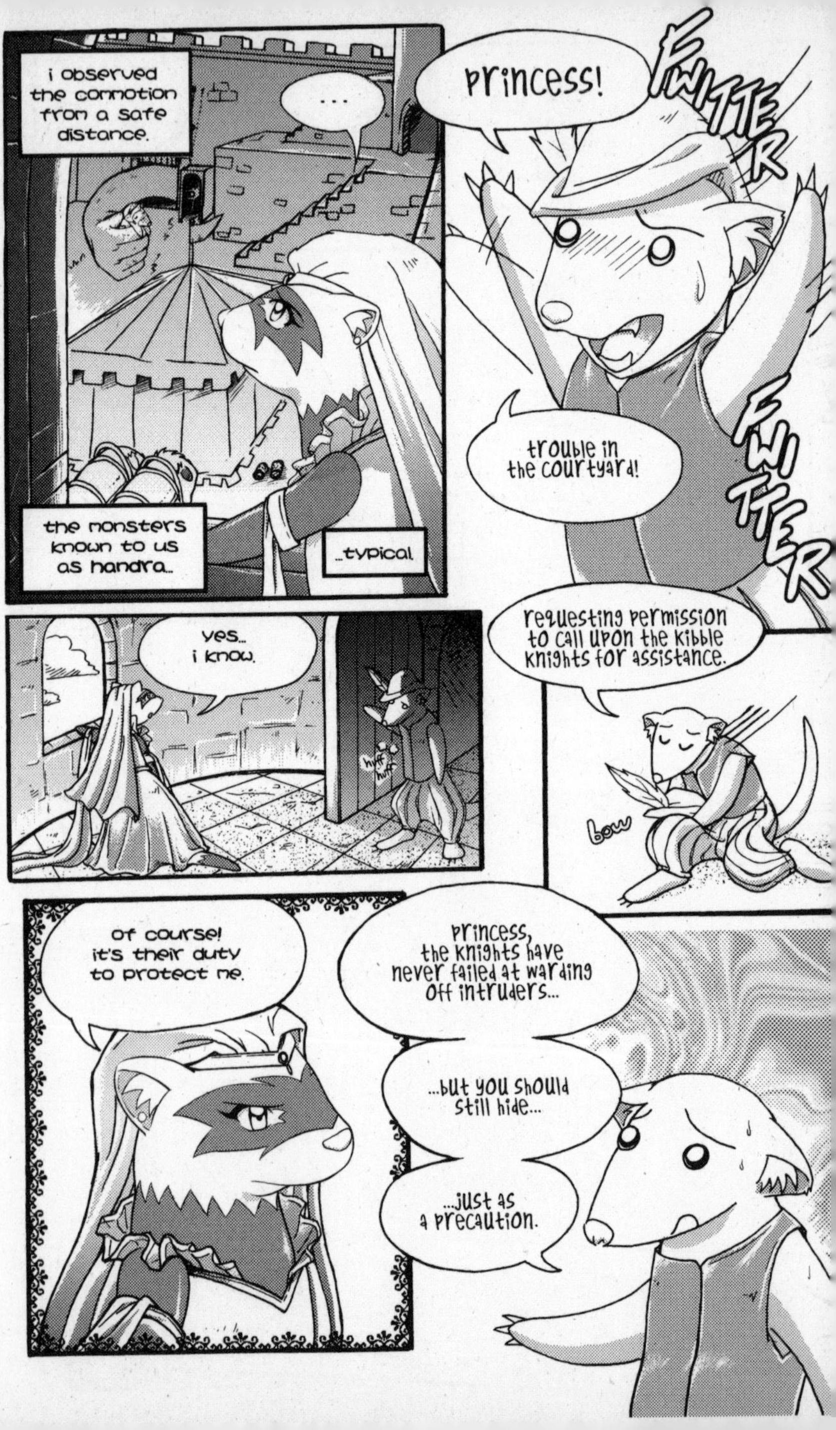
i observed the commotion from a safe distance.
...
the monsters known to us as handra...
...typical.
princess!
FWITTER
trouble in the courtyard!
FWITTER
yes... i know.
huff huff
requesting permission to call upon the kibble knights for assistance.
bow
of course! it's their duty to protect me.
princess, the knights have never failed at warding off intruders...
...but you should still hide...
...just as a precaution.

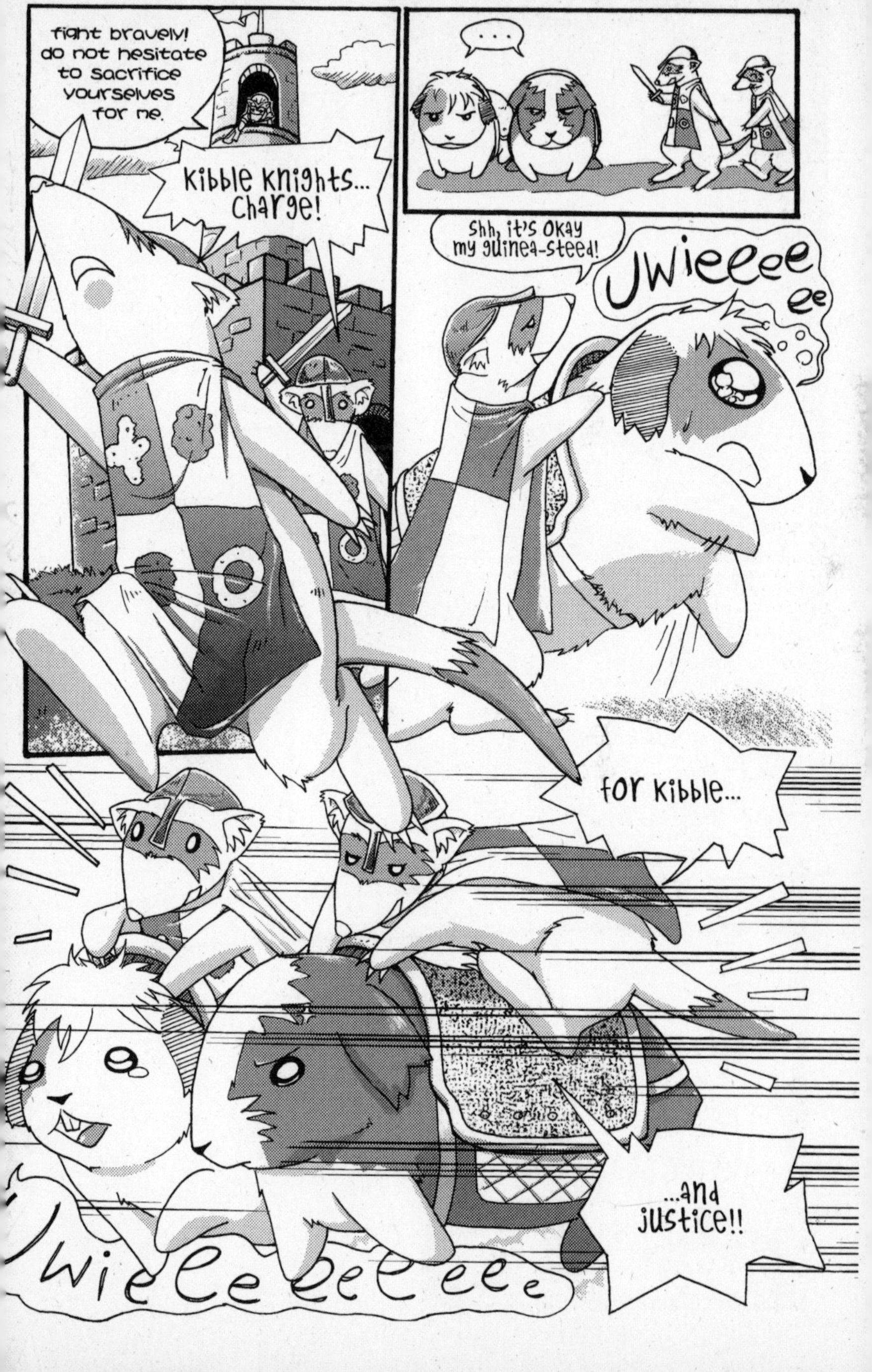
fight bravely! do not hesitate to sacrifice yourselves for me.
Kibble knights... charge!
. . .
Shh, it's okay my guinea-steed!
Uwieeee ee
for kibble...
...and justice!!
Wieeeeeeeeee

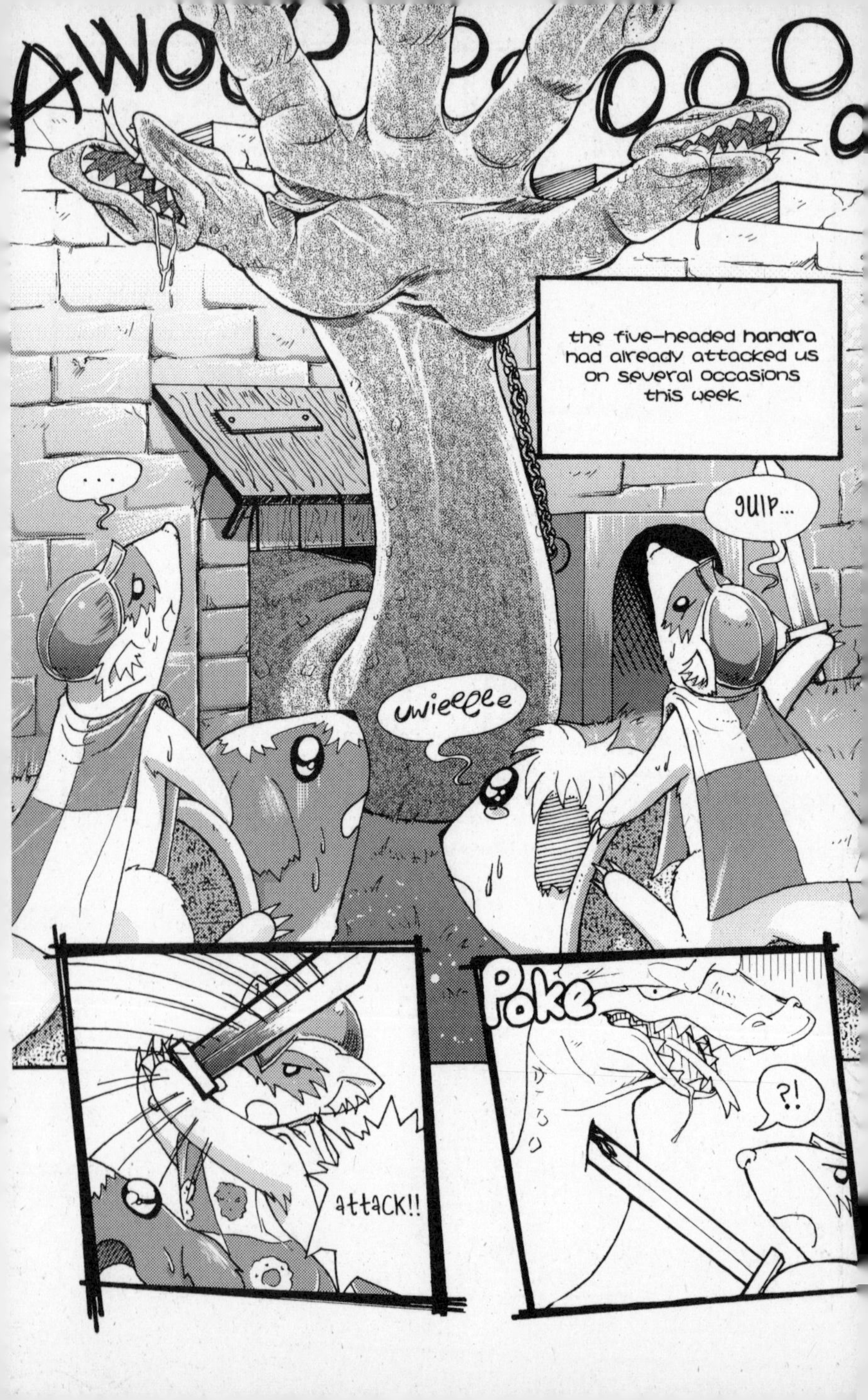
AWOOOOOOOOOO
the five-headed handra had already attacked us on several occasions this week.
...
gulp...
uwiellle
attack!!
Poke
?!

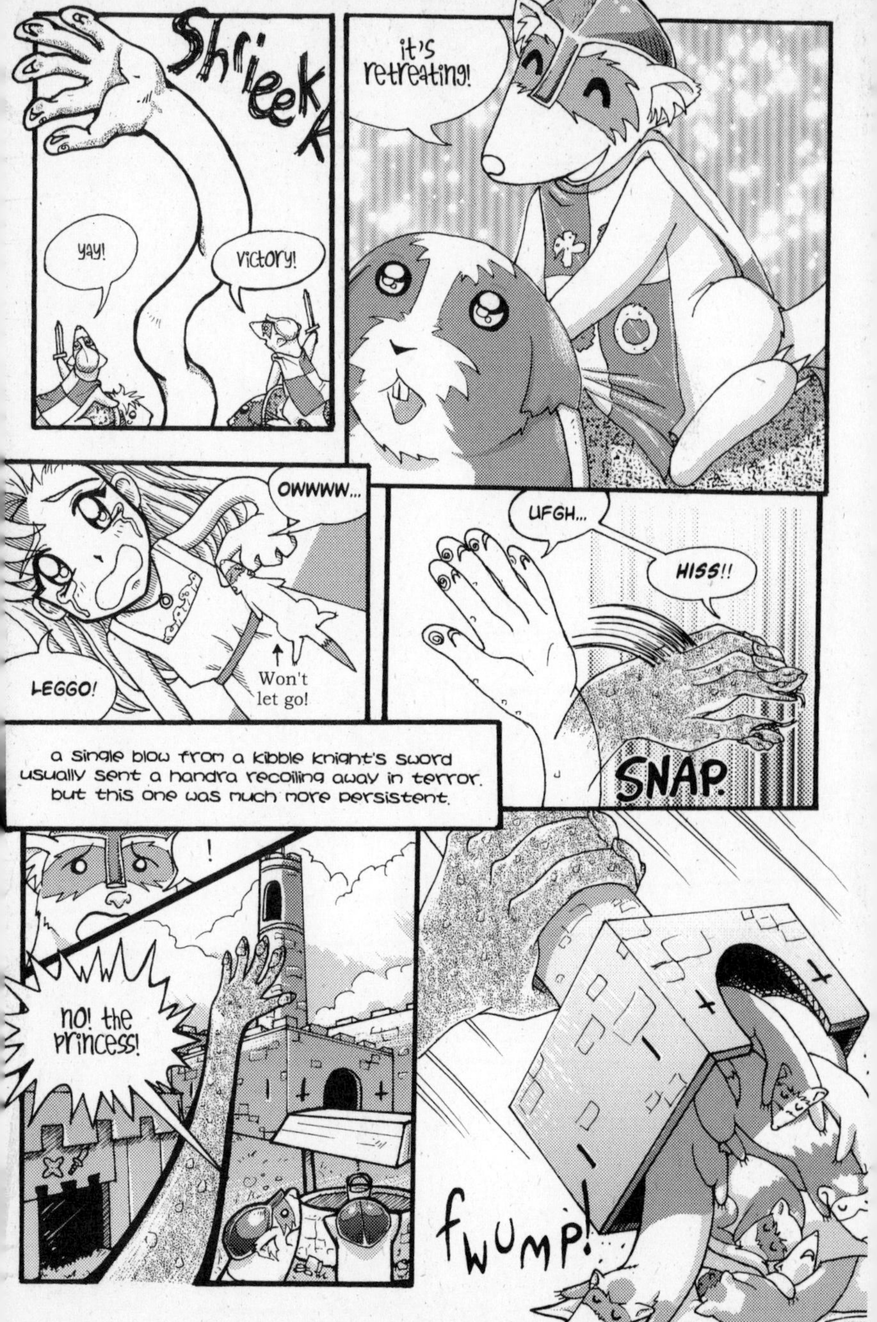
Shrieeek
yay!
victory!
it's retreating!
OWWWW...
LEGGO!
Won't let go!
UFGH...
HISS!!
SNAP.
a single blow from a kibble knight's sword usually sent a handra recoiling away in terror. but this one was much more persistent.
!
no! the princess!
fwump!

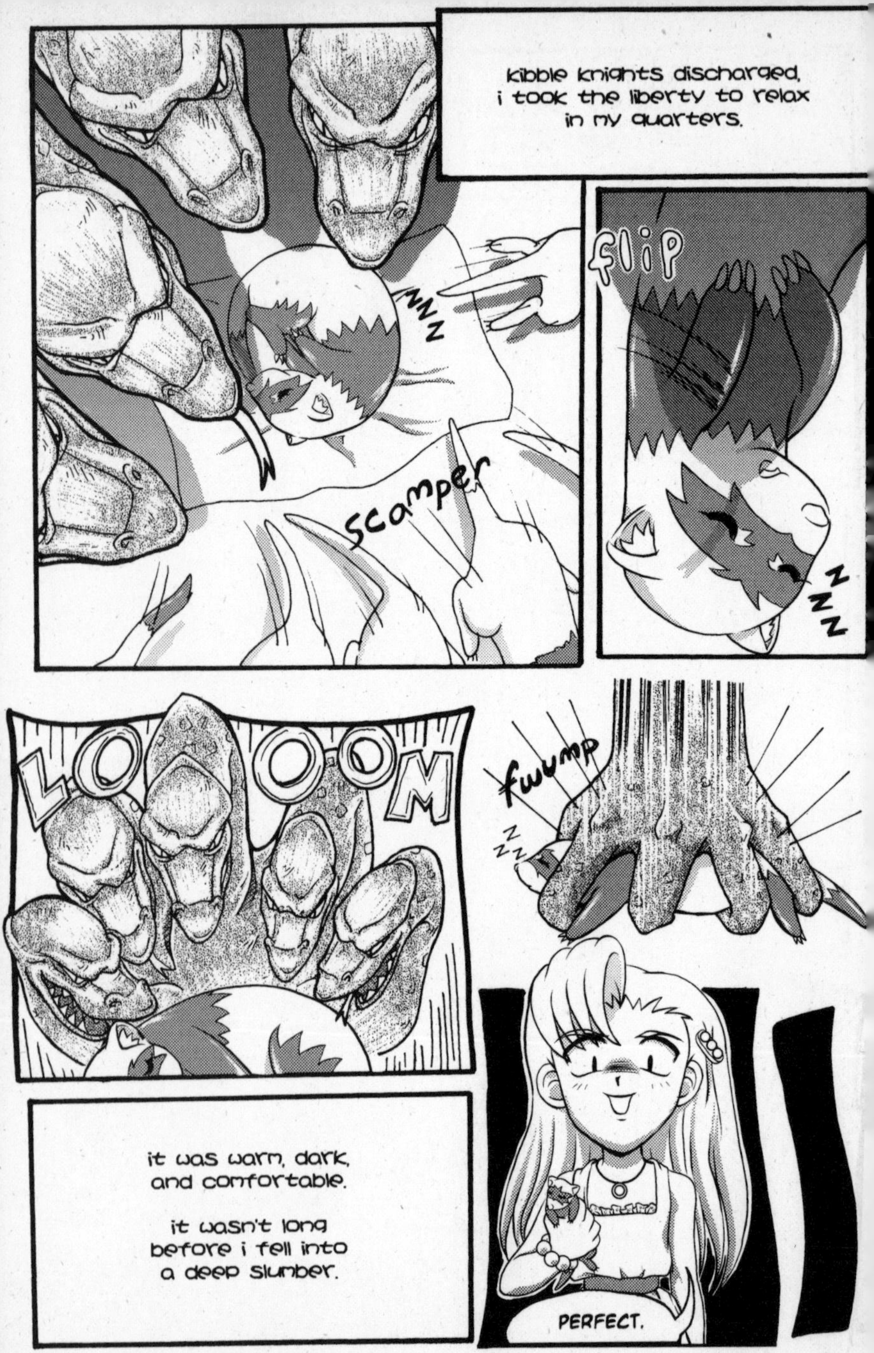
kibble knights discharged, i took the liberty to relax in my quarters.
ZZZ
scamper
flip
ZZZ
LOOOOM
fwump
ZZZ
it was warm, dark, and comfortable.
it wasn't long before i fell into a deep slumber.
PERFECT.

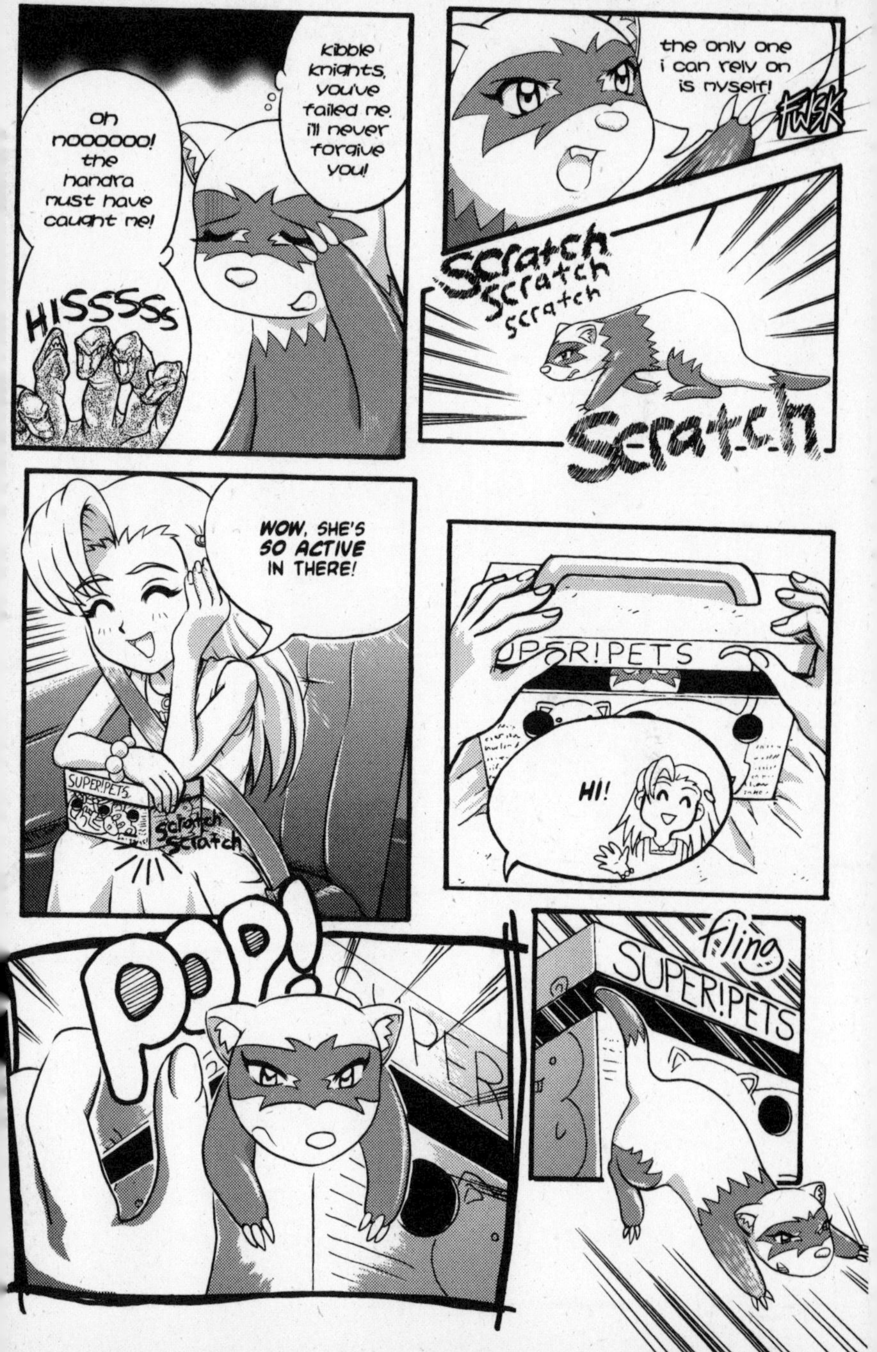
oh nooooooo! the handra must have caught me!
kibble knights, you've failed me. i'll never forgive you!
HISSSSSS
the only one i can rely on is myself!
FWSK
Scratch Scratch Scratch
Scratch
WOW, SHE'S SO ACTIVE IN THERE!
SUPER!PETS
scratch scratch
SUPER!PETS
HI!
POP!
fling
SUPER!PETS

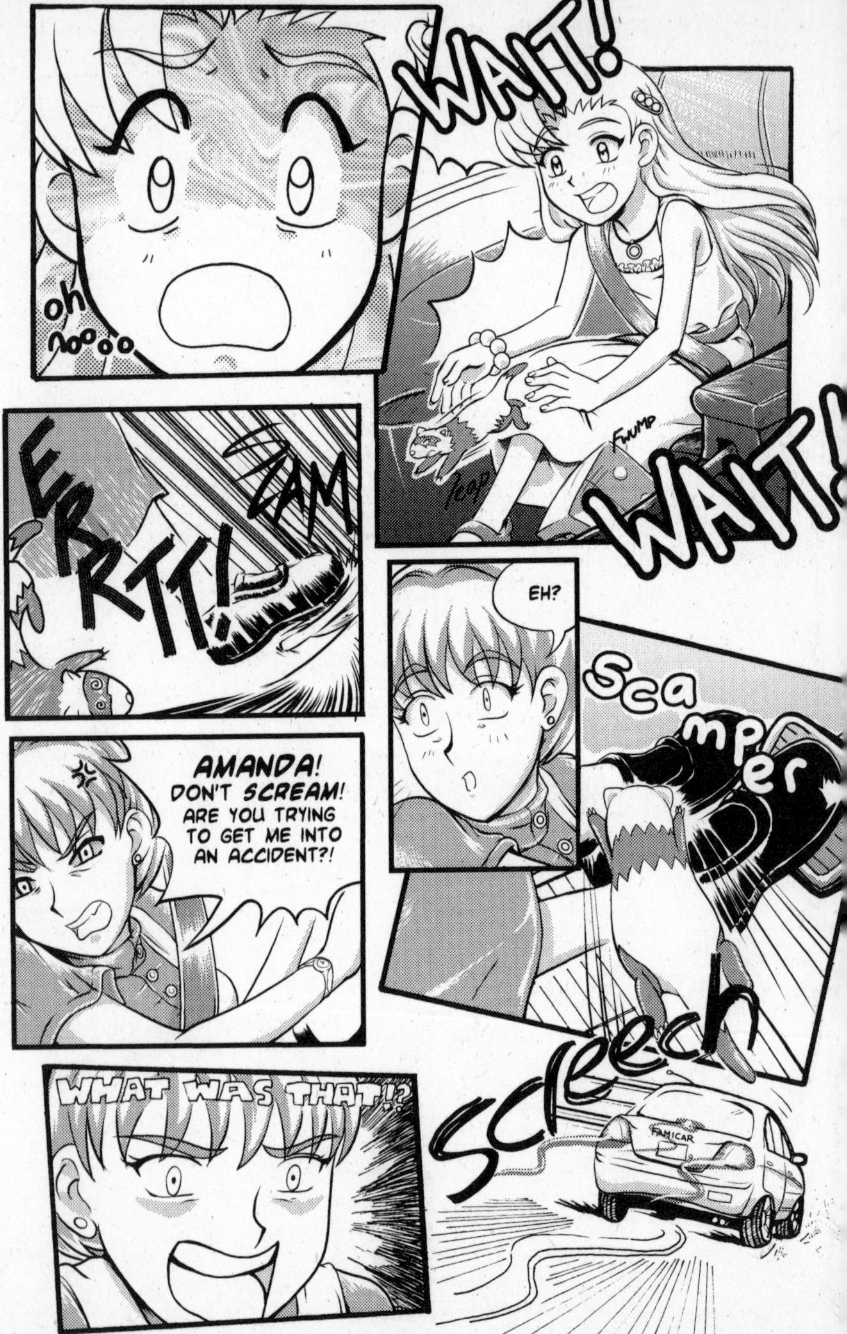
oh nooooo
WAIT!
FWUMP
WAIT!
ERRTT!
ZAM
EH?
AMANDA! DON'T SCREAM! ARE YOU TRYING TO GET ME INTO AN ACCIDENT?!
Scamper
WHAT WAS THAT!?
SCREECH
FAMICAR

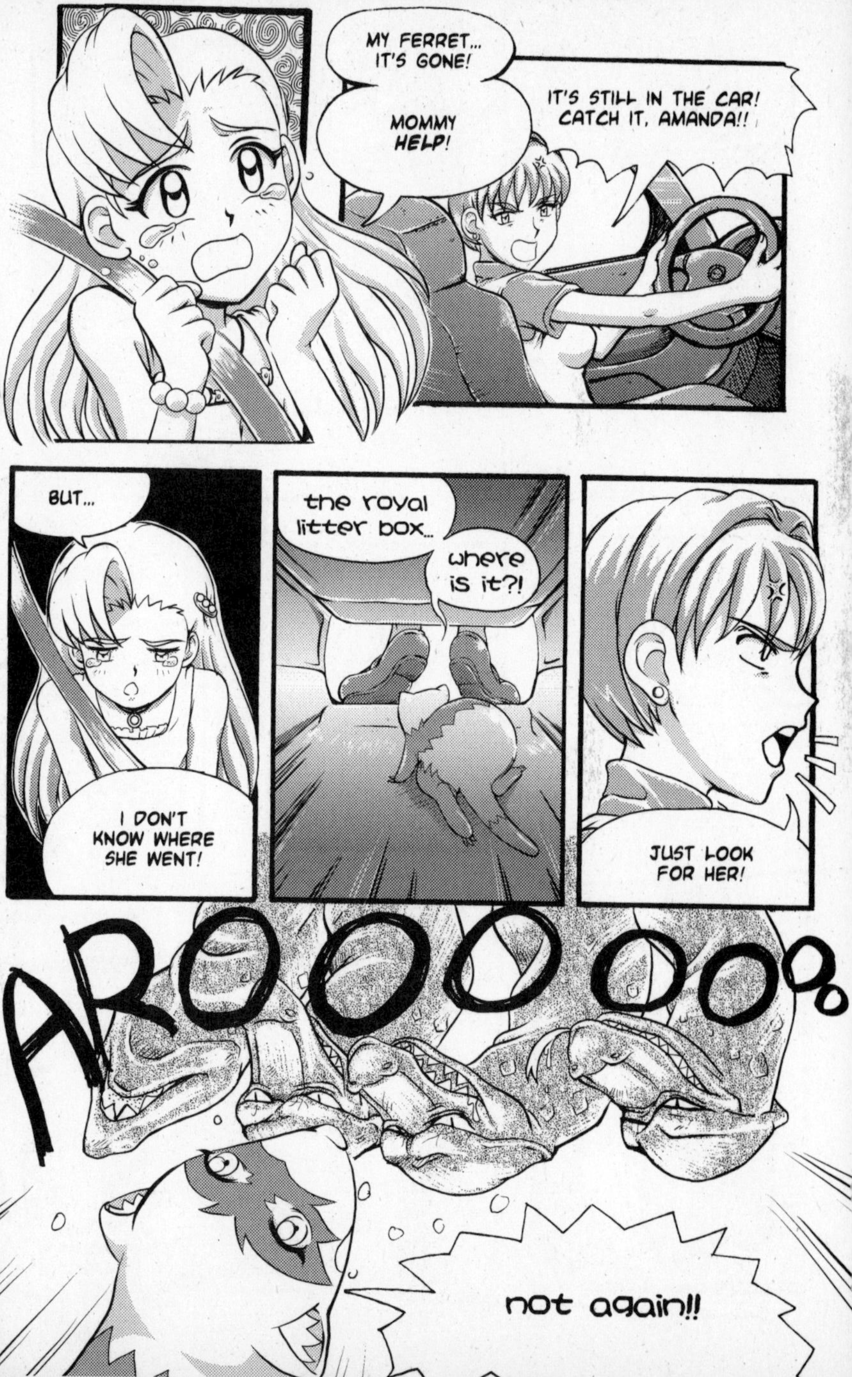
MY FERRET... IT'S GONE!
MOMMY HELP!
IT'S STILL IN THE CAR! CATCH IT, AMANDA!!
BUT...
I DON'T KNOW WHERE SHE WENT!
the royal litter box...
where is it?!
JUST LOOK FOR HER!
AROOOOOo
not again!!

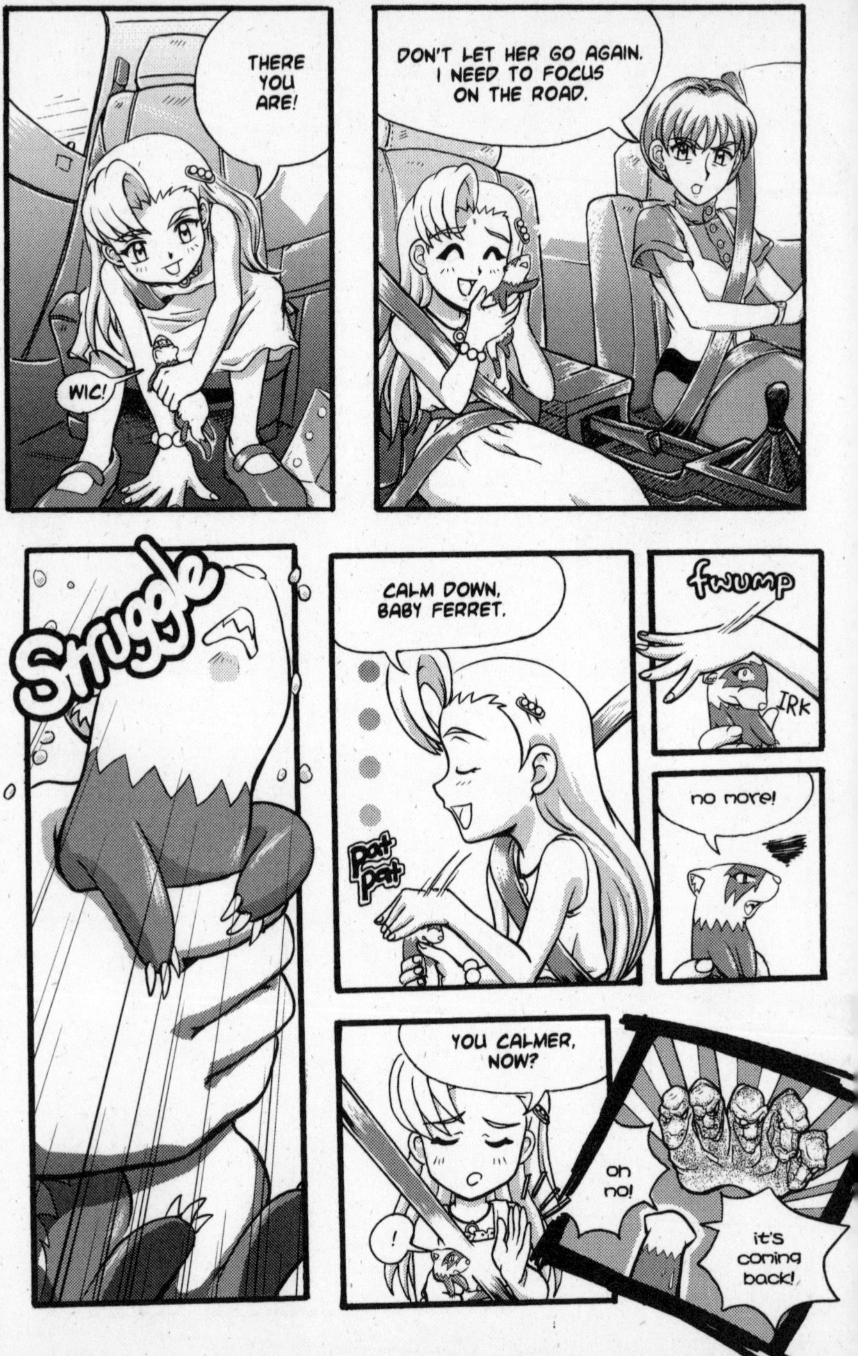
THERE YOU ARE!
WIC!
DON'T LET HER GO AGAIN. I NEED TO FOCUS ON THE ROAD.
Struggle
CALM DOWN, BABY FERRET.
pat pat
fwump
IRK
no more!
YOU CALMER, NOW?
!
oh no!
it's coming back!

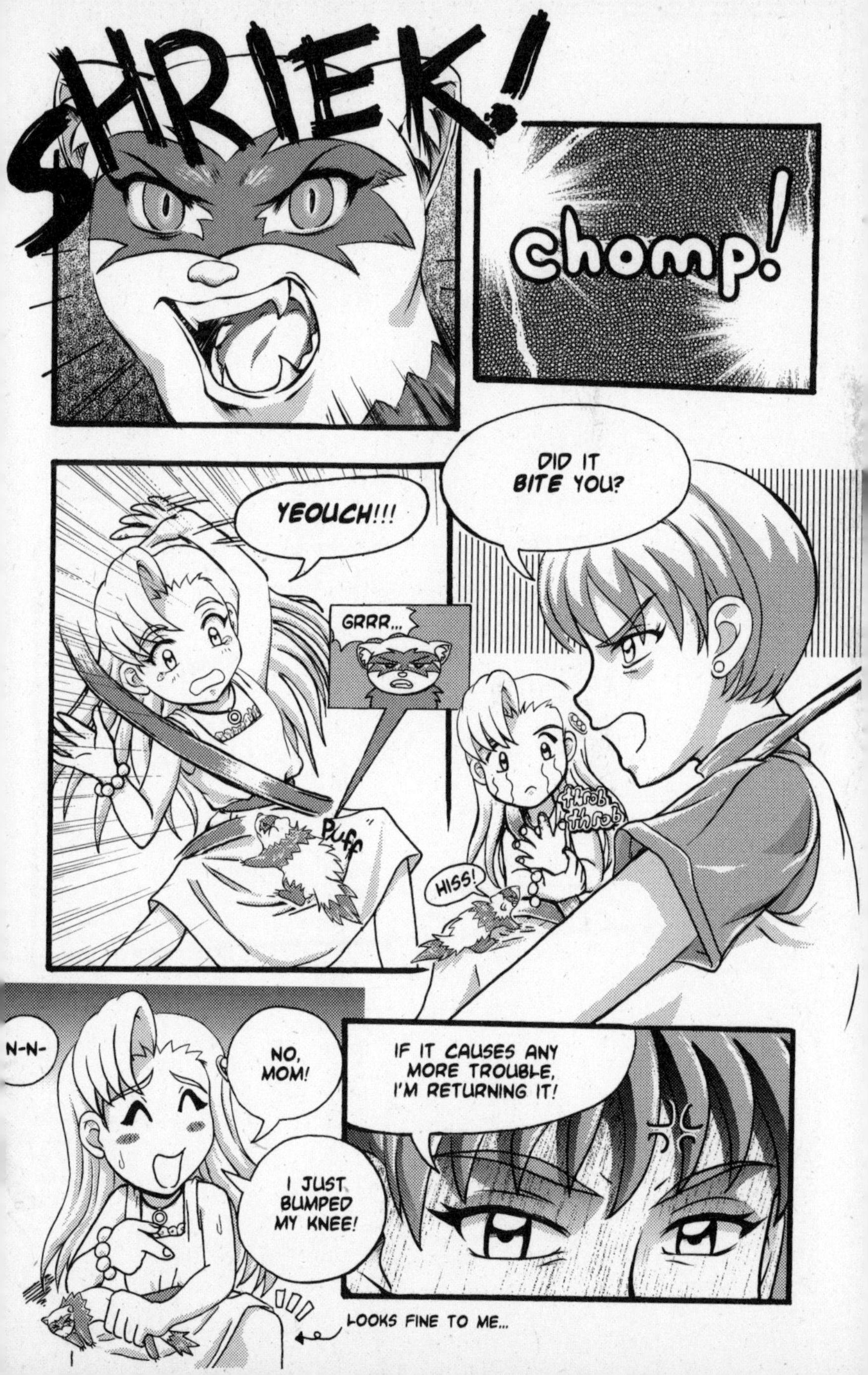
SHRIEK!
chomp!
YEOUCH!!!
GRRR...
Puff
DID IT BITE YOU?
throb throb
HISS!
N-N-
NO, MOM!
I JUST BUMPED MY KNEE!
LOOKS FINE TO ME...
IF IT CAUSES ANY MORE TROUBLE, I'M RETURNING IT!

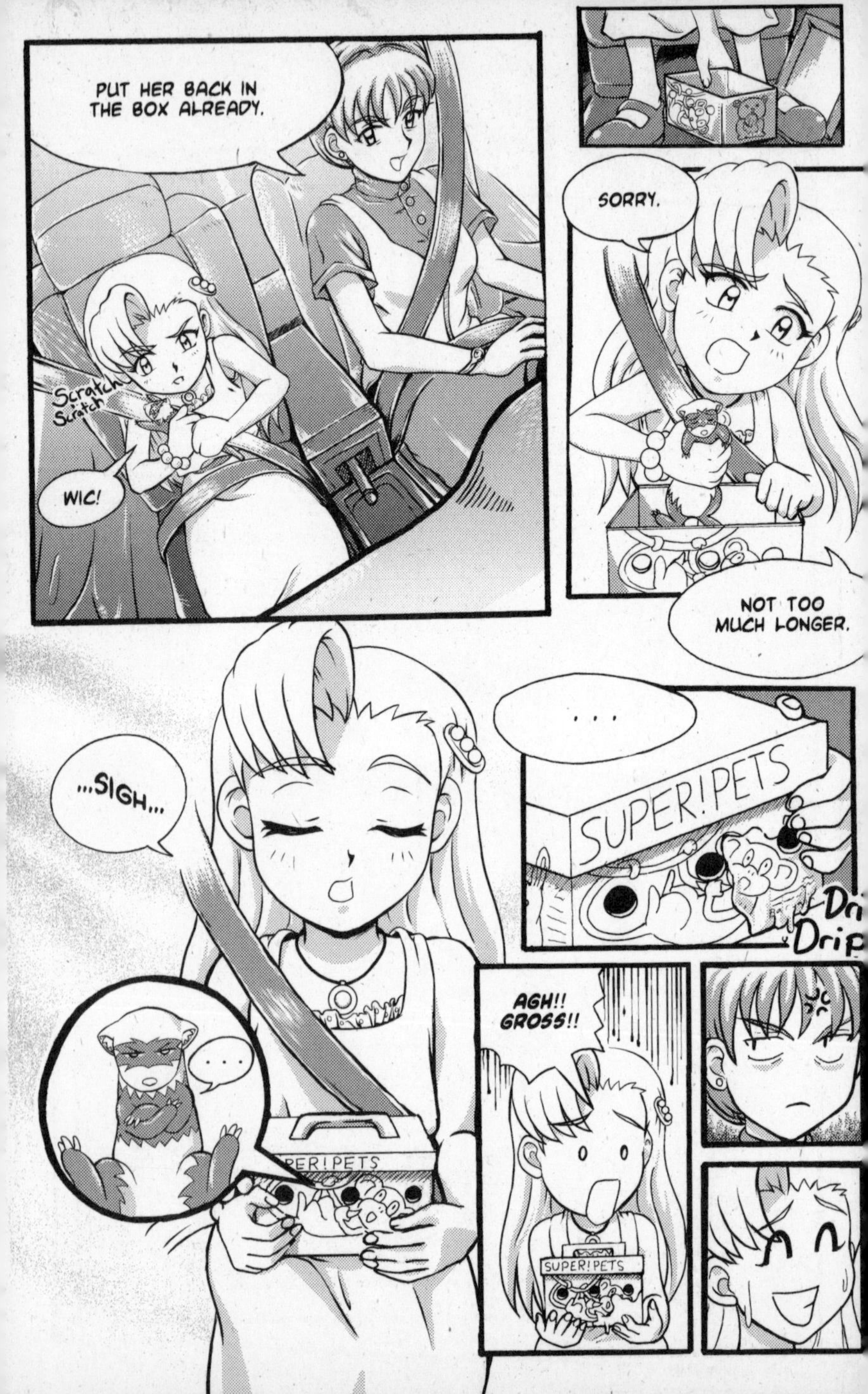
PUT HER BACK IN THE BOX ALREADY.
Scratch Scratch
WIC!
SORRY.
NOT TOO MUCH LONGER.
...SIGH...
. . .
SUPER!PETS
. . .
SUPER!PETS
Dri
Drip
AGH!! GROSS!!
SUPER!PETS

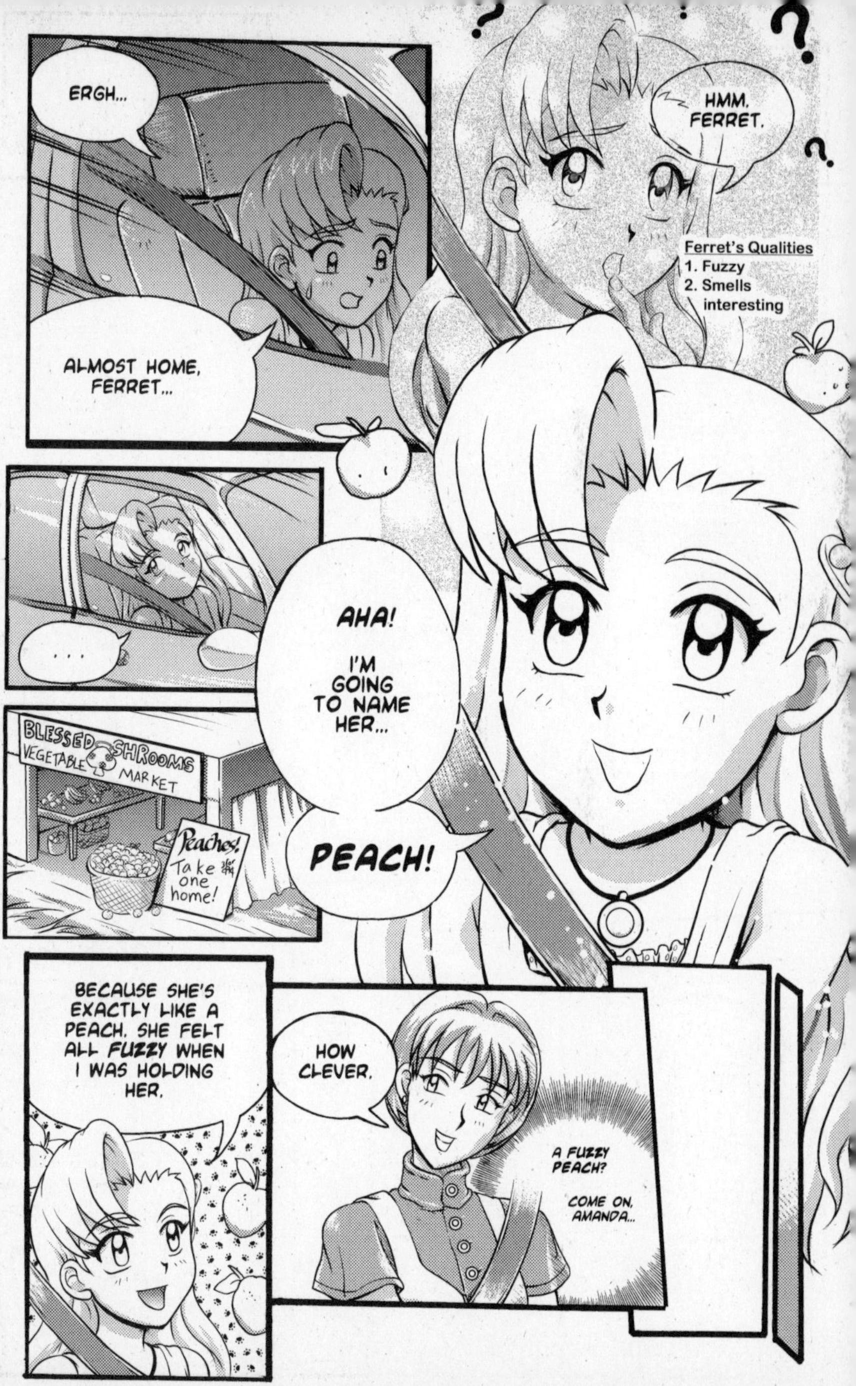
ERGH...
ALMOST HOME, FERRET...
HMM. FERRET.
Ferret's Qualities
1. Fuzzy
2. Smells interesting
...
BLESSED SHROOMS
VEGETABLE MARKET
Peaches!
Take one home!
AHA!
I'M GOING TO NAME HER...
PEACH!
BECAUSE SHE'S EXACTLY LIKE A PEACH. SHE FELT ALL FUZZY WHEN I WAS HOLDING HER.
HOW CLEVER.
A FUZZY PEACH?
COME ON, AMANDA...

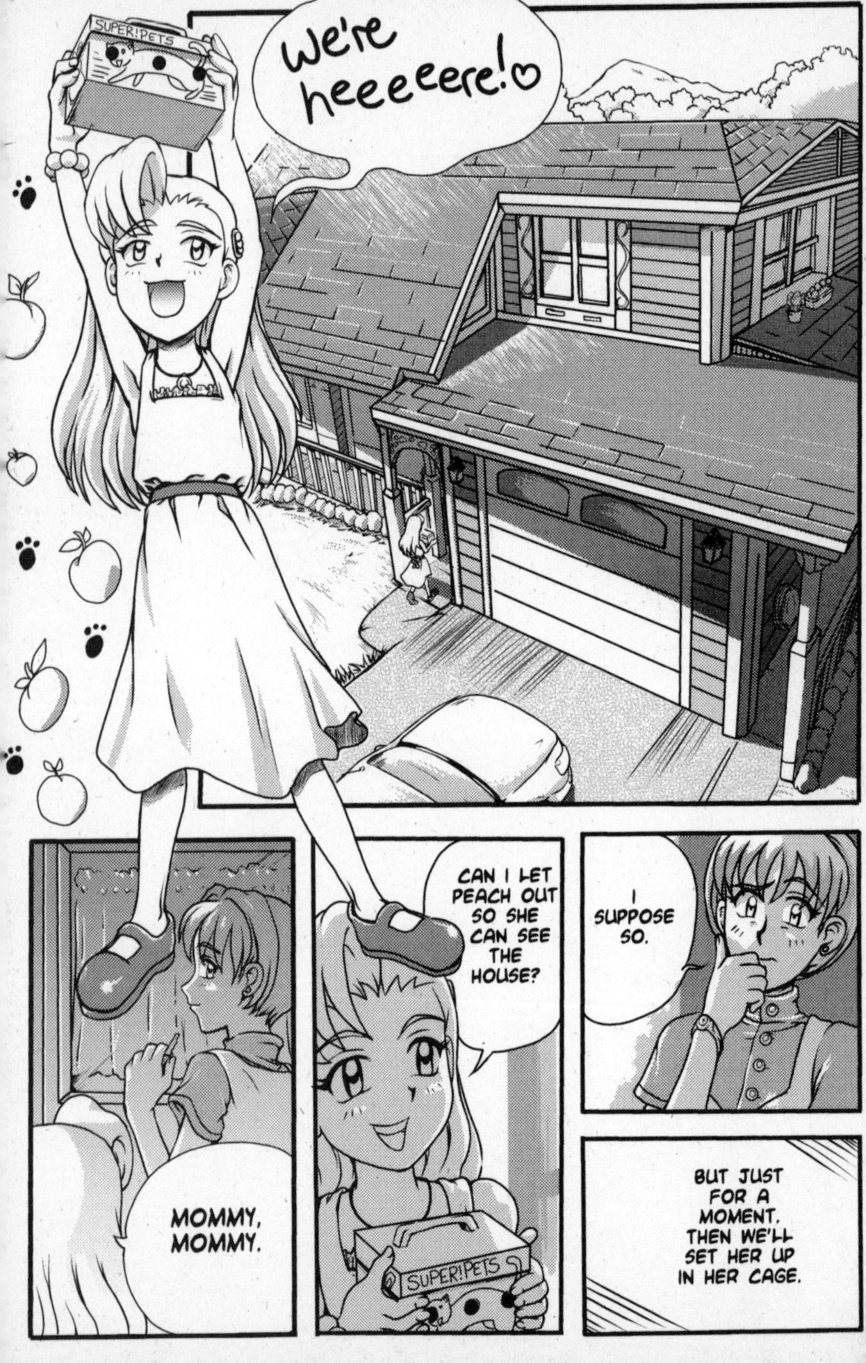
SUPER!PETS
We're heeeeere!♡
MOMMY, MOMMY.
CAN I LET PEACH OUT SO SHE CAN SEE THE HOUSE?
SUPER!PETS
I SUPPOSE SO.
BUT JUST FOR A MOMENT. THEN WE'LL SET HER UP IN HER CAGE.

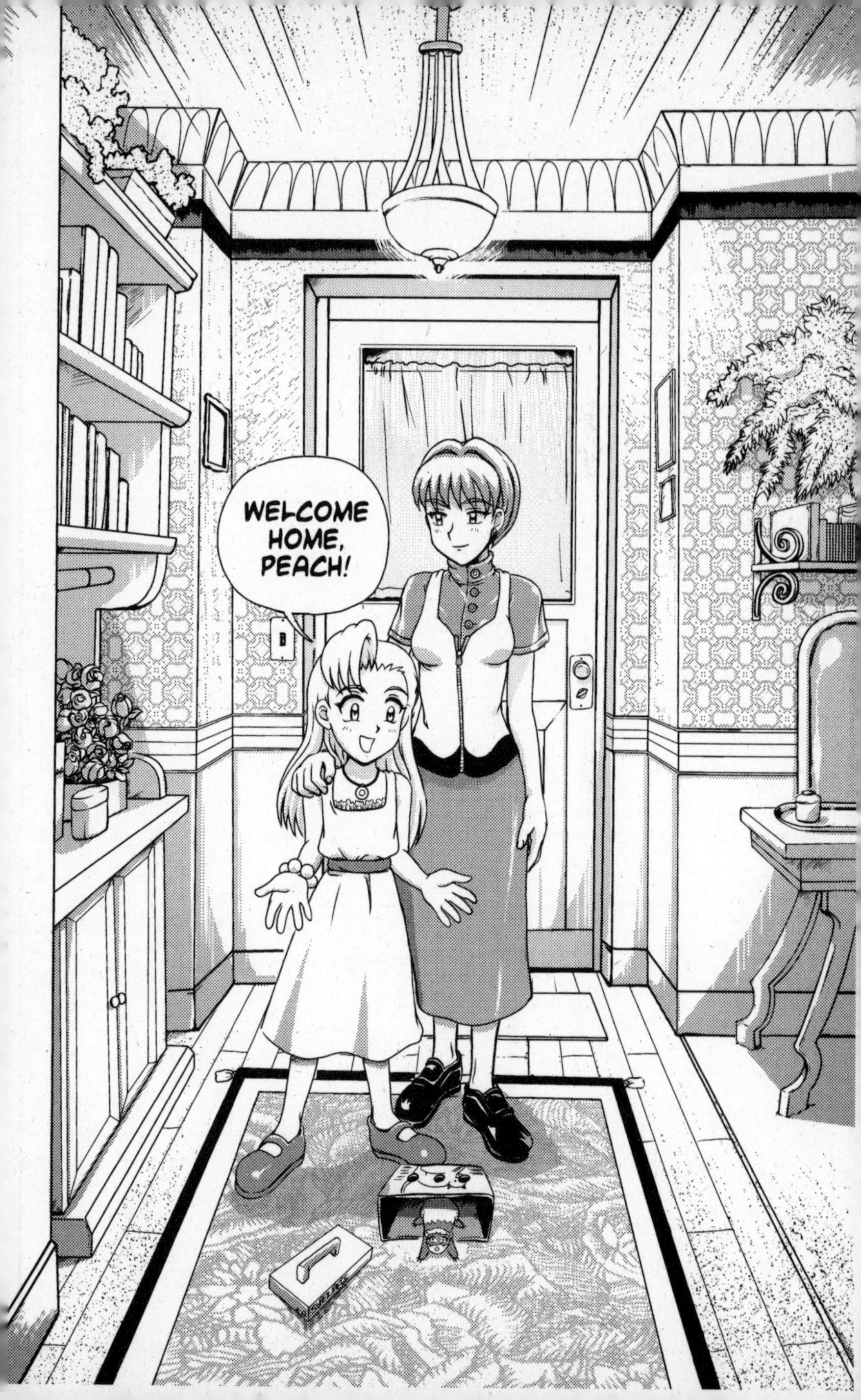
WELCOME HOME, PEACH!

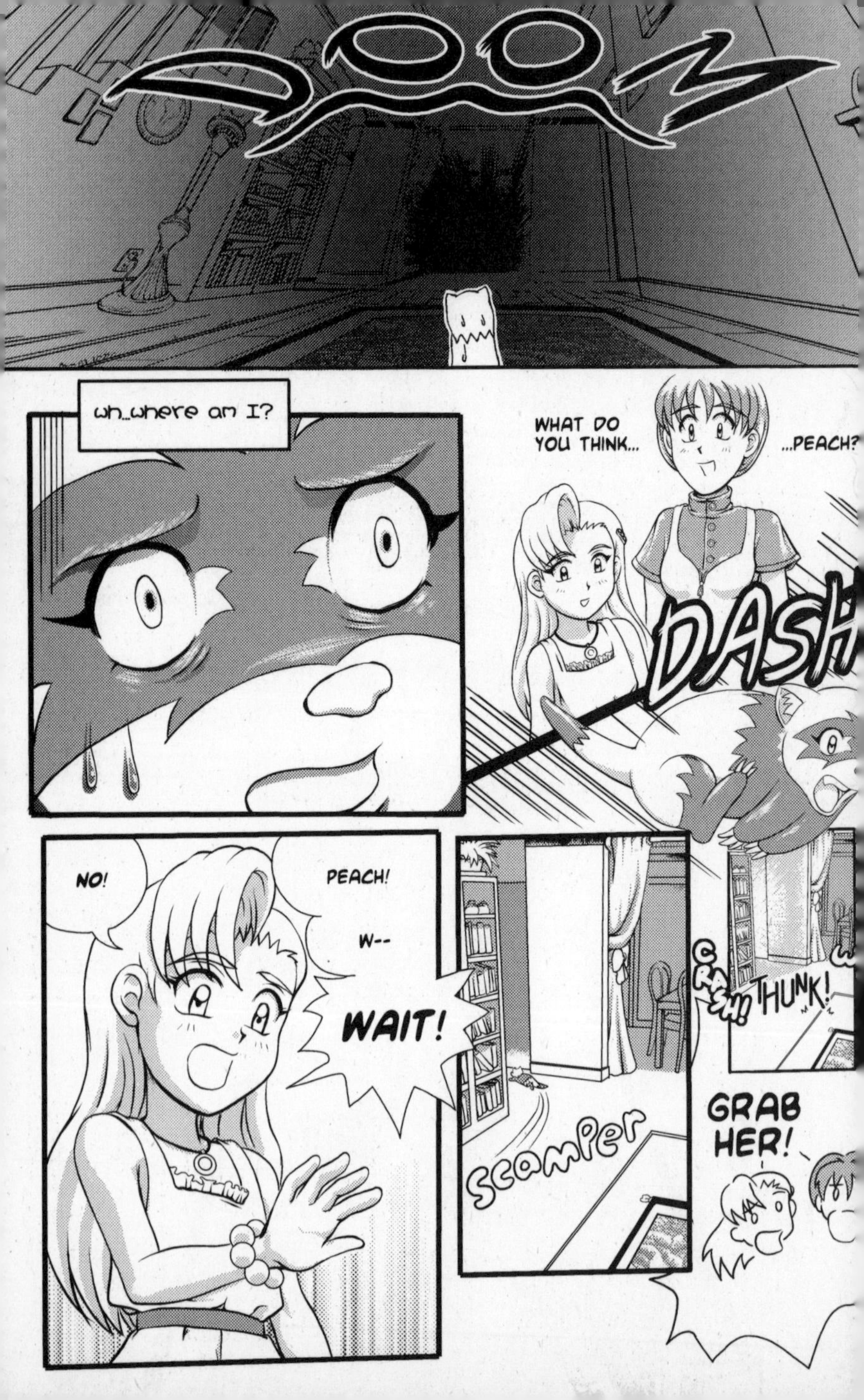
DOOM
wh..where am I?
WHAT DO YOU THINK...
...PEACH?
DASH
NO!
PEACH!
W--
WAIT!
scamper
CRASH!
THUNK!
GRAB HER!

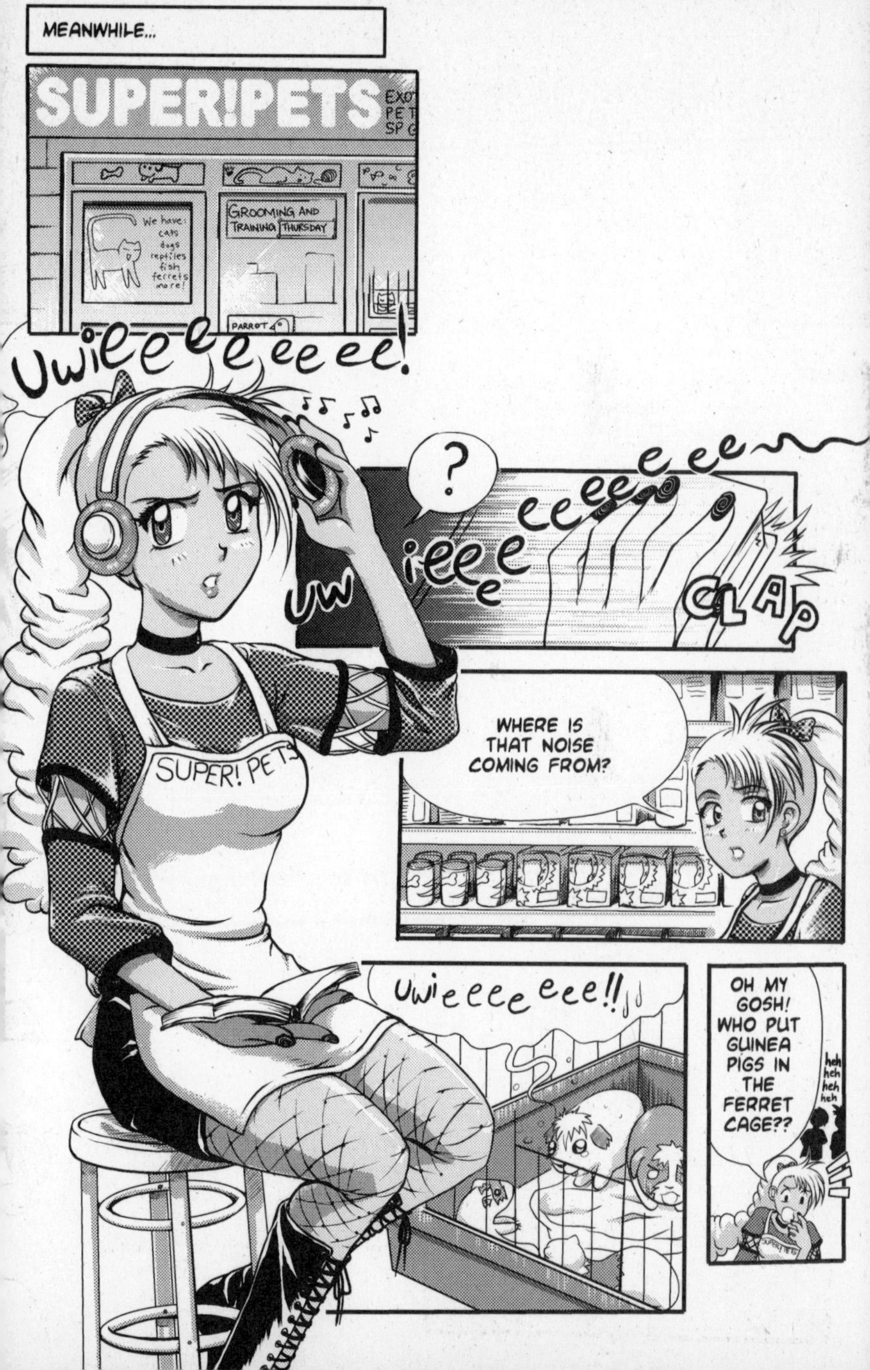
MEANWHILE...
SUPER!PETS
GROOMING AND TRAINING THURSDAY
We have: cats dogs reptiles fish ferrets more!
PARROT
Uwieeeeeeee!
?
Uwieeeeeeeeeee
CLAP
WHERE IS THAT NOISE COMING FROM?
SUPER! PETS
Uwieeeeeee!!
OH MY GOSH! WHO PUT GUINEA PIGS IN THE FERRET CAGE??
heh heh heh heh

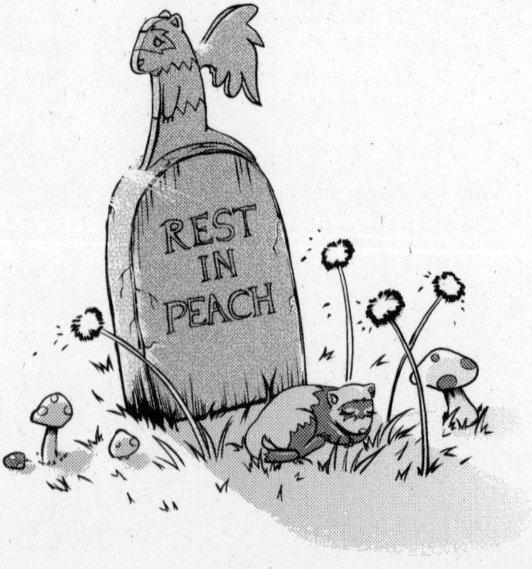
REST
IN
PEACH

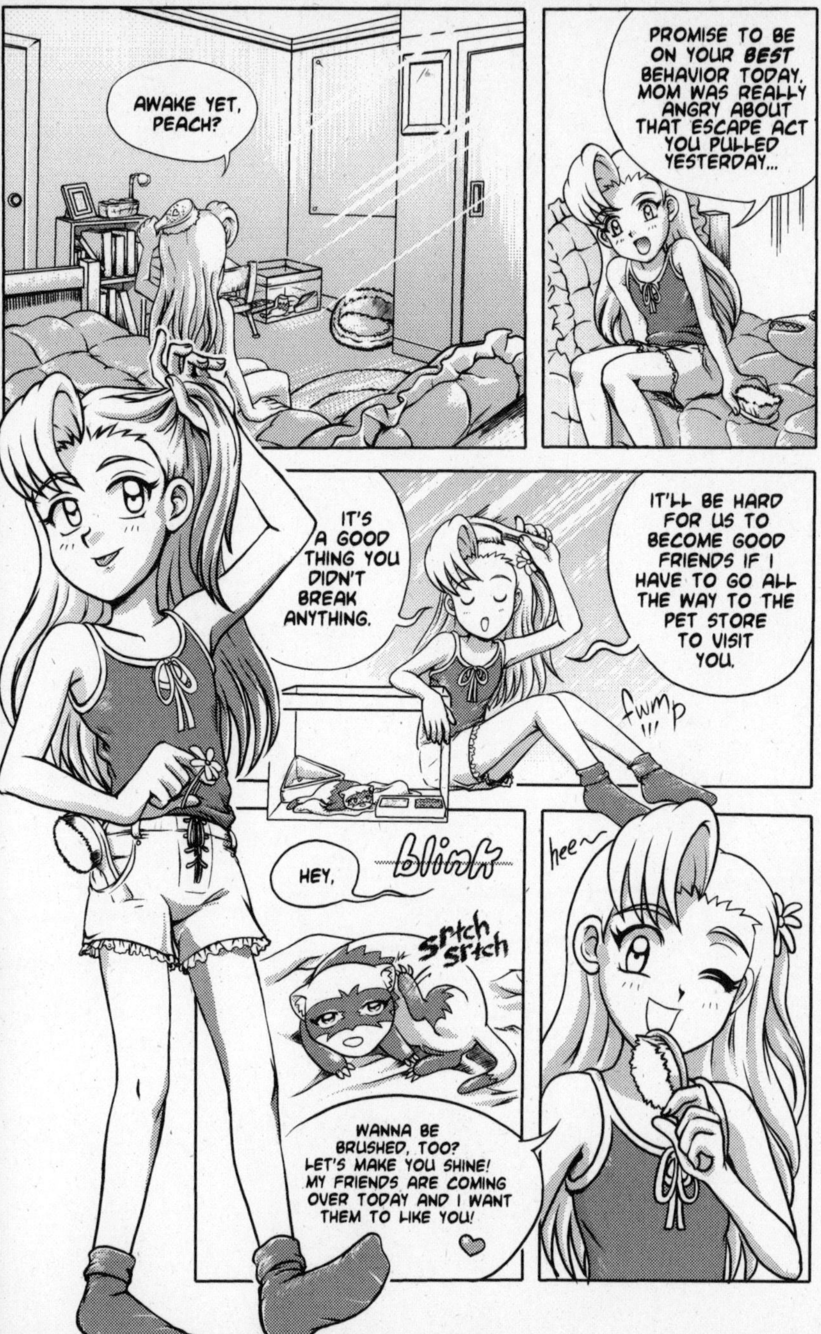
AWAKE YET, PEACH?
PROMISE TO BE ON YOUR BEST BEHAVIOR TODAY. MOM WAS REALLY ANGRY ABOUT THAT ESCAPE ACT YOU PULLED YESTERDAY...
IT'S A GOOD THING YOU DIDN'T BREAK ANYTHING.
IT'LL BE HARD FOR US TO BECOME GOOD FRIENDS IF I HAVE TO GO ALL THE WAY TO THE PET STORE TO VISIT YOU.
fwmp !!!
HEY,
blink
srtch srtch
hee~
WANNA BE BRUSHED, TOO? LET'S MAKE YOU SHINE! MY FRIENDS ARE COMING OVER TODAY AND I WANT THEM TO LIKE YOU!

Chapter 2
R.I.P. van Ferret

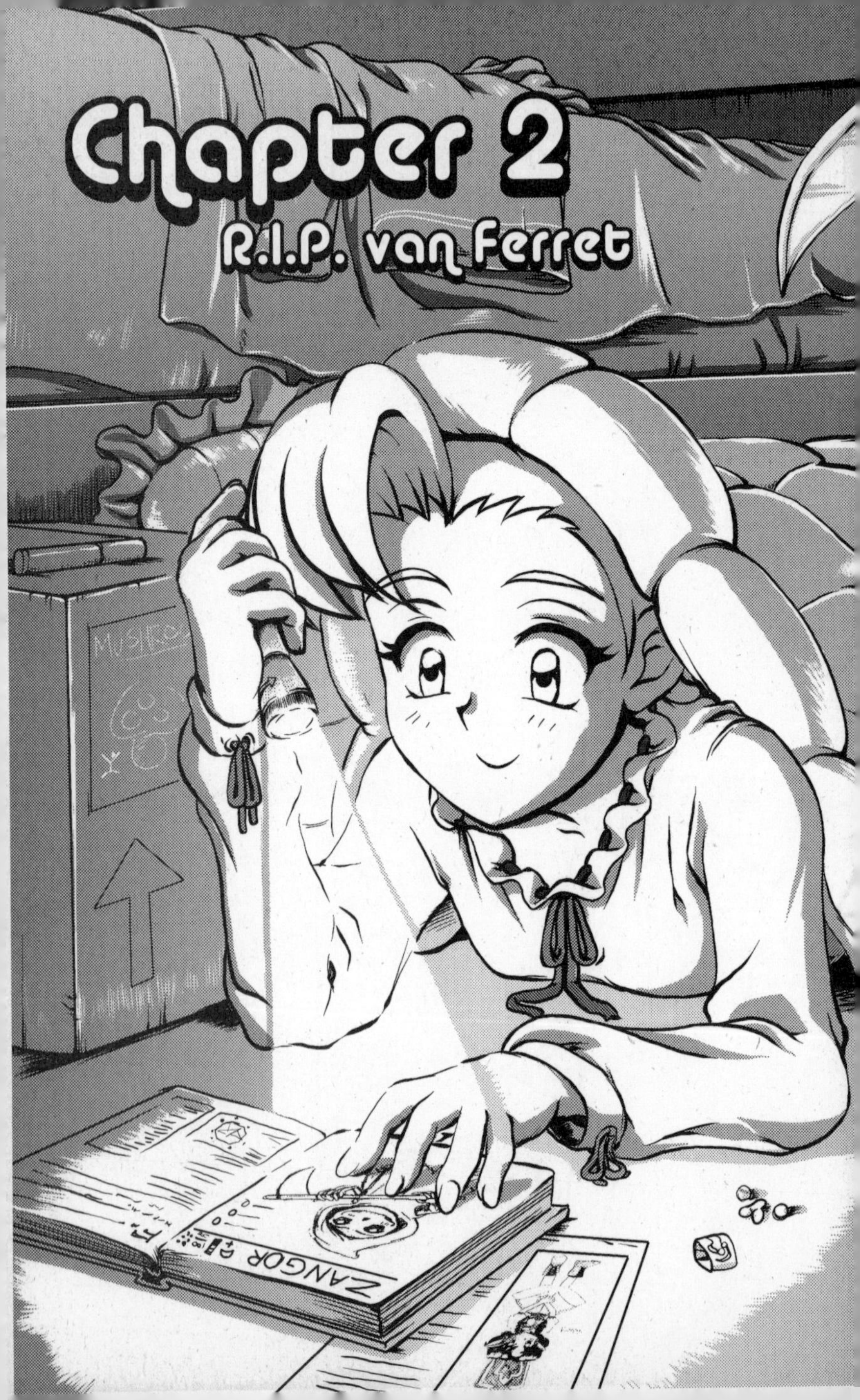
ZANGOR

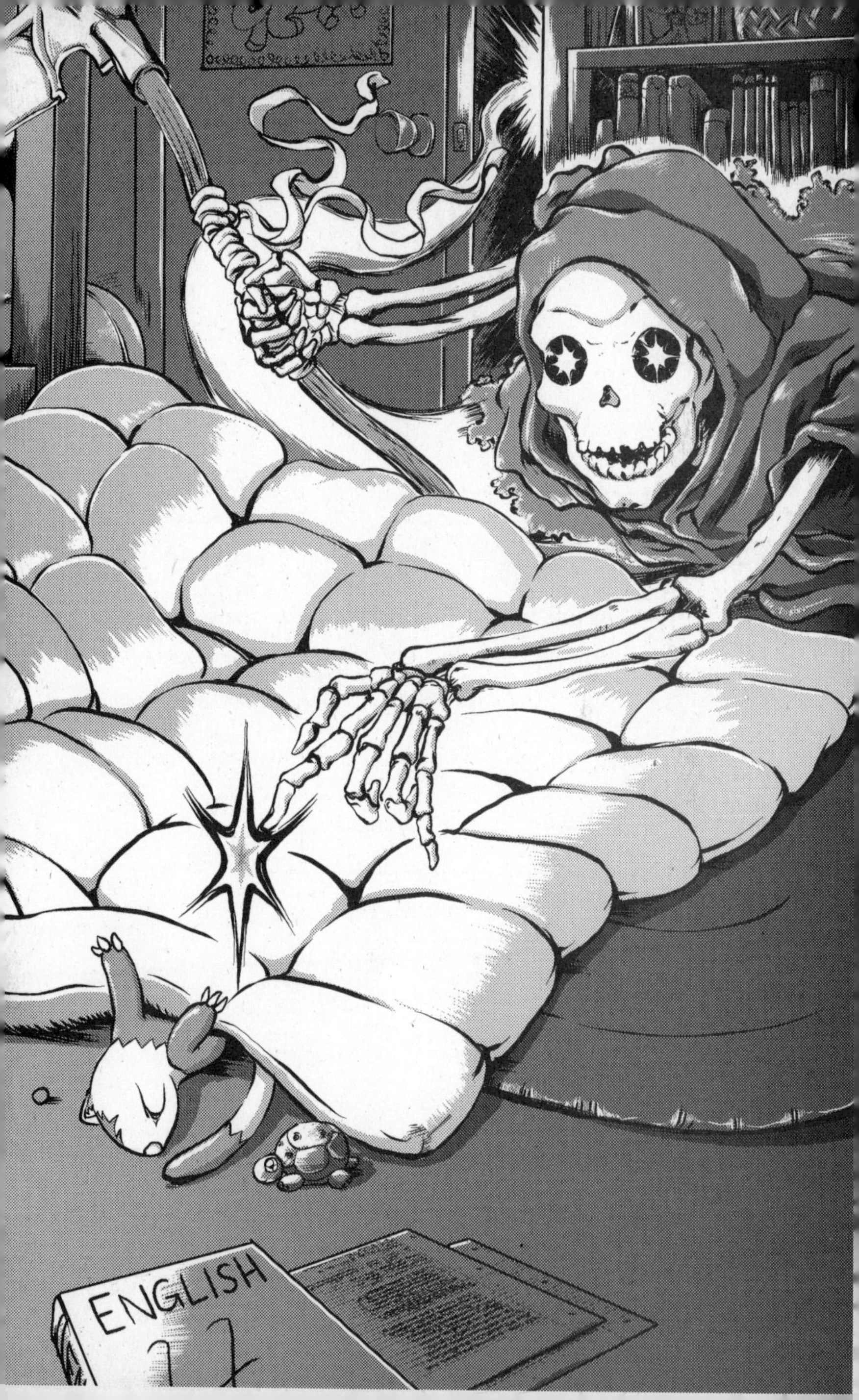
ENGLISH

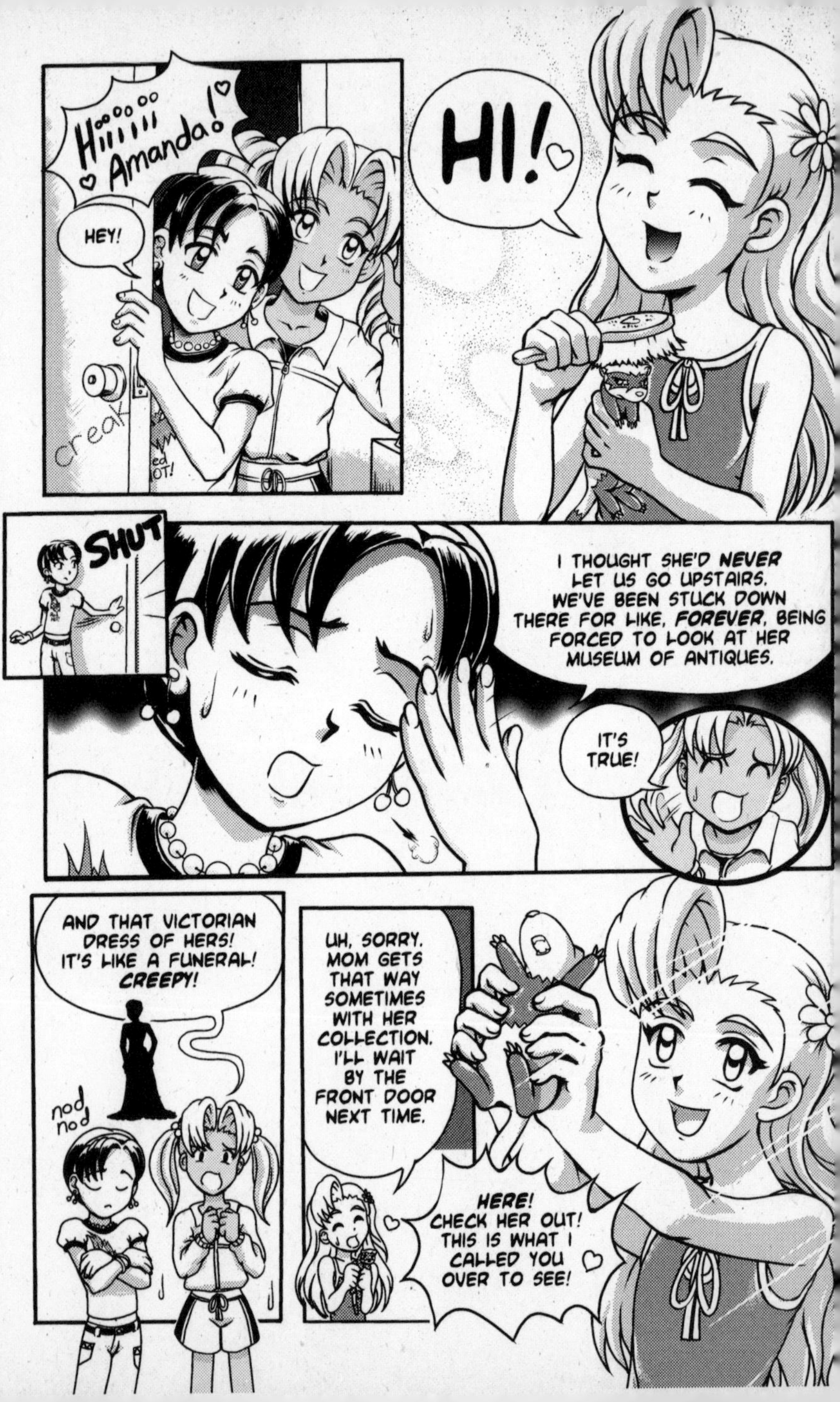

Hiiiiii Amanda!
HEY!
creak
HI!
SHUT
I THOUGHT SHE'D NEVER LET US GO UPSTAIRS. WE'VE BEEN STUCK DOWN THERE FOR LIKE, FOREVER, BEING FORCED TO LOOK AT HER MUSEUM OF ANTIQUES.
IT'S TRUE!
AND THAT VICTORIAN DRESS OF HERS! IT'S LIKE A FUNERAL! CREEPY!
nod nod
UH, SORRY. MOM GETS THAT WAY SOMETIMES WITH HER COLLECTION. I'LL WAIT BY THE FRONT DOOR NEXT TIME.
HERE! CHECK HER OUT! THIS IS WHAT I CALLED YOU OVER TO SEE!

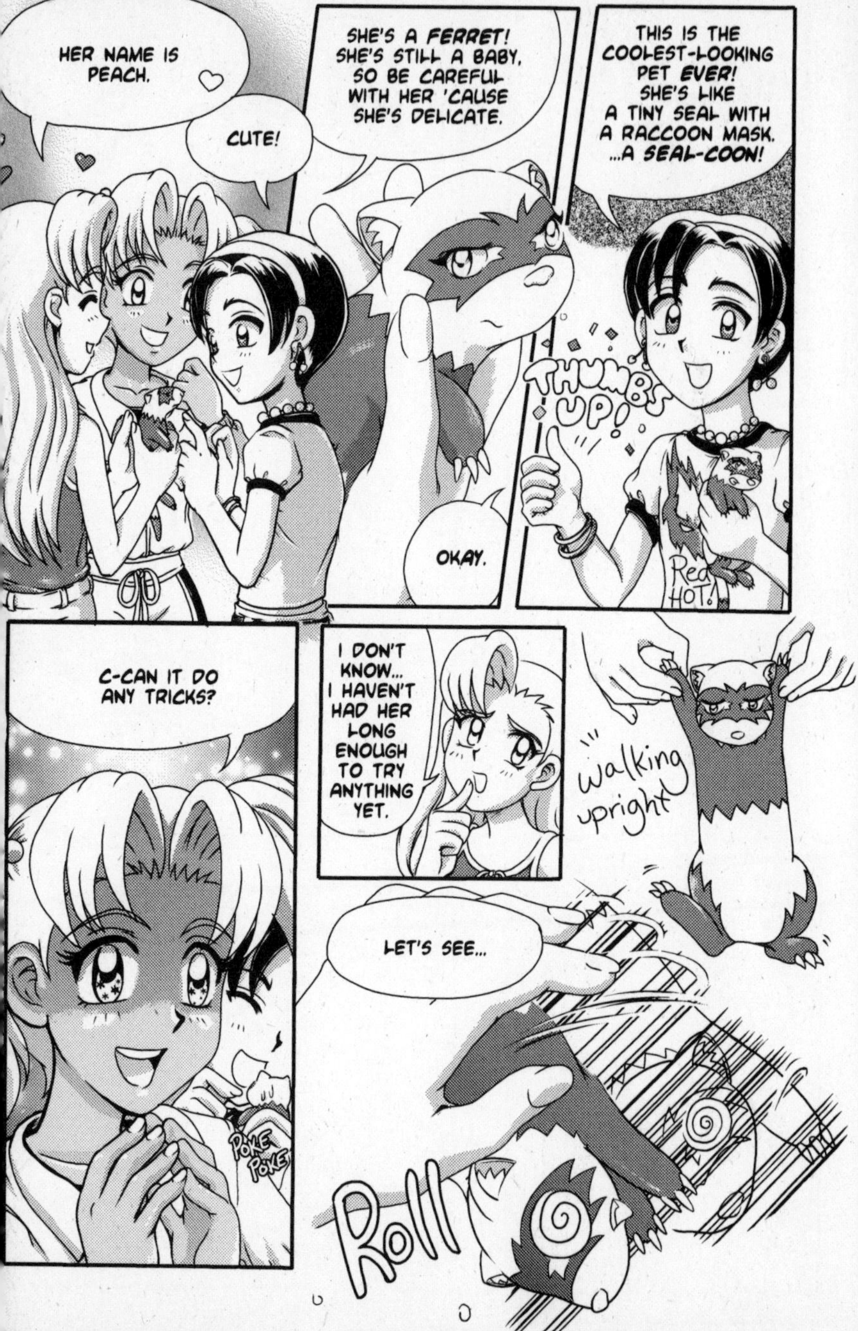
HER NAME IS PEACH.
CUTE!
SHE'S A FERRET! SHE'S STILL A BABY, SO BE CAREFUL WITH HER 'CAUSE SHE'S DELICATE.
OKAY.
THIS IS THE COOLEST-LOOKING PET EVER! SHE'S LIKE A TINY SEAL WITH A RACCOON MASK. ...A SEAL-COON!
THUMBS UP!
Red HOT!
C-CAN IT DO ANY TRICKS?
POKE POKE
I DON'T KNOW... I HAVEN'T HAD HER LONG ENOUGH TO TRY ANYTHING YET.
walking upright
LET'S SEE...
Roll

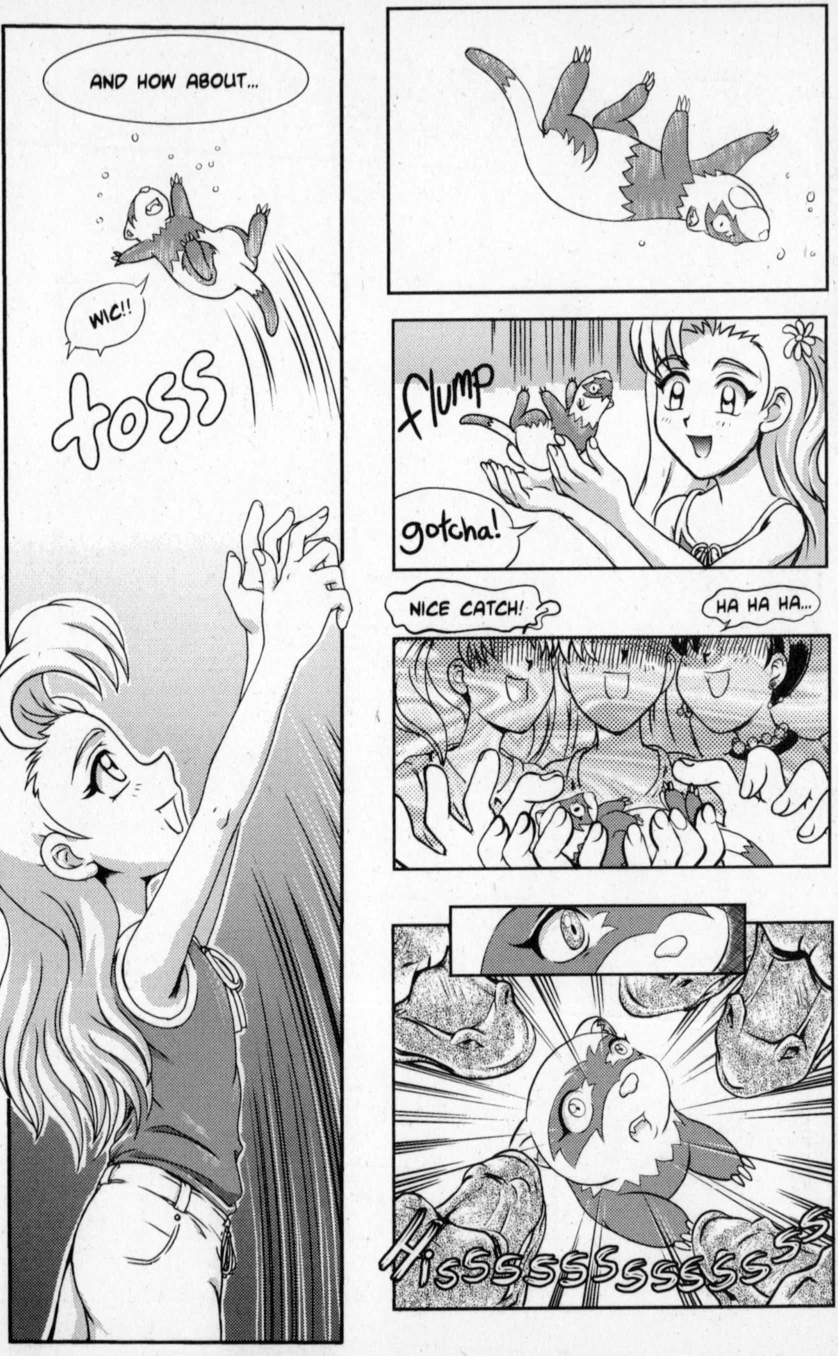
AND HOW ABOUT...
WIC!!
toss
flump
gotcha!
NICE CATCH!
HA HA HA...
HiSSSSSSSSSSSSSS

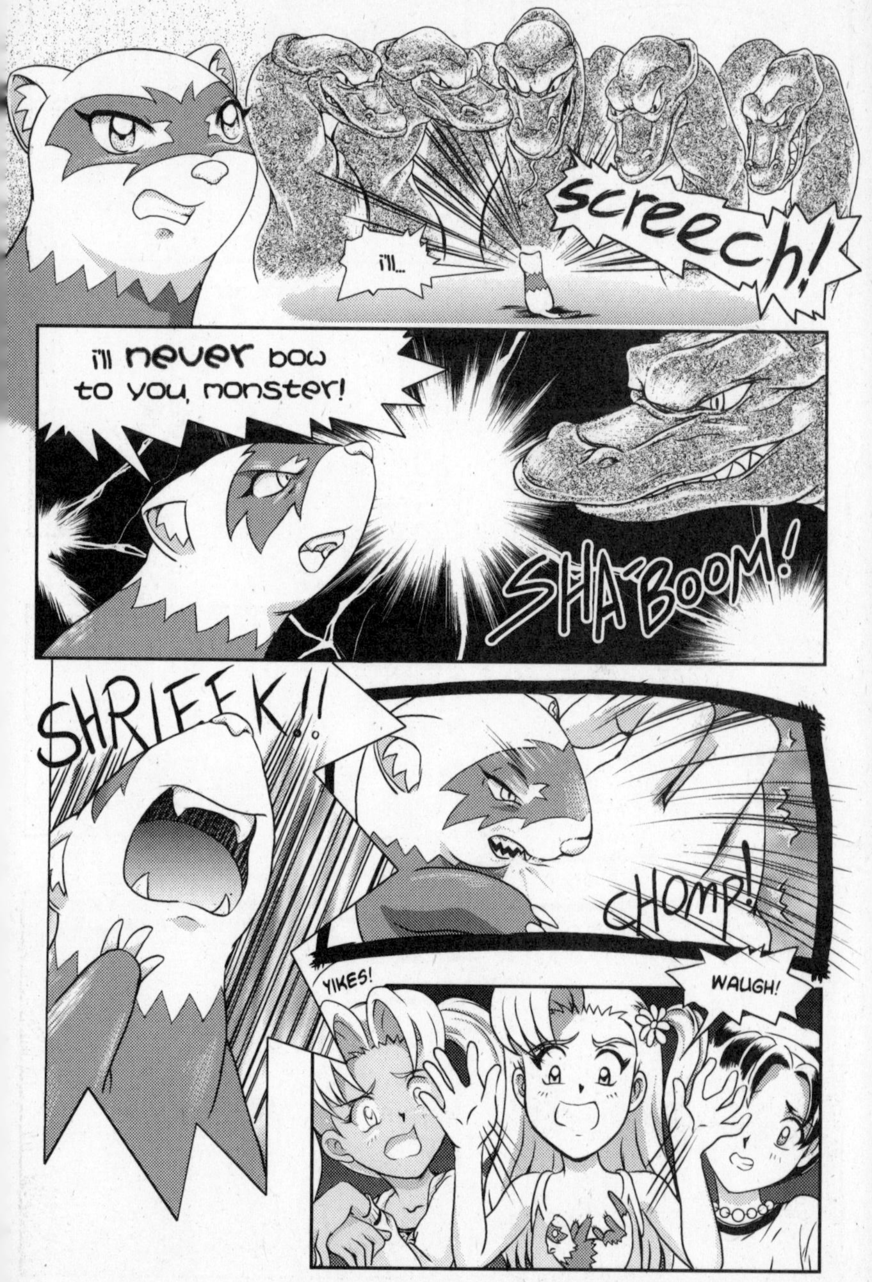

i'll...
screech!
i'll never bow to you, monster!
SHA-BOOM!
SHRIEEK!!
CHOMP!
YIKES!
WAUGH!

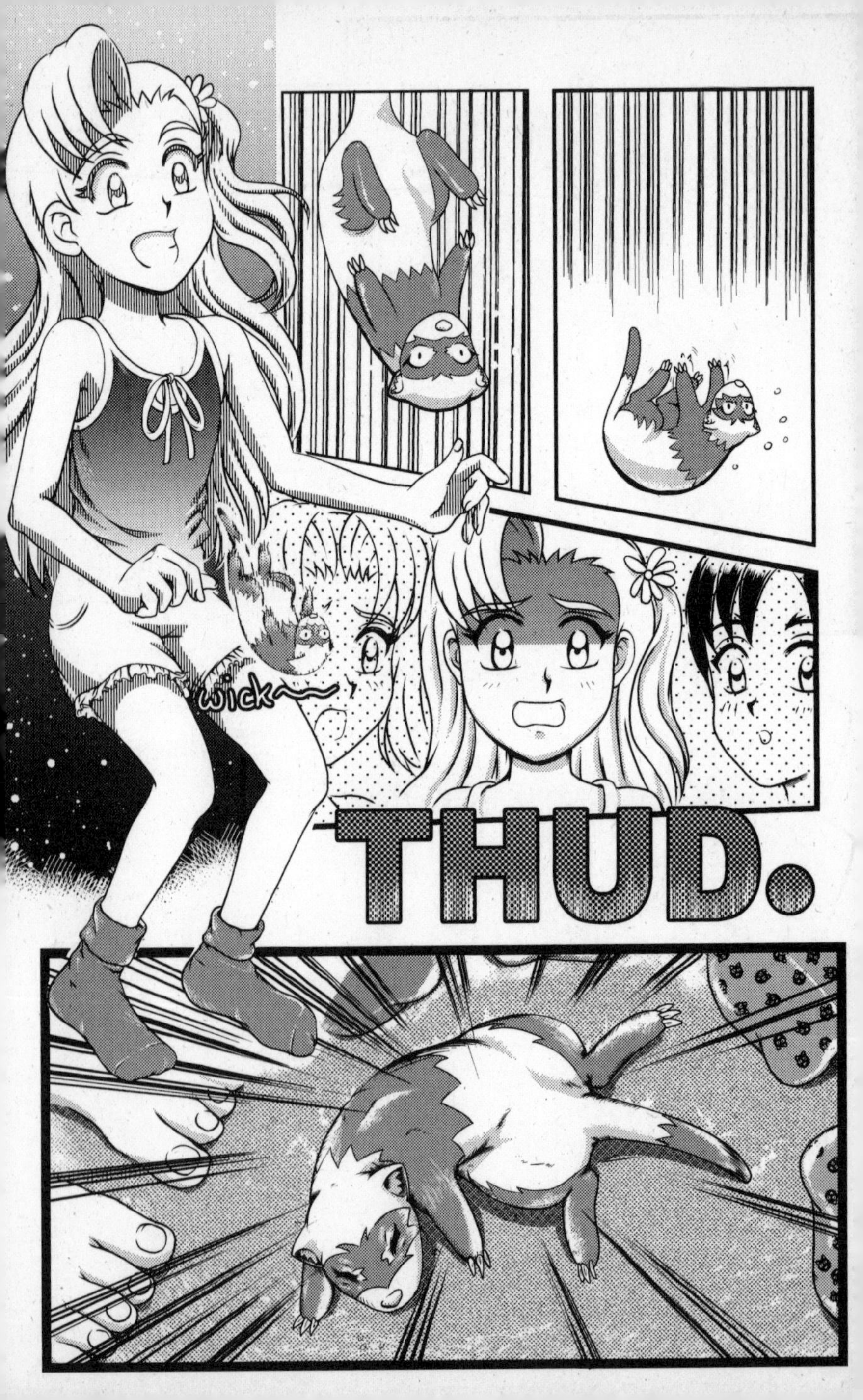
wick~~
THUD.

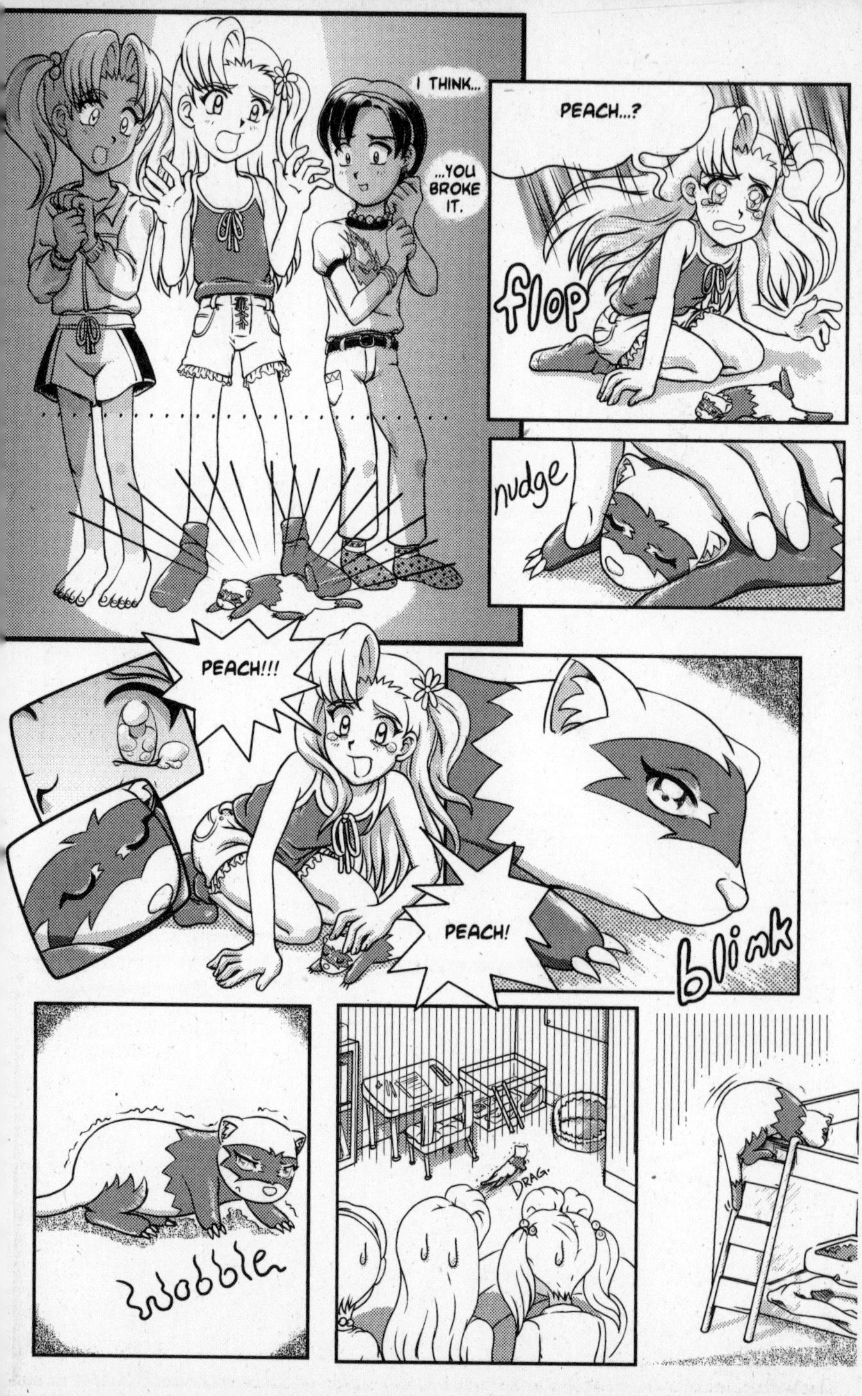
I THINK...
...YOU BROKE IT.
PEACH...?
flop
nudge
PEACH!!!
PEACH!
blink
wobble
DRAG.

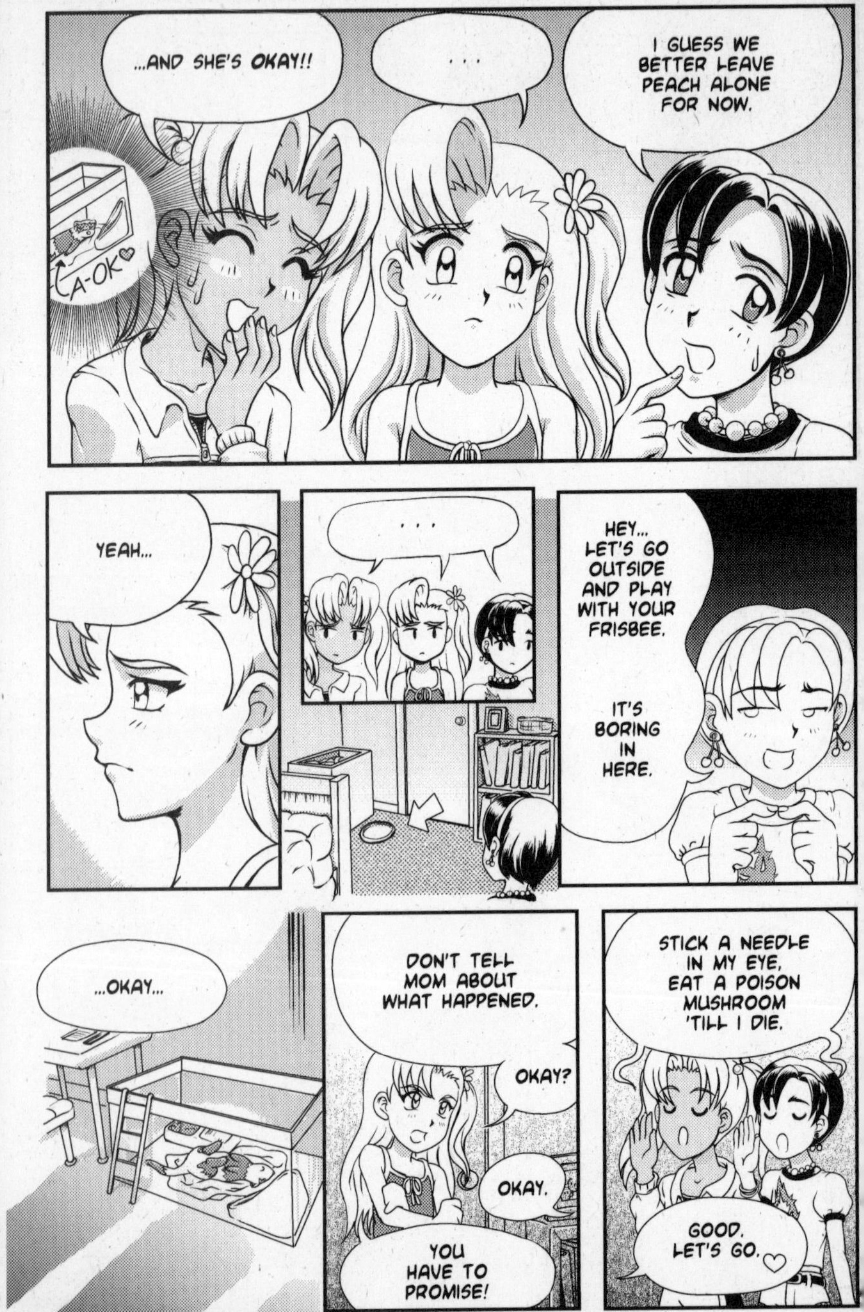

...AND SHE'S **OKAY**!!
A-OK
...
I GUESS WE BETTER LEAVE PEACH ALONE FOR NOW.
YEAH...
...
HEY... LET'S GO OUTSIDE AND PLAY WITH YOUR FRISBEE.
IT'S BORING IN HERE.
...OKAY...
DON'T TELL MOM ABOUT WHAT HAPPENED.
OKAY?
OKAY.
YOU HAVE TO PROMISE!
STICK A NEEDLE IN MY EYE, EAT A POISON MUSHROOM 'TILL I DIE.
GOOD. LET'S GO.

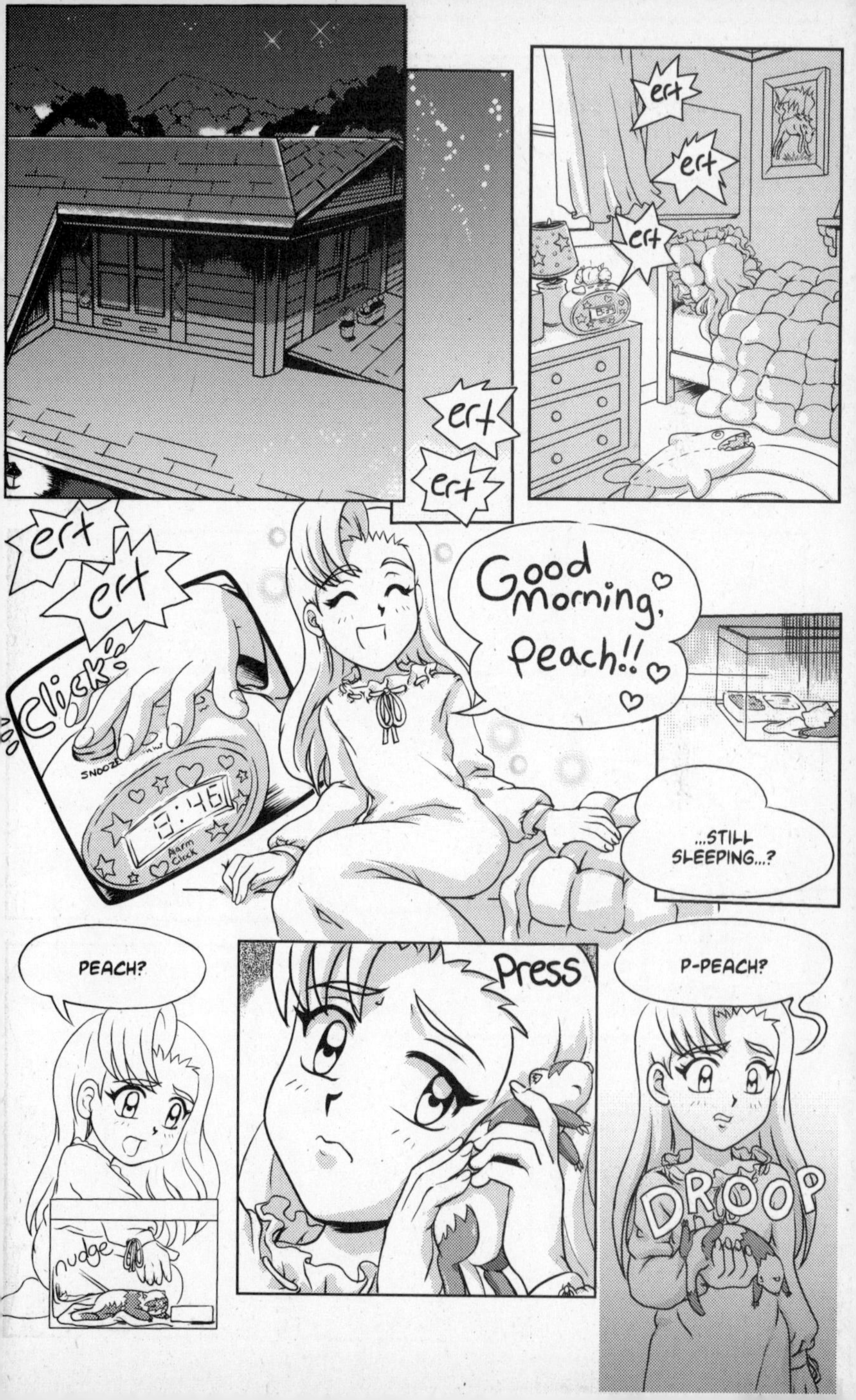
ert
ert
ert
ert
ert
ert
ert
Click
SNOOZE
Alarm Clock
Good morning, peach!!
...STILL SLEEPING...?
PEACH?
nudge
Press
P-PEACH?
DROOP

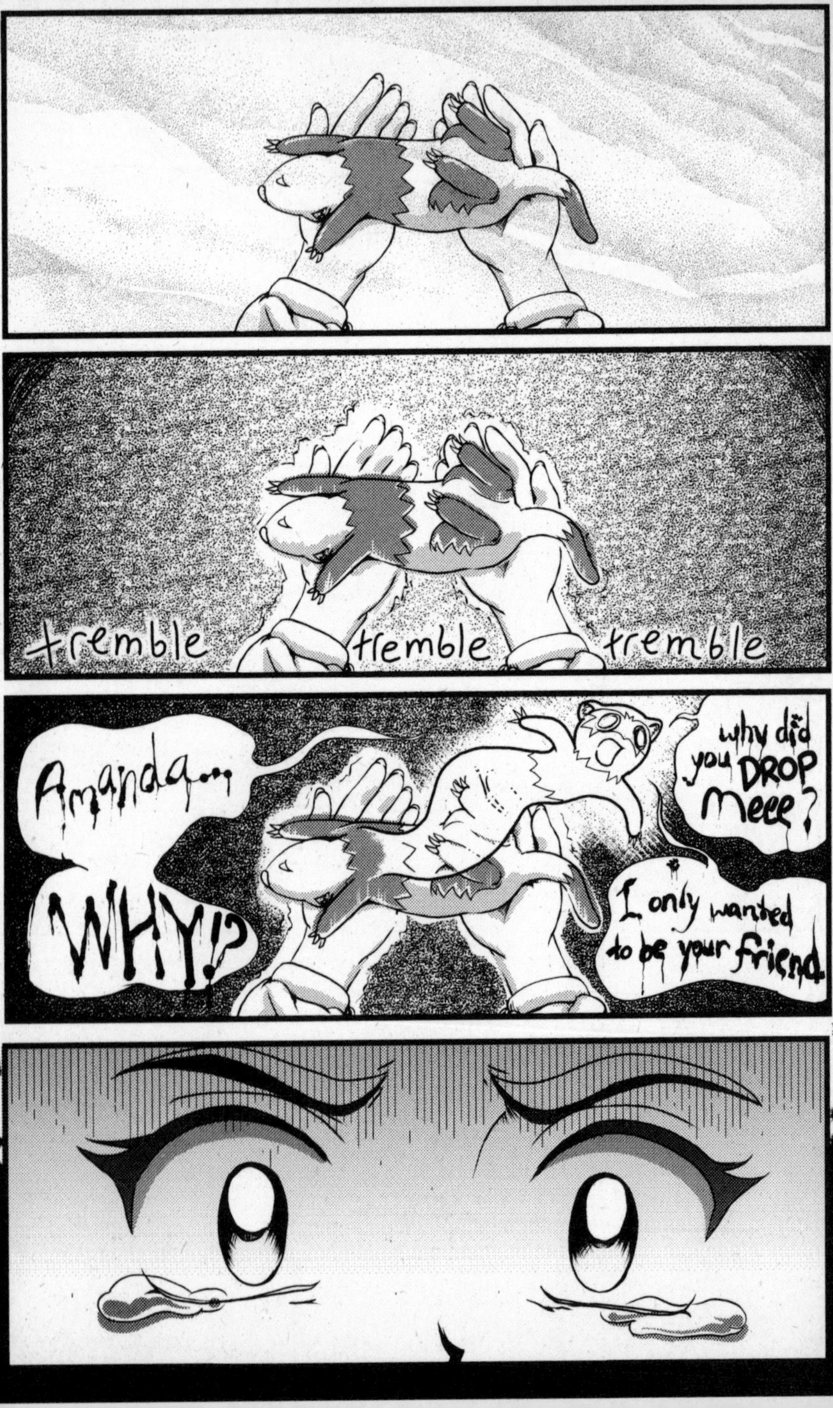

tremble
tremble
tremble
Amanda...
WHY!?
why did you DROP meee?
I only wanted to be your friend.

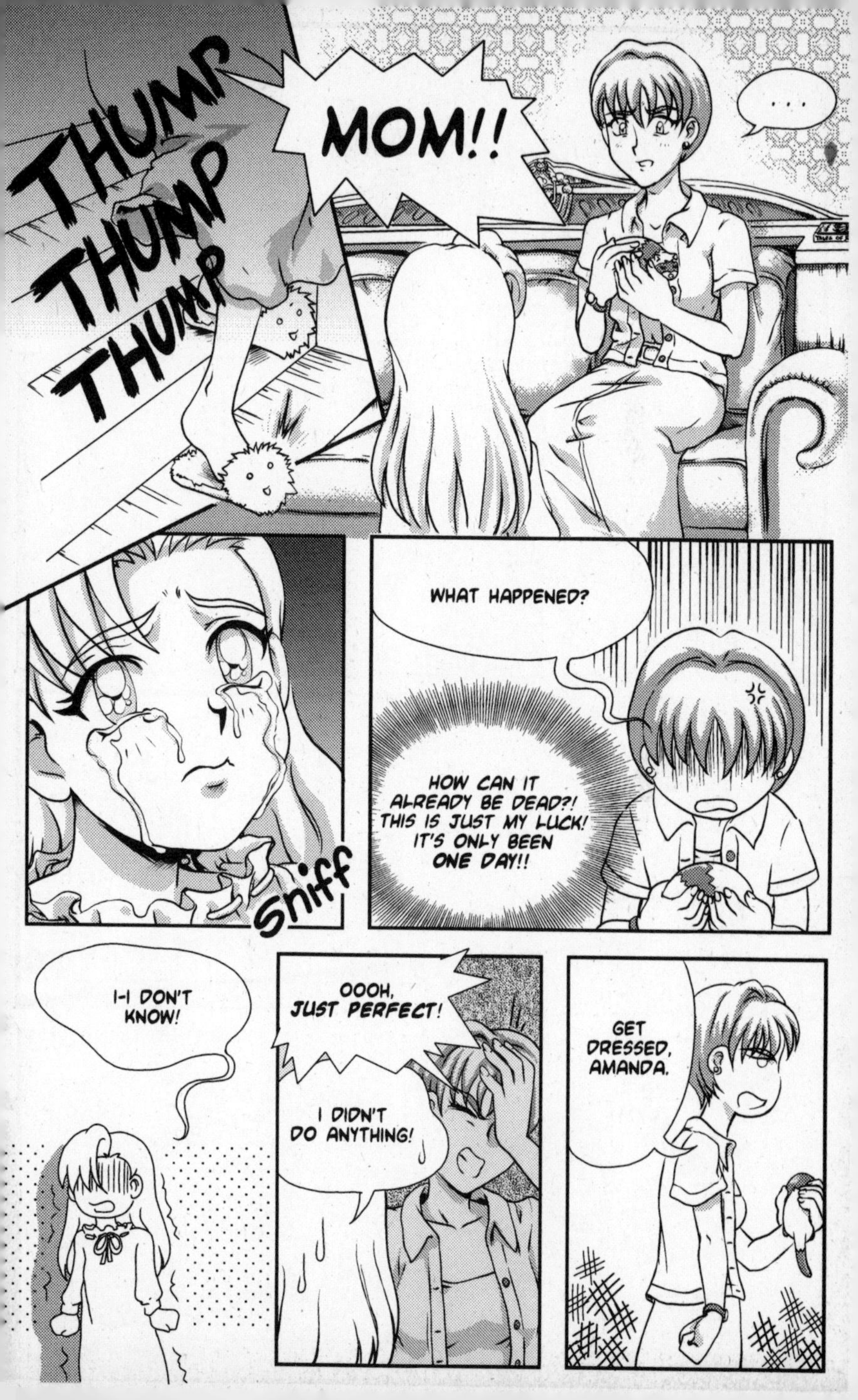
THUMP THUMP THUMP THUMP
MOM!!
...
Sniff
WHAT HAPPENED?
HOW CAN IT ALREADY BE DEAD?! THIS IS JUST MY LUCK! IT'S ONLY BEEN ONE DAY!!
I-I DON'T KNOW!
OOOH, JUST PERFECT!
I DIDN'T DO ANYTHING!
GET DRESSED, AMANDA.

MUSHROOM
VALLEY
ANIMAL CLINIC

Walk-ins
WELCOME ♡

I CAN'T PLACE WHERE I'VE SEEN HER BEFORE, BUT SHE LOOKS FAMILIAR.

MOM!! HURRY!

...MEGAN?

MEGAN KELLER?

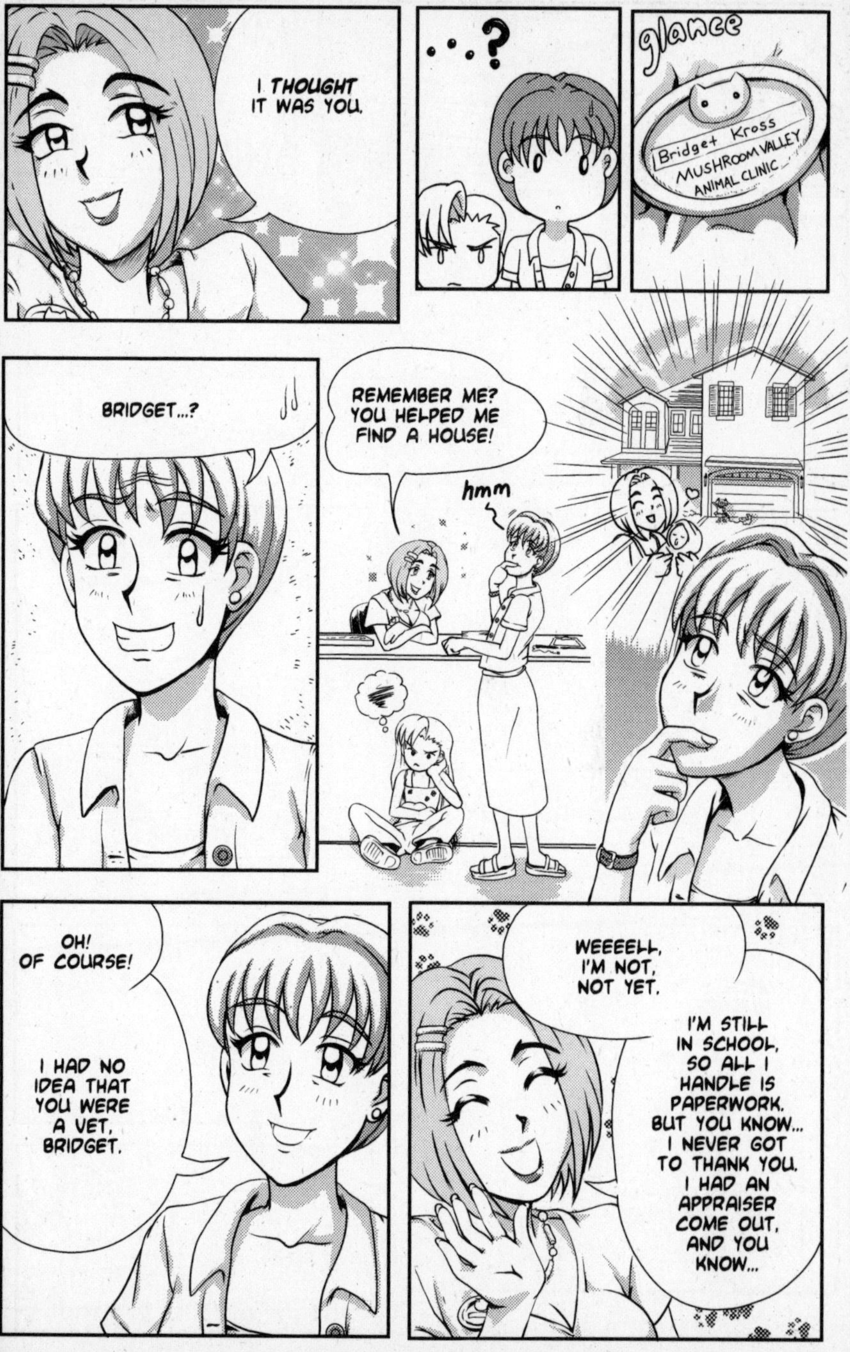
I THOUGHT IT WAS YOU.
...?
glance
Bridget Kross
MUSHROOM VALLEY ANIMAL CLINIC
BRIDGET...?
REMEMBER ME? YOU HELPED ME FIND A HOUSE!
hmm
OH! OF COURSE!
I HAD NO IDEA THAT YOU WERE A VET, BRIDGET.
WEEEELL, I'M NOT, NOT YET.
I'M STILL IN SCHOOL, SO ALL I HANDLE IS PAPERWORK. BUT YOU KNOW... I NEVER GOT TO THANK YOU. I HAD AN APPRAISER COME OUT, AND YOU KNOW...

NO. IT'S THE ONE ON MUSHROOM GROVES DRIVE.

"SUPER!PETS"

REALLY?

THAT'S A NICE SHOP FOR A NON-CHAIN STORE. THEY'RE SMALL, BUT...

WHAT DID YOU THINK OF THE CLERK WHO WORKS THERE?

whisper

THE SUPER!PETS STORE CLERK...?

MOOOOM!!

TUG!

A BIT OUTRAGEOUS, BUT NOT TOO BAD, RIGHT?

W-INK

EH HEH HEH HEH.

PEACH, REMEMBER?

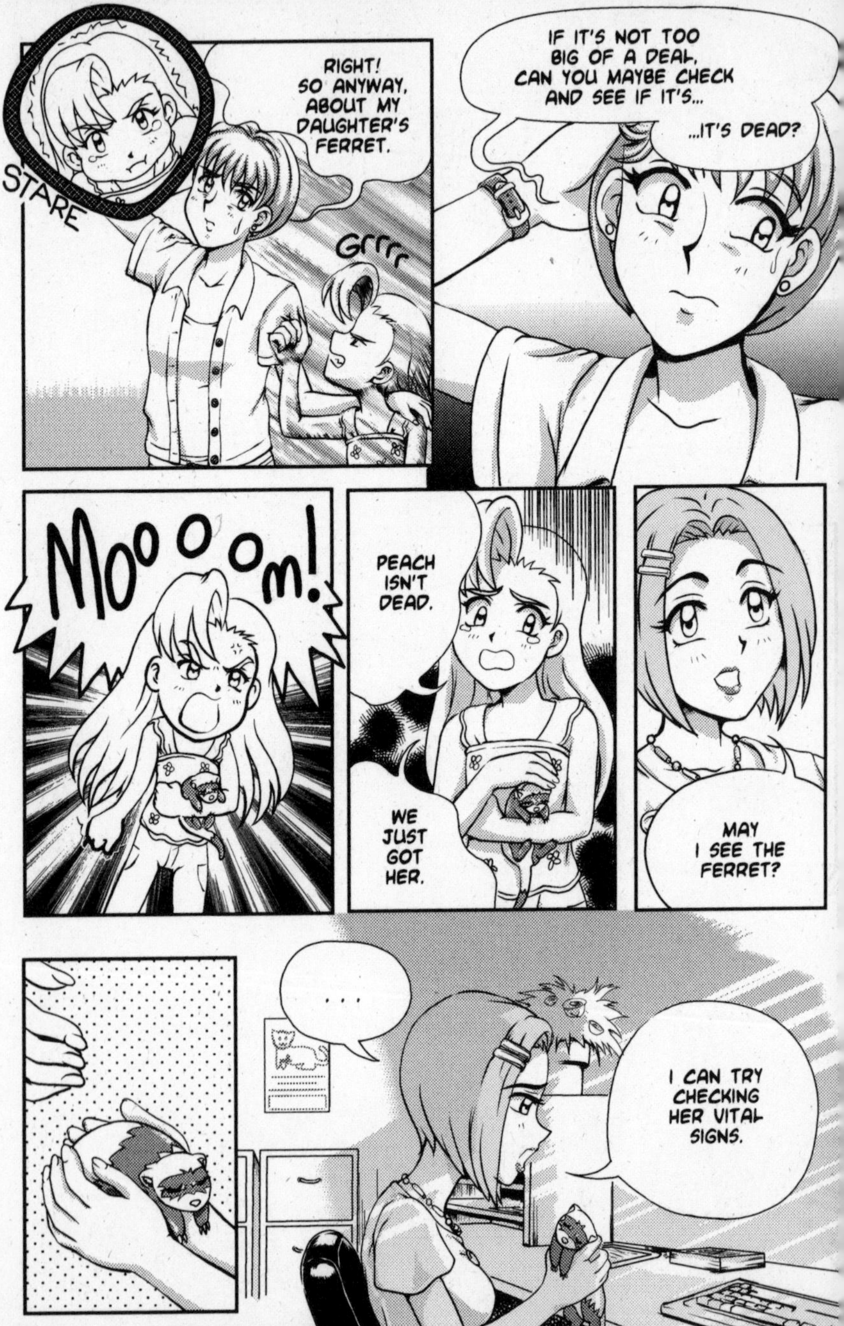
STARE
RIGHT! SO ANYWAY, ABOUT MY DAUGHTER'S FERRET.
Grrrr
IF IT'S NOT TOO BIG OF A DEAL, CAN YOU MAYBE CHECK AND SEE IF IT'S...
...IT'S DEAD?
Moo o om!
PEACH ISN'T DEAD.
WE JUST GOT HER.
MAY I SEE THE FERRET?
. . .
I CAN TRY CHECKING HER VITAL SIGNS.

I...

....

swfff

MURDERER!

...DON'T KNOW!!

Sob!

Sob
Sob

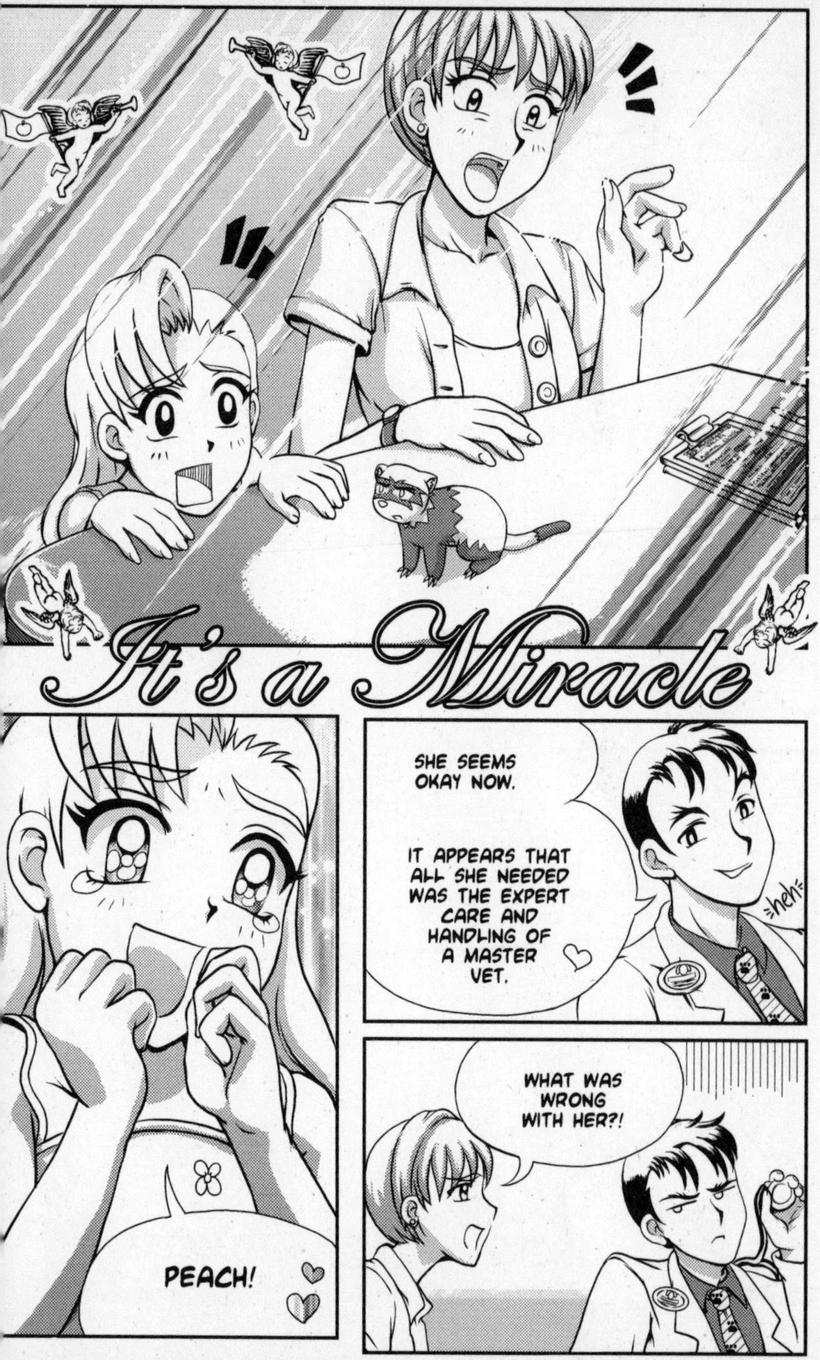
It's a Miracle
PEACH!
SHE SEEMS OKAY NOW.
IT APPEARS THAT ALL SHE NEEDED WAS THE EXPERT CARE AND HANDLING OF A MASTER VET.
heh
WHAT WAS WRONG WITH HER?!

I HAVE NO IDEA.

I JUST DEAL WITH DOGS AND CATS.

WE DON'T GENERALLY DEAL WITH--

WILD AND EXOTIC CREATURES.

IT BIT ME!! THIS THING BETTER HAVE ALL ITS RABIES SHOTS!

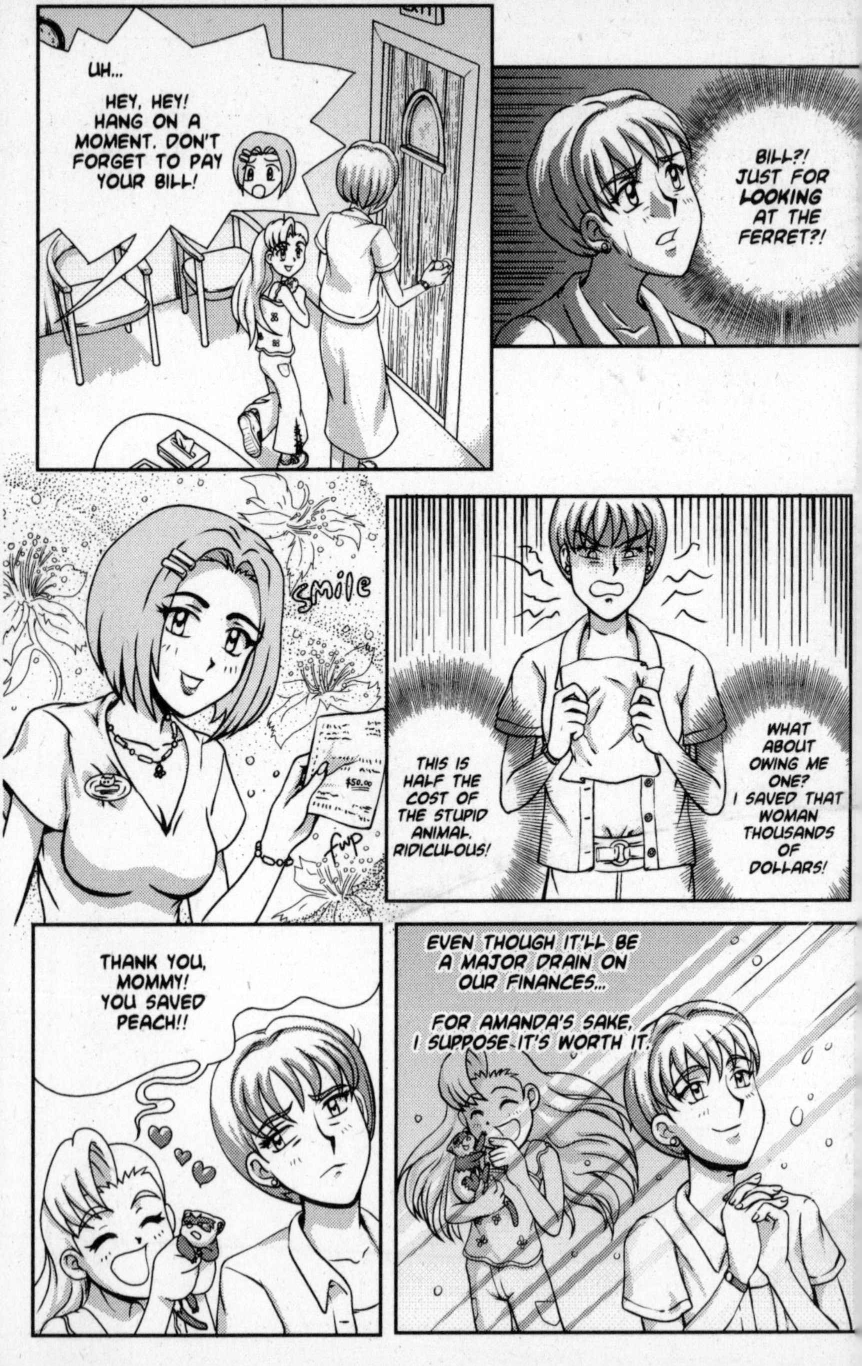
UH...
HEY, HEY! HANG ON A MOMENT. DON'T FORGET TO PAY YOUR BILL!
BILL?! JUST FOR LOOKING AT THE FERRET?!
smile
$50.00
fwp
THIS IS HALF THE COST OF THE STUPID ANIMAL. RIDICULOUS!
WHAT ABOUT OWING ME ONE? I SAVED THAT WOMAN THOUSANDS OF DOLLARS!
THANK YOU, MOMMY! YOU SAVED PEACH!!
EVEN THOUGH IT'LL BE A MAJOR DRAIN ON OUR FINANCES...
FOR AMANDA'S SAKE, I SUPPOSE IT'S WORTH IT.

HONEY... WE NEED TO TALK.

...COMING UP NEXT ON AFTERNOON TOONS...

OKAY...

fwp

fwp

MUSHROOM VALLEY BANK

Account Statement

SUPER!PETS

Fuzzy farm feed ... 35.49

Kitty litter ... 10.99

total 45.98
tax 3.22
49.20

YOUR FERRET.

IT'S PUT SOME STRAIN ON THE FAMILY FINANCES WITH ALL THE EXPENSES IT'S RACKED UP SO FAR.

UH HUH?

CAGE, FOOD, TREATS, TOYS, SUPPLIES, LITTER, THAT VET VISIT...

AMANDA, ARE YOU LISTENING TO ME?!

click

YES, MOOOOM.

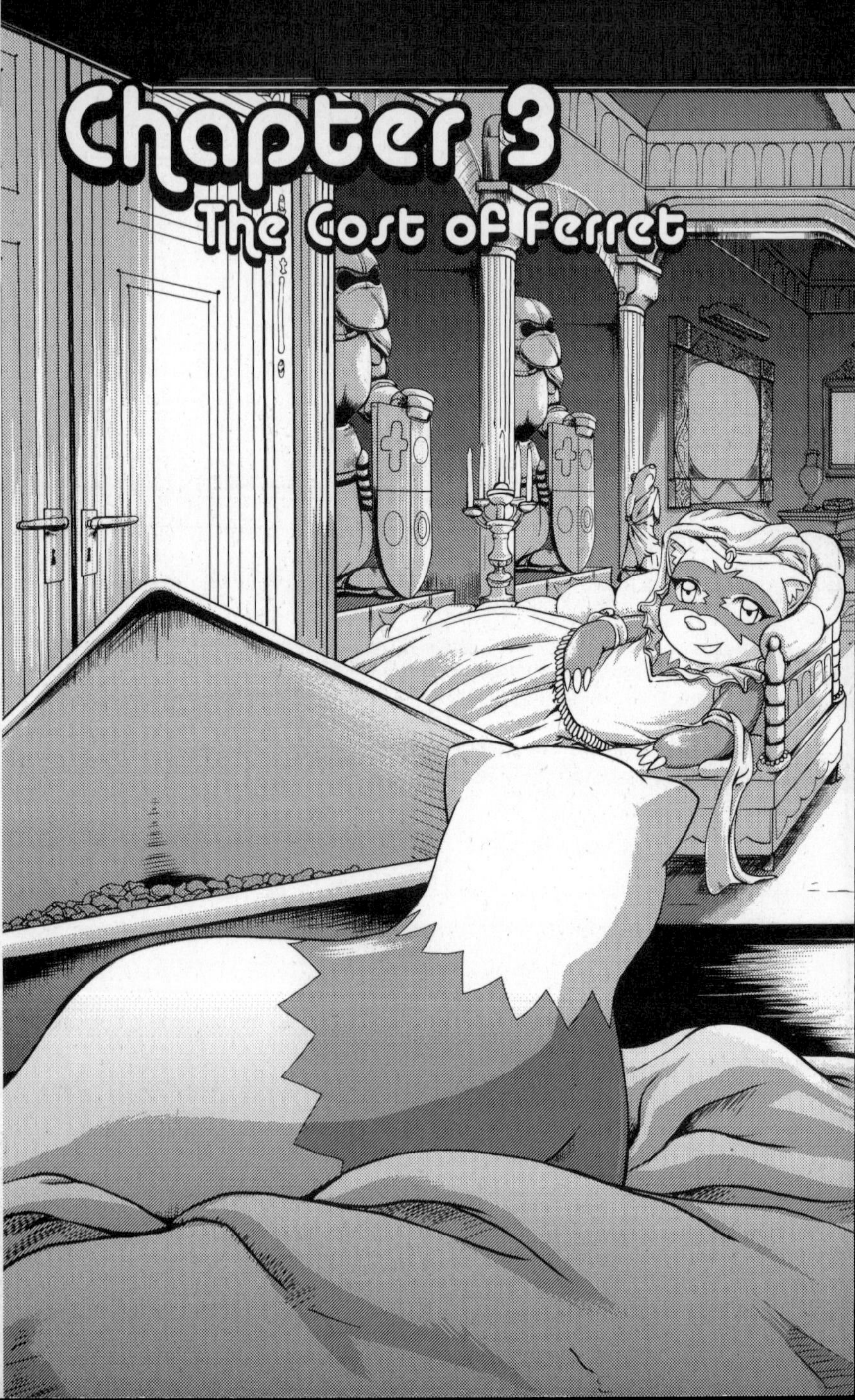
Chapter 3
The Cost of Ferret

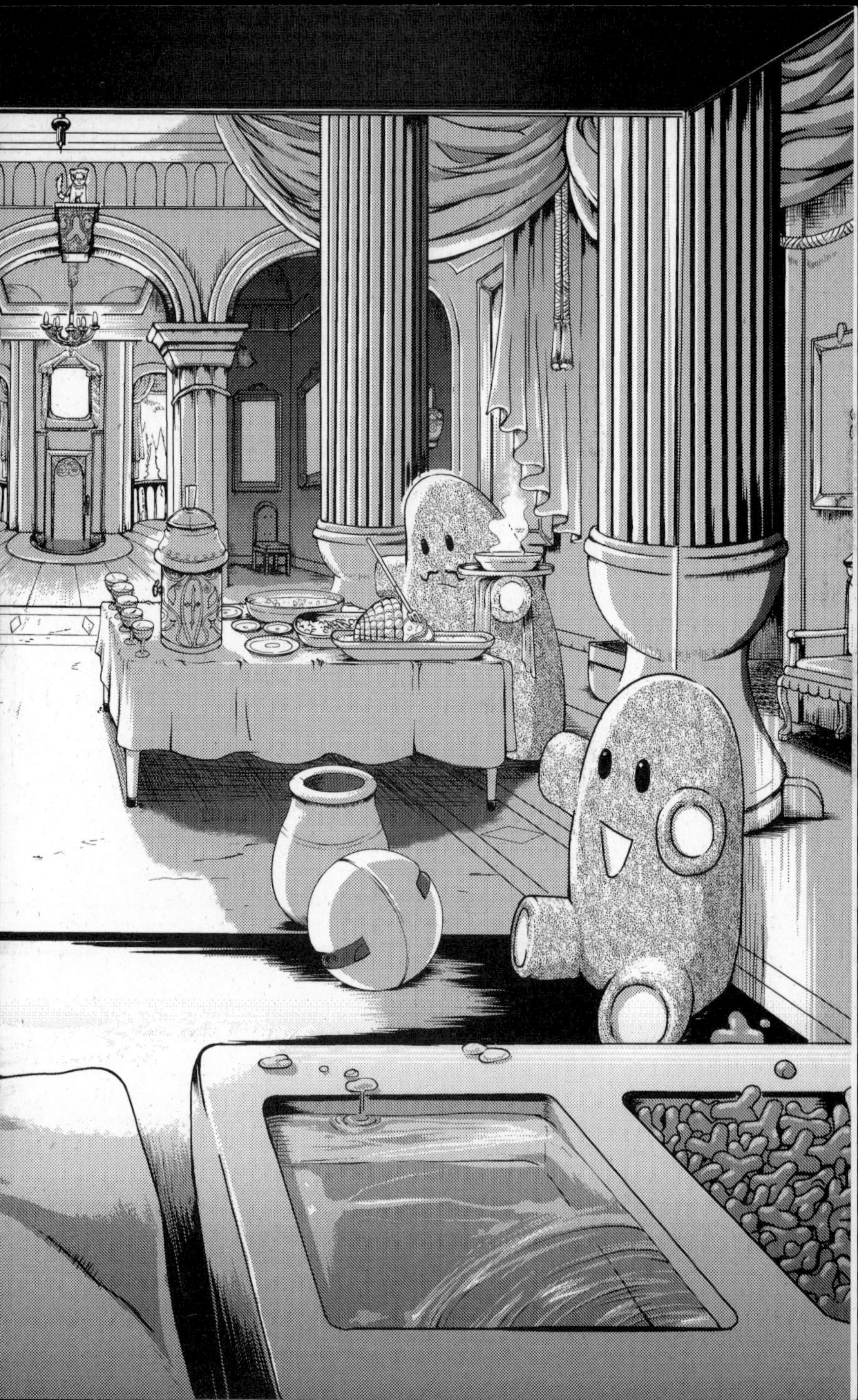

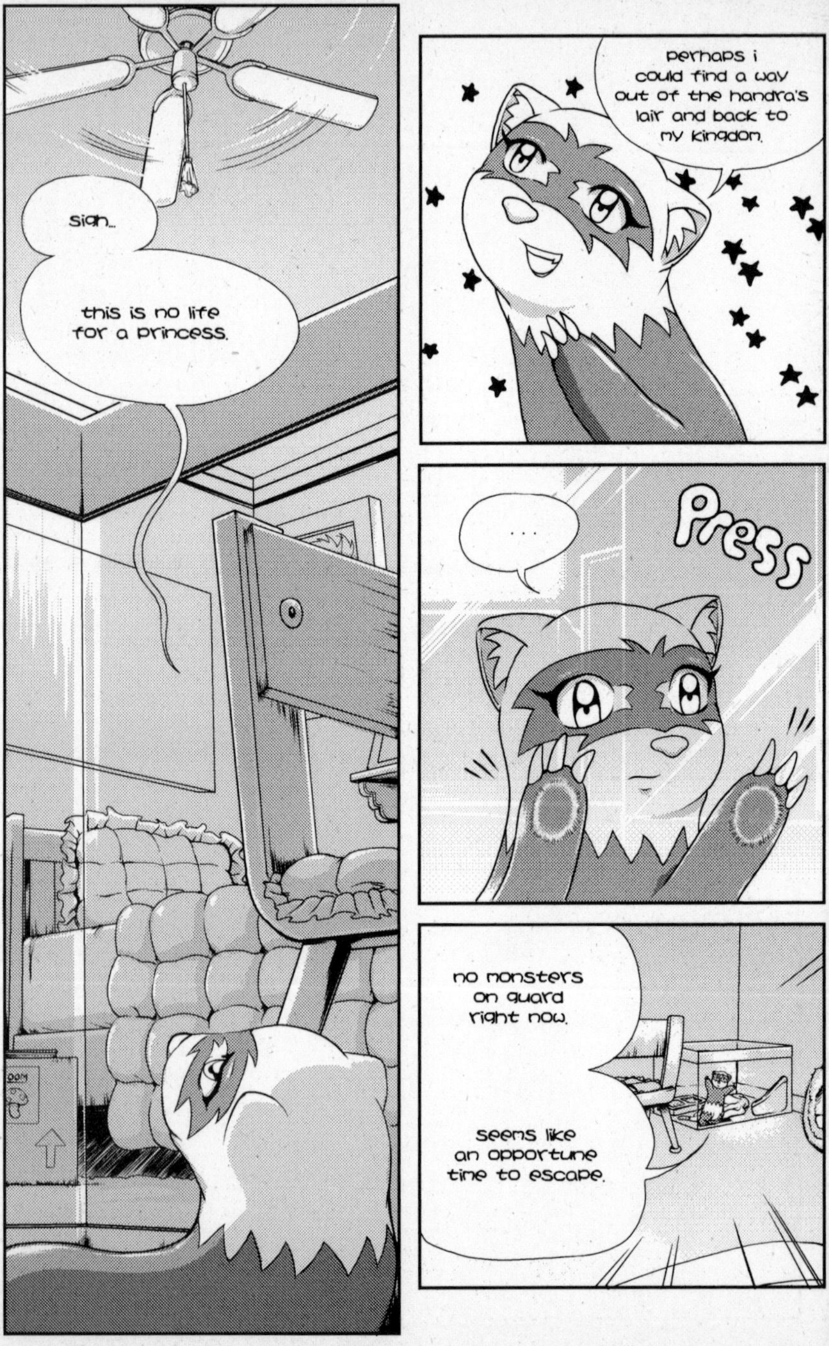
sigh...
this is no life for a princess.
perhaps i could find a way out of the handra's lair and back to my kingdom.
. . .
Press
no monsters on guard right now.
seems like an opportune time to escape.

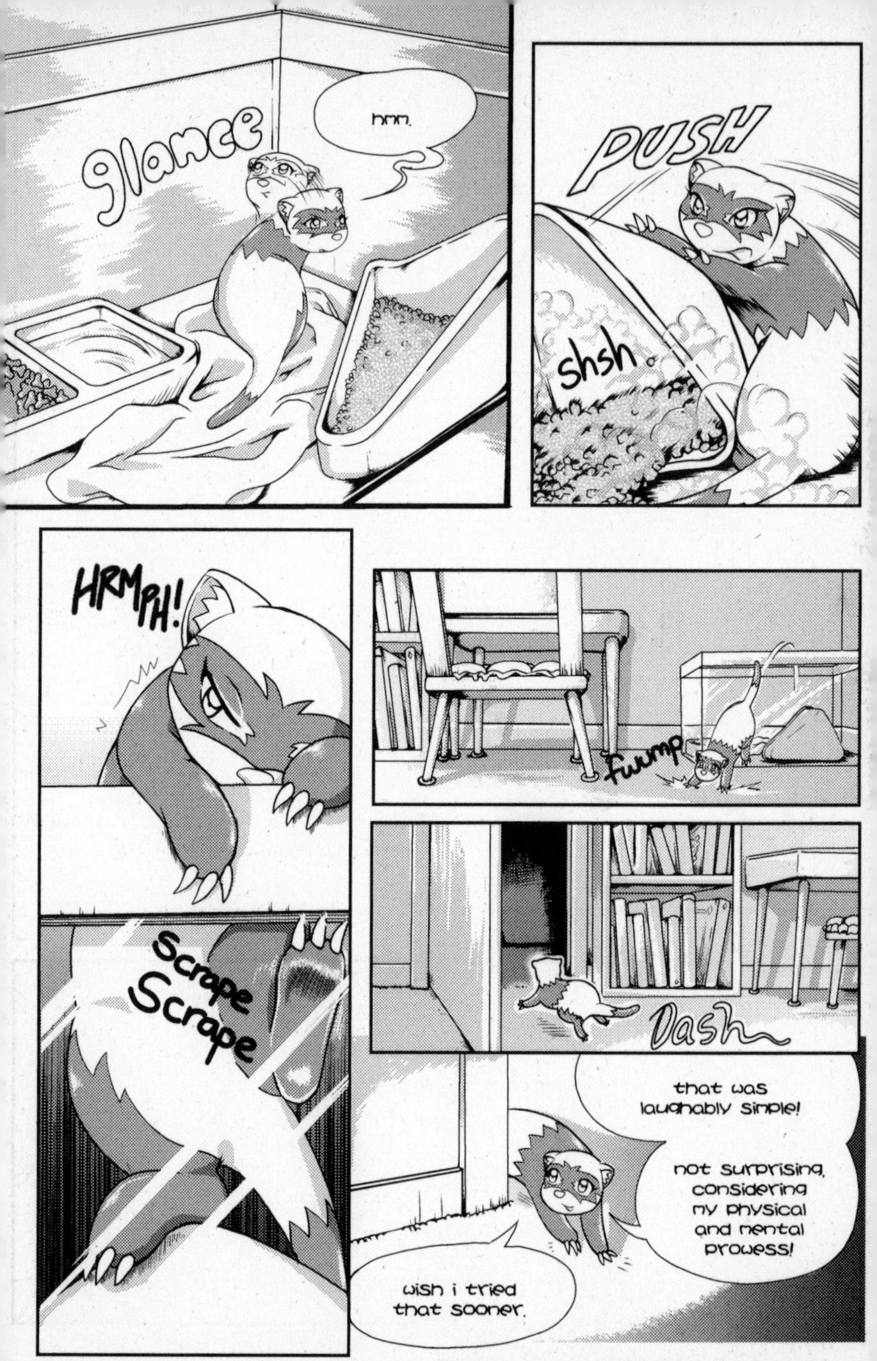
glance
hnn.
PUSH
shsh
HRMPH!
fwump
Scrape
Scrape
Dash
that was laughably simple!
not surprising, considering my physical and mental prowess!
wish i tried that sooner.

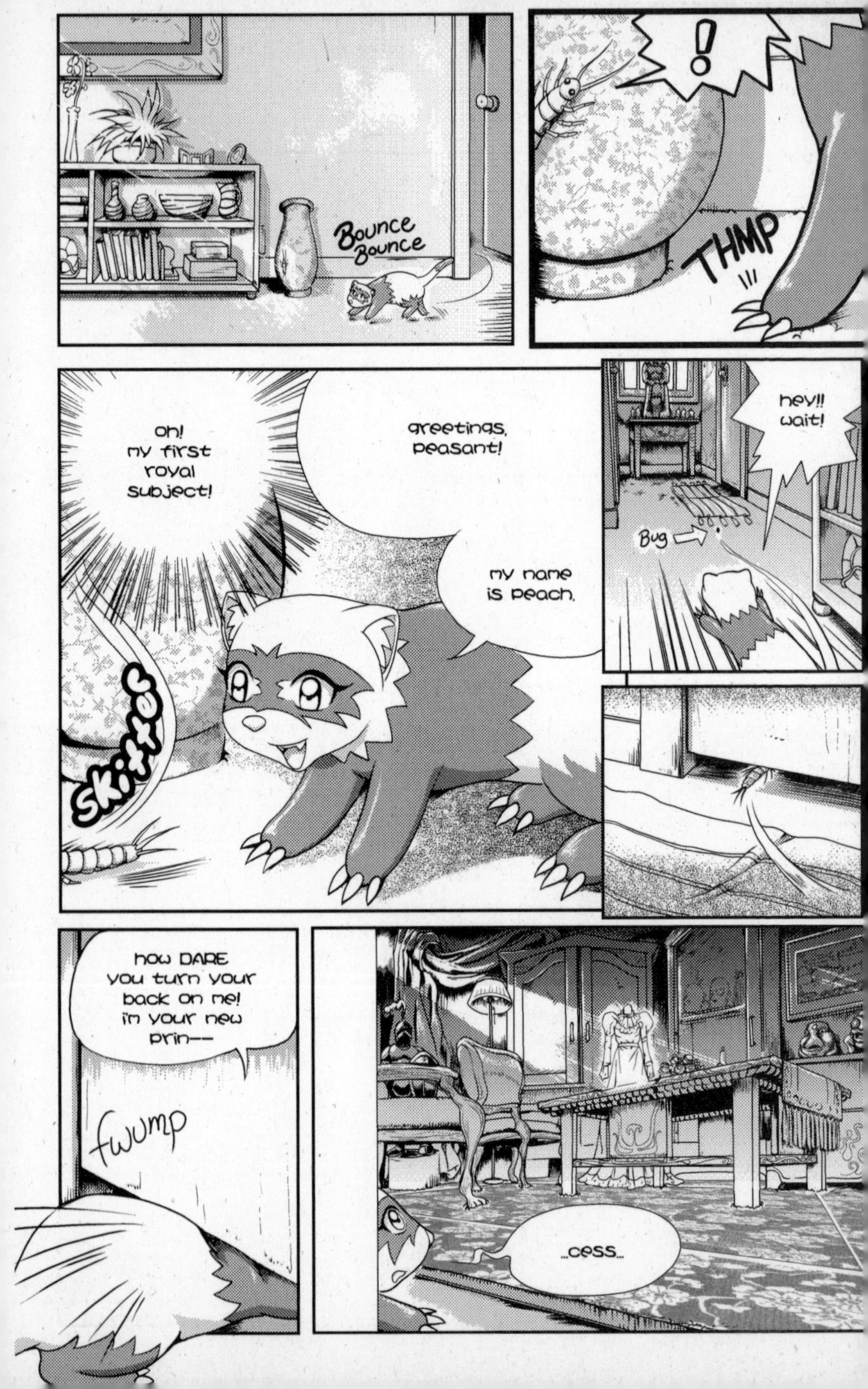
Bounce Bounce
!
THMP
oh! my first royal subject!
greetings, peasant!
my name is peach.
skitter
hey!! wait!
Bug
how DARE you turn your back on me! i'm your new prin--
fwump
...cess...

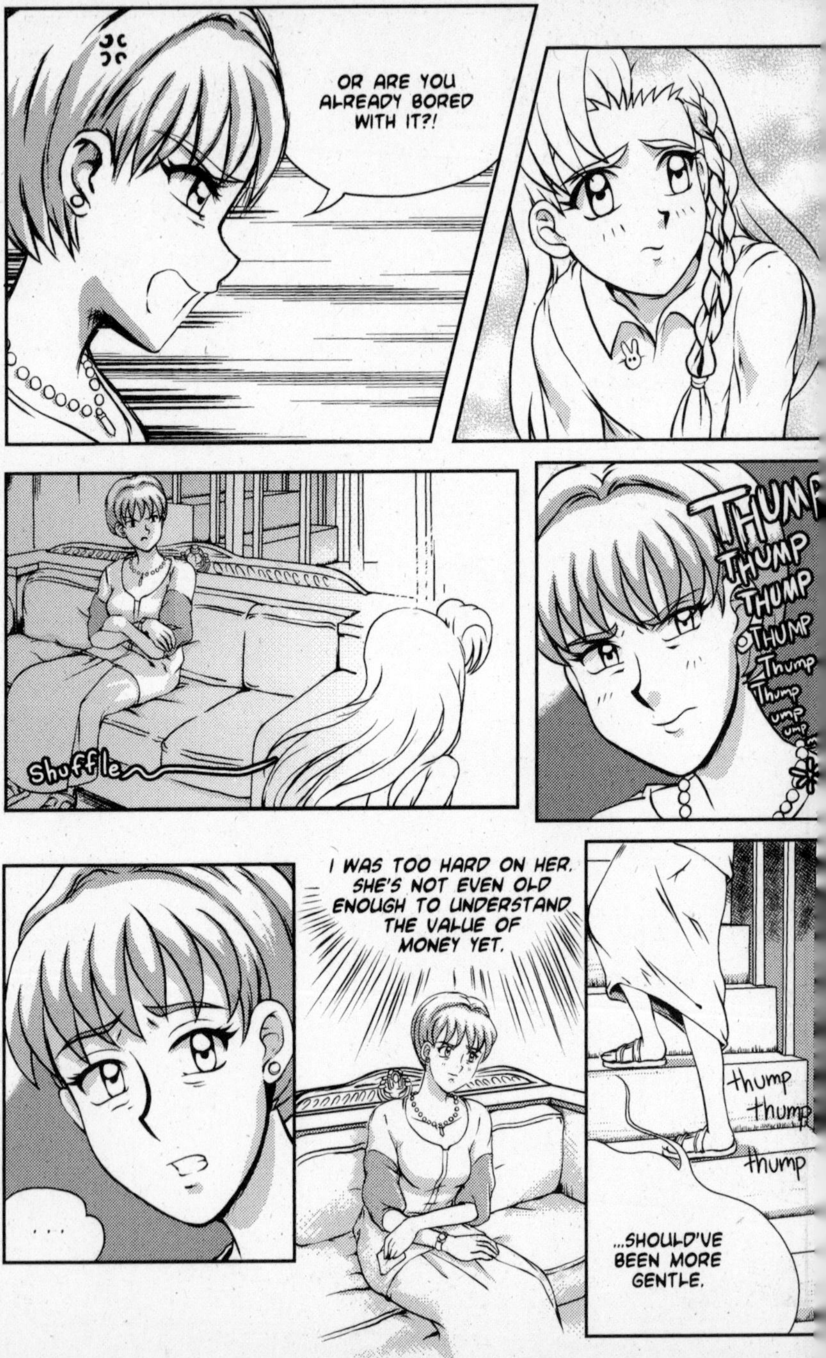
OR ARE YOU ALREADY BORED WITH IT?!
Shuffle
THUMP
THUMP
THUMP
THUMP
Thump
Thump
ump
ump
...
I WAS TOO HARD ON HER. SHE'S NOT EVEN OLD ENOUGH TO UNDERSTAND THE VALUE OF MONEY YET.
thump
thump
thump
...SHOULD'VE BEEN MORE GENTLE.

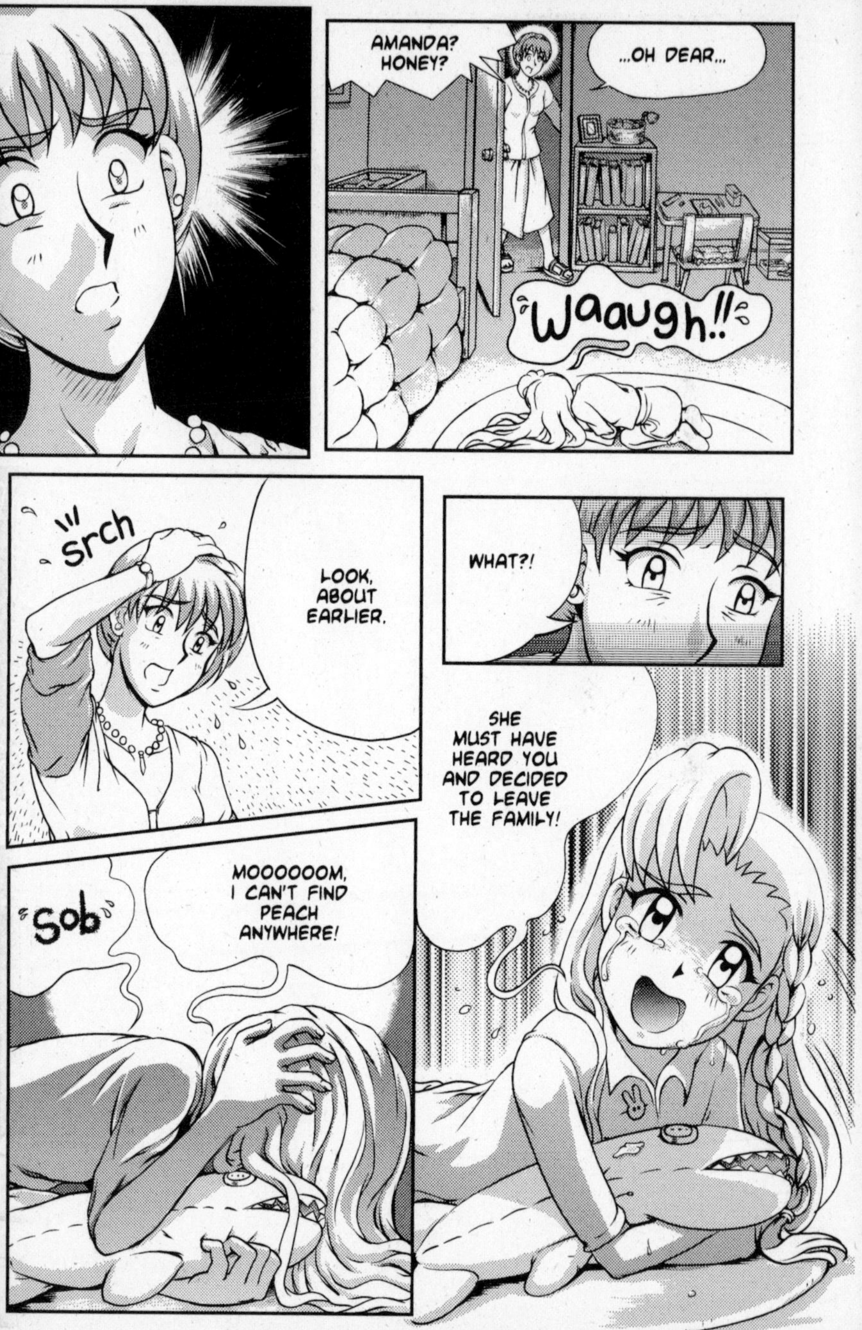
AMANDA? HONEY?
...OH DEAR...
Waaugh!!
srch
LOOK, ABOUT EARLIER.
WHAT?!
SHE MUST HAVE HEARD YOU AND DECIDED TO LEAVE THE FAMILY!
Sob
MOOOOOOM, I CAN'T FIND PEACH ANYWHERE!

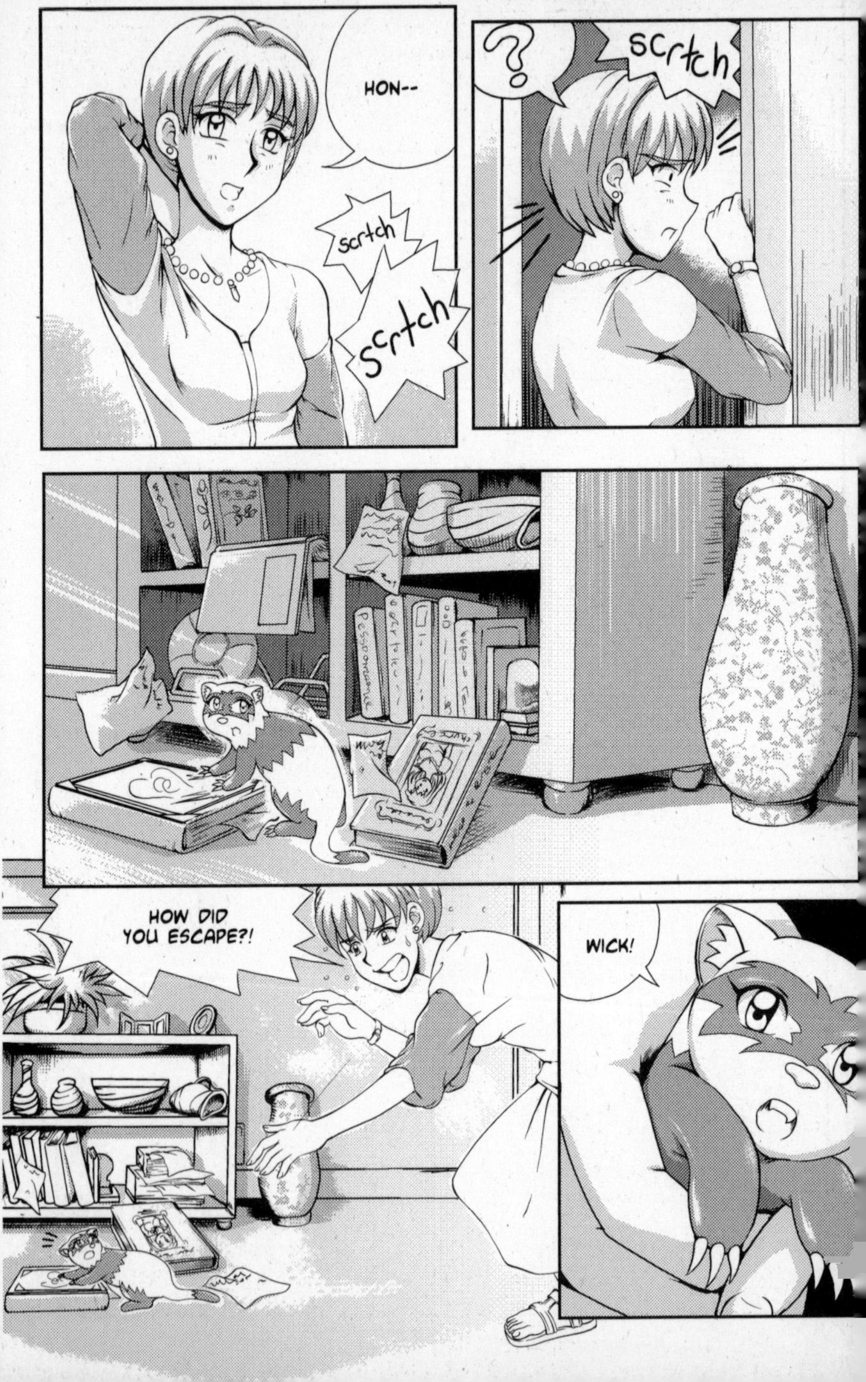
HON--
scrtch
scrtch
?
scrtch
HOW DID YOU ESCAPE?!
WICK!

big heavy rock.

spare plywood.

masking tape.

fish tank.

suffocating ferret.

IT'S HARDLY USED.

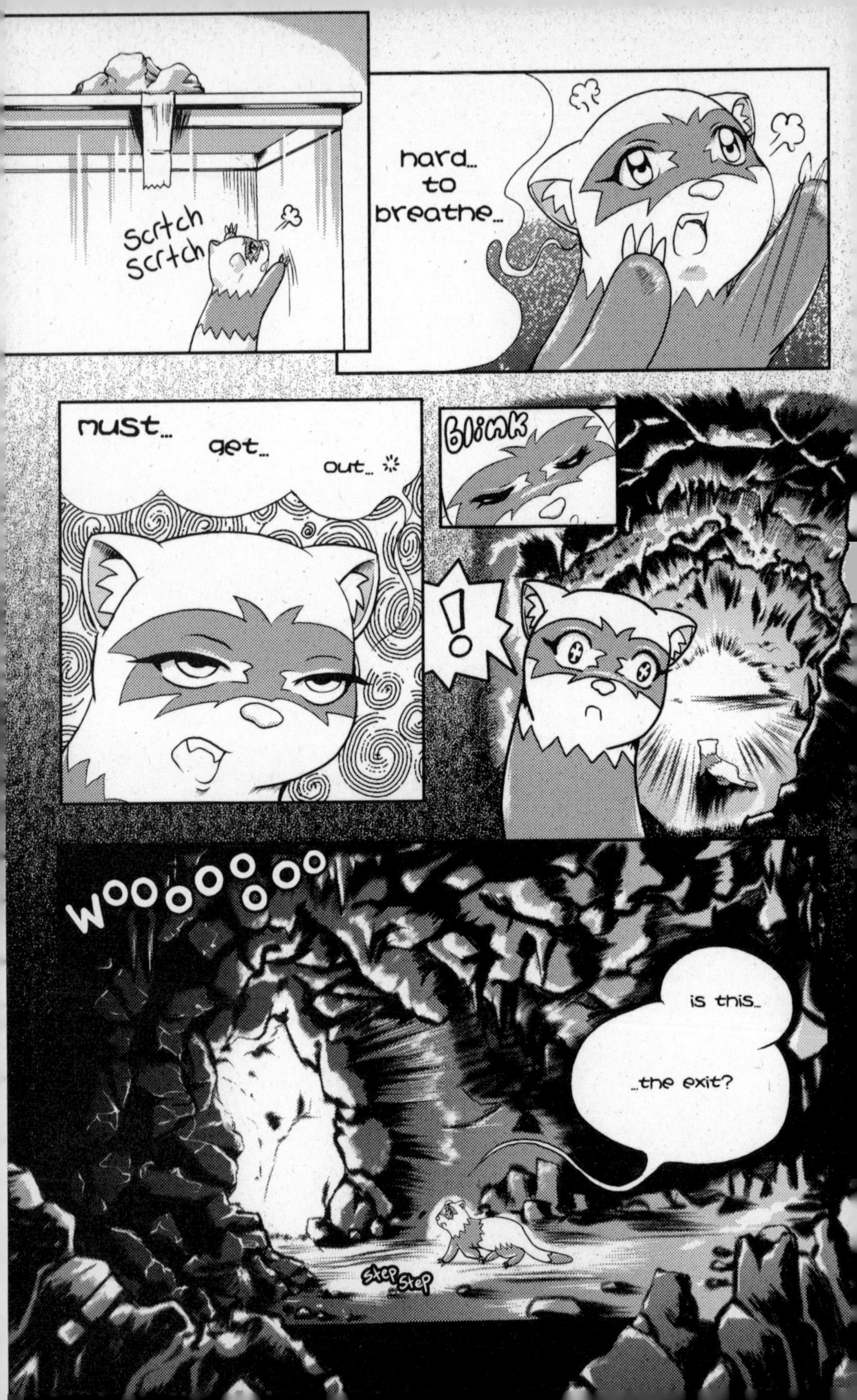
scrtch scrtch
hard... to breathe...
must... get... out...
Blink
!
WOOOOOOO
is this...
...the exit?
step step

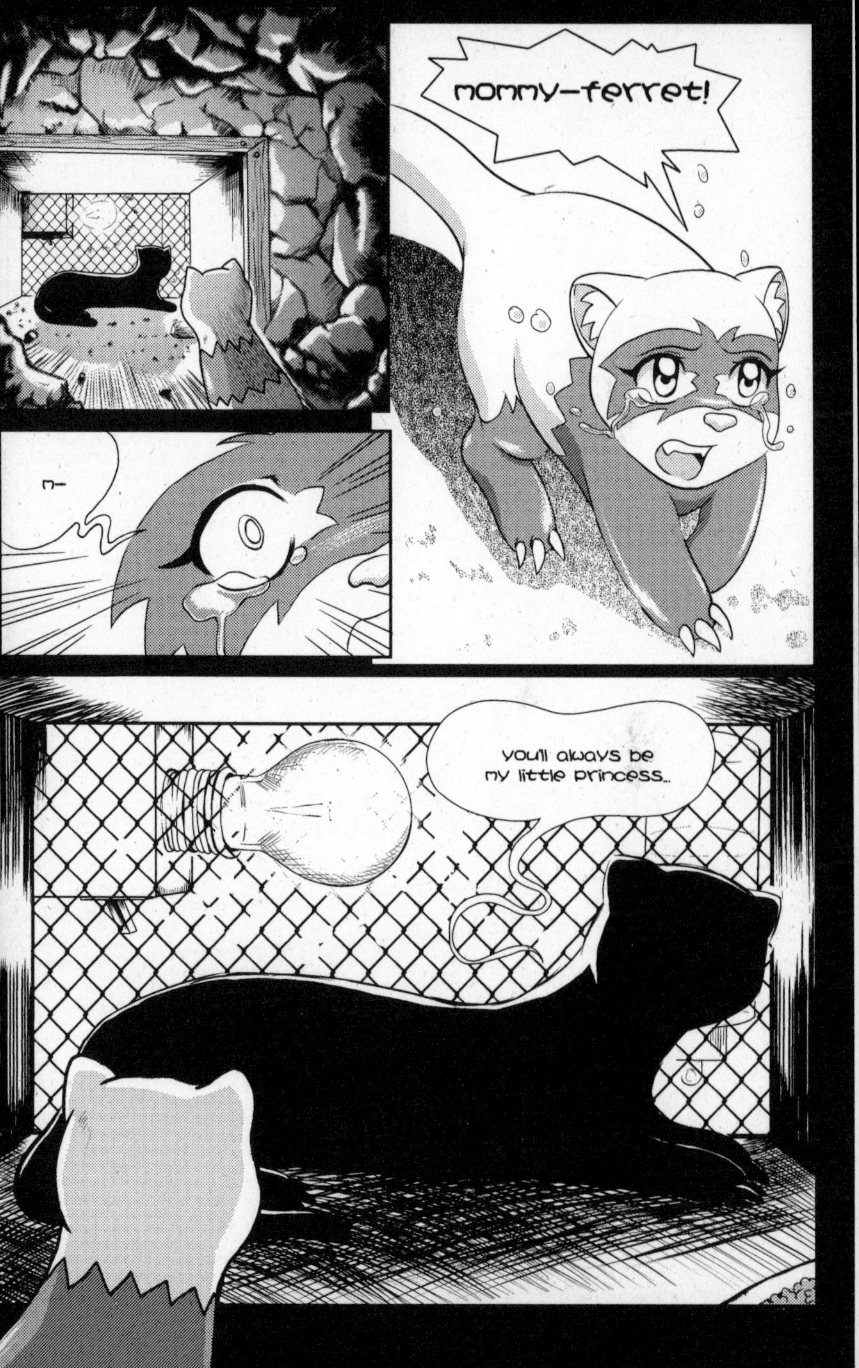
mommy-ferret!
you'll always be
my little princess..

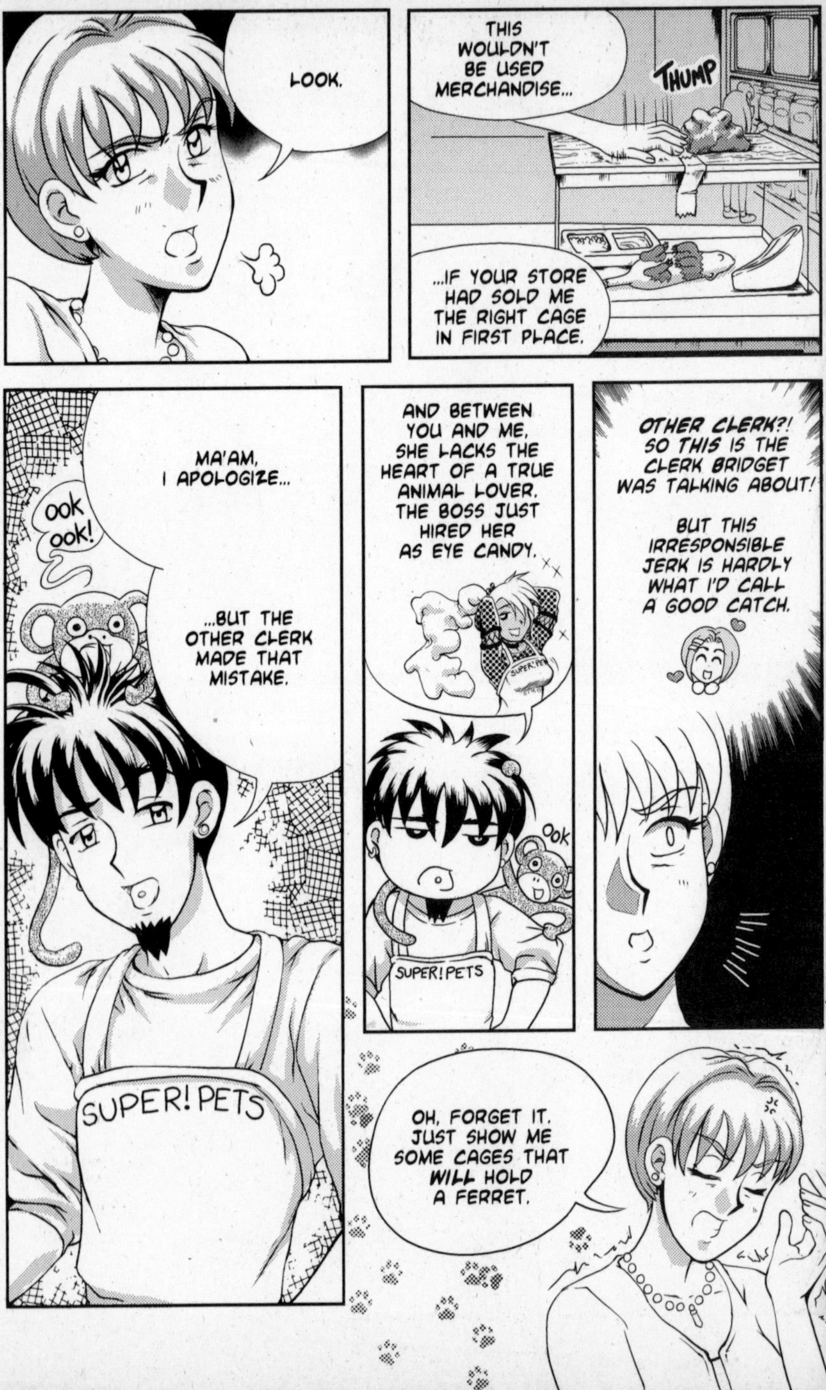
LOOK.
THIS WOULDN'T BE USED MERCHANDISE...
THUMP
...IF YOUR STORE HAD SOLD ME THE RIGHT CAGE IN FIRST PLACE.
OOK OOK!
MA'AM, I APOLOGIZE...
...BUT THE OTHER CLERK MADE THAT MISTAKE.
SUPER! PETS
AND BETWEEN YOU AND ME, SHE LACKS THE HEART OF A TRUE ANIMAL LOVER. THE BOSS JUST HIRED HER AS EYE CANDY.
OOK
SUPER! PETS
OTHER CLERK?! SO THIS IS THE CLERK BRIDGET WAS TALKING ABOUT!
BUT THIS IRRESPONSIBLE JERK IS HARDLY WHAT I'D CALL A GOOD CATCH.
OH, FORGET IT. JUST SHOW ME SOME CAGES THAT WILL HOLD A FERRET.

WHY NOT PICK OUT SOME FISH FOR YOURSELF?

OOK OOK

HUH?

YOUR FISH TANK! YOU MIGHT AS WELL PUT SOMETHING IN IT.

UH...

fish Paradise

I RECOMMEND OUR TROPICAL FISH.

THEY'RE SCIENTIFICALLY PROVEN TO REDUCE STRESS LEVELS.

...

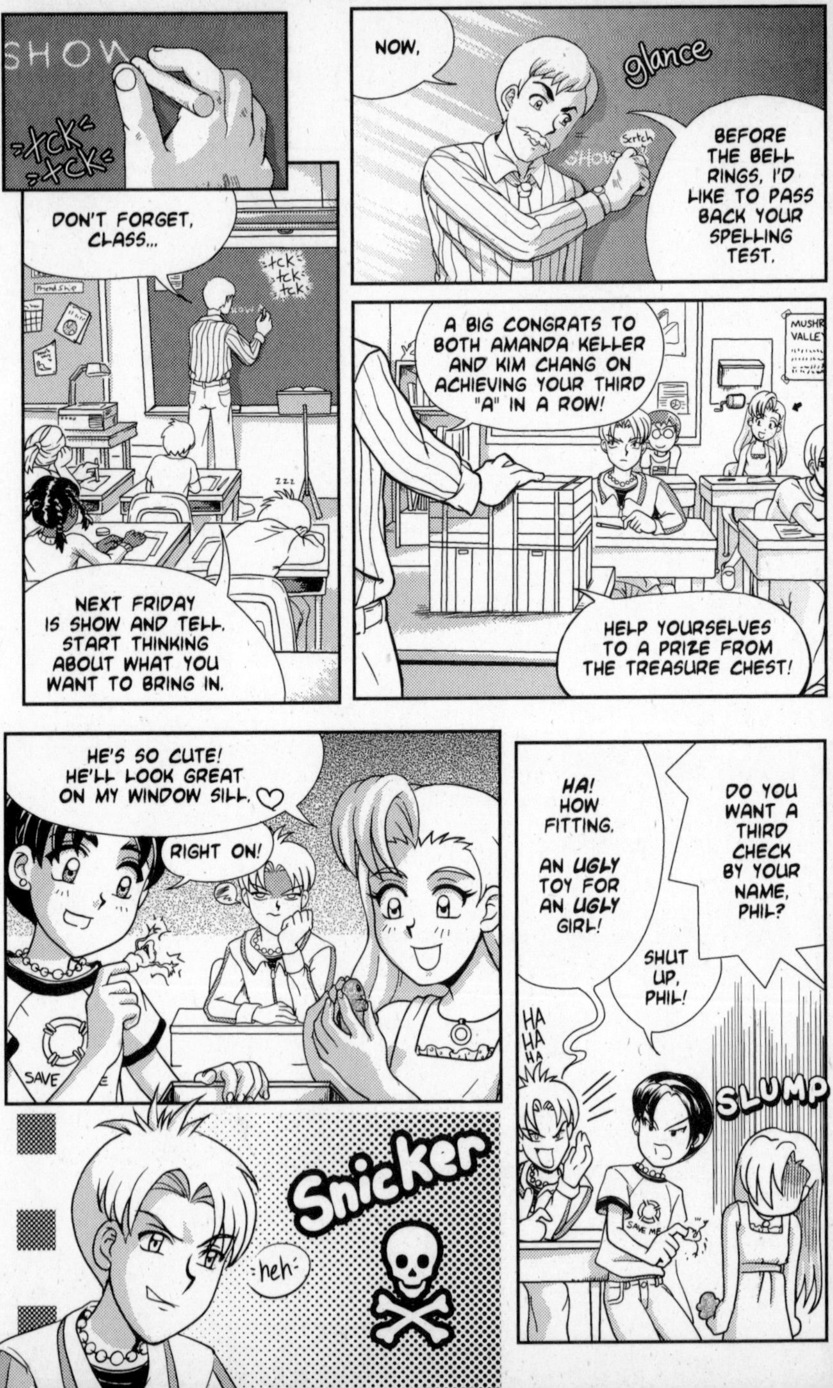
SHOW
tck tck
DON'T FORGET, CLASS...
tck tck tck
zzz
NEXT FRIDAY IS SHOW AND TELL. START THINKING ABOUT WHAT YOU WANT TO BRING IN.
NOW,
glance
Scrtch
BEFORE THE BELL RINGS, I'D LIKE TO PASS BACK YOUR SPELLING TEST.
A BIG CONGRATS TO BOTH AMANDA KELLER AND KIM CHANG ON ACHIEVING YOUR THIRD "A" IN A ROW!
HELP YOURSELVES TO A PRIZE FROM THE TREASURE CHEST!
HE'S SO CUTE! HE'LL LOOK GREAT ON MY WINDOW SILL.
RIGHT ON!
SAVE
Snicker
heh
HA! HOW FITTING.
AN UGLY TOY FOR AN UGLY GIRL!
DO YOU WANT A THIRD CHECK BY YOUR NAME, PHIL?
SHUT UP, PHIL!
HA HA HA
SLUMP
SAVE ME

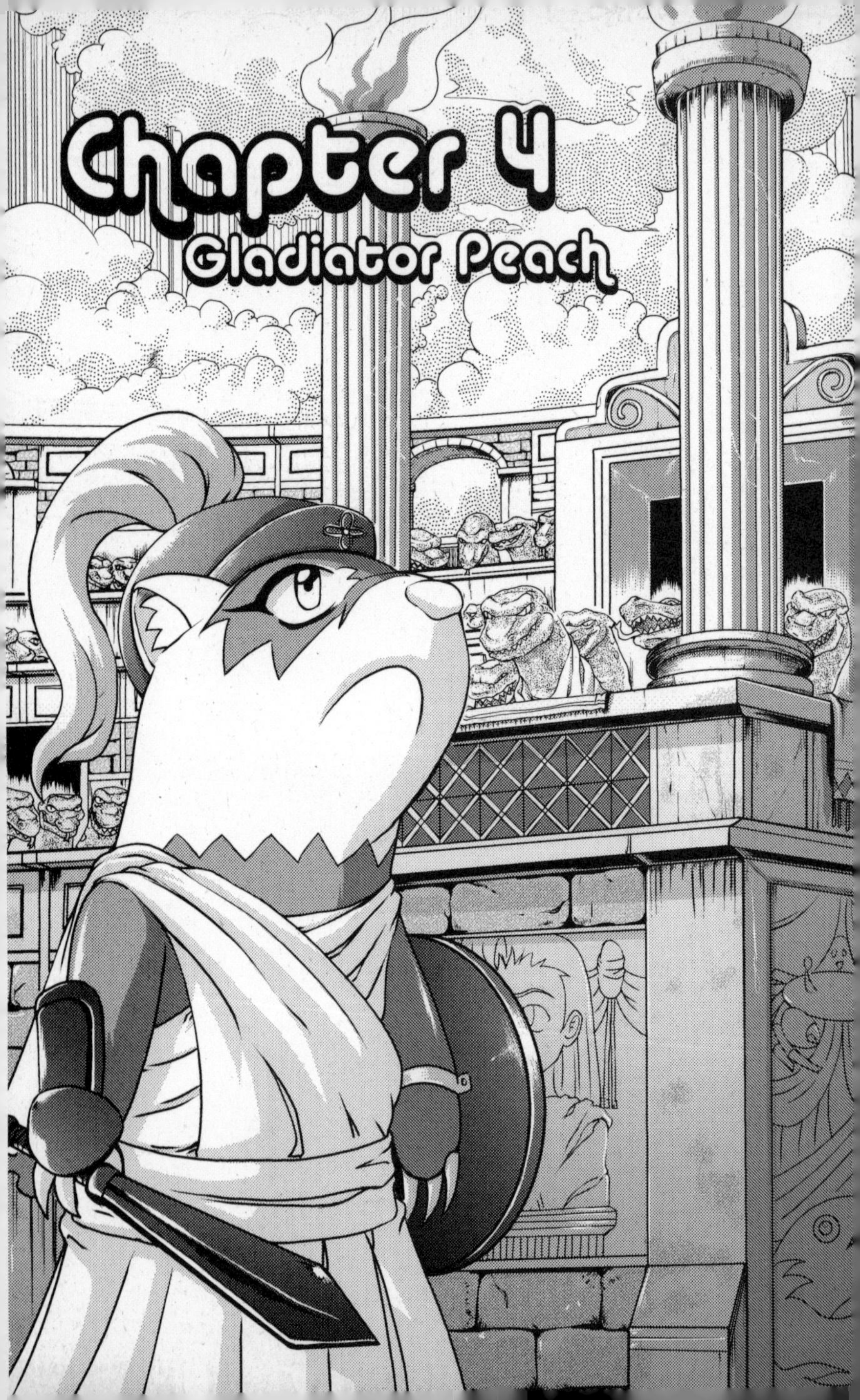
Chapter 4
Gladiator Peach

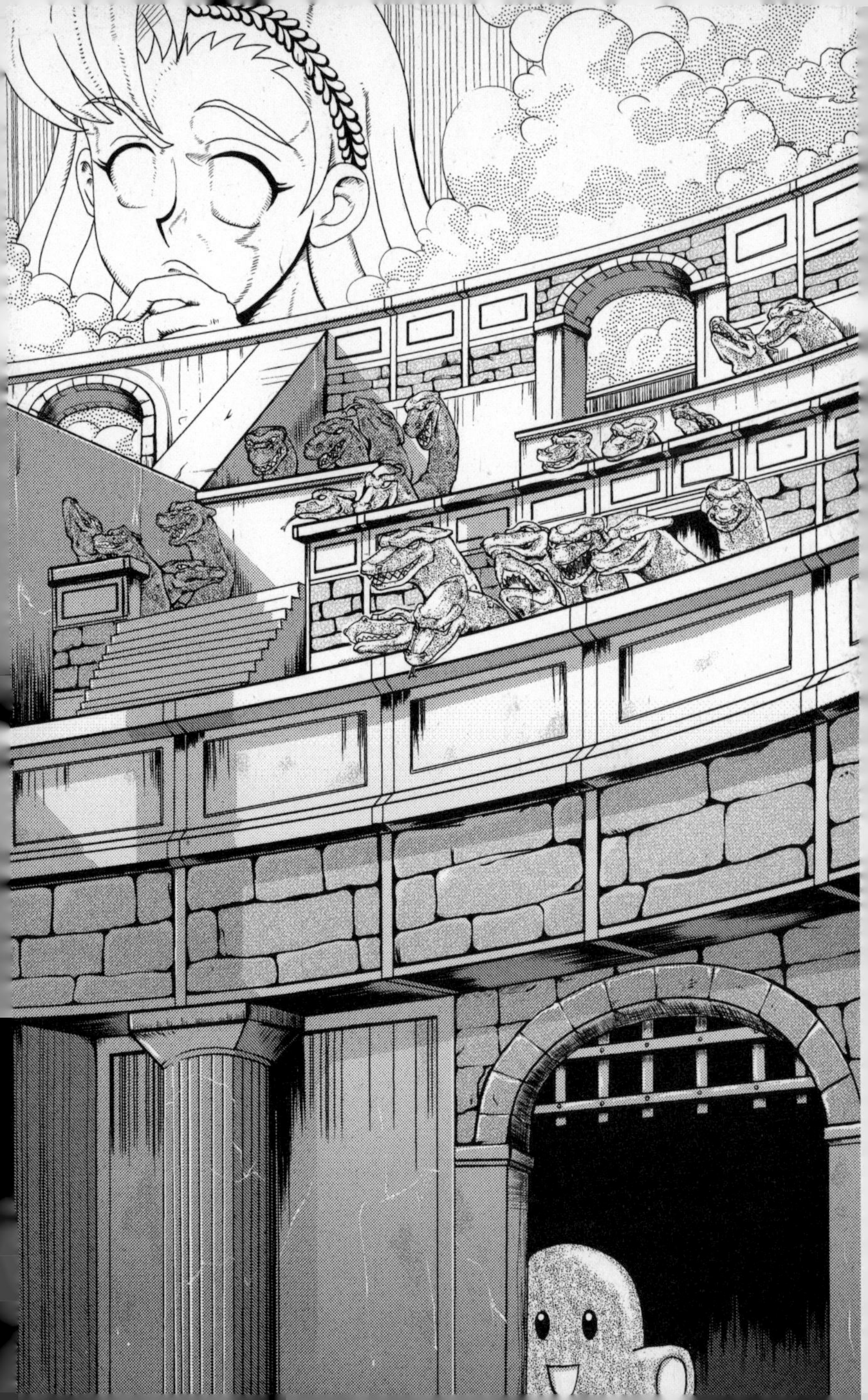

thump
Thump
THUMP

cla. chk

BAM

tok

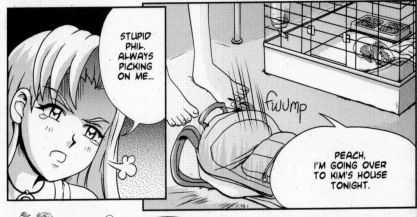

STUPID PHIL. ALWAYS PICKING ON ME...

fwump

PEACH, I'M GOING OVER TO KIM'S HOUSE TONIGHT.

fwp

NOT THAT *YOU'D* NOTICE SINCE YOU'RE *ALWAYS* SLEEPING.

rustle rustle

UGH.

HERE! I DON'T WANT THIS *UGLY* THING, SO YOU CAN HAVE IT.

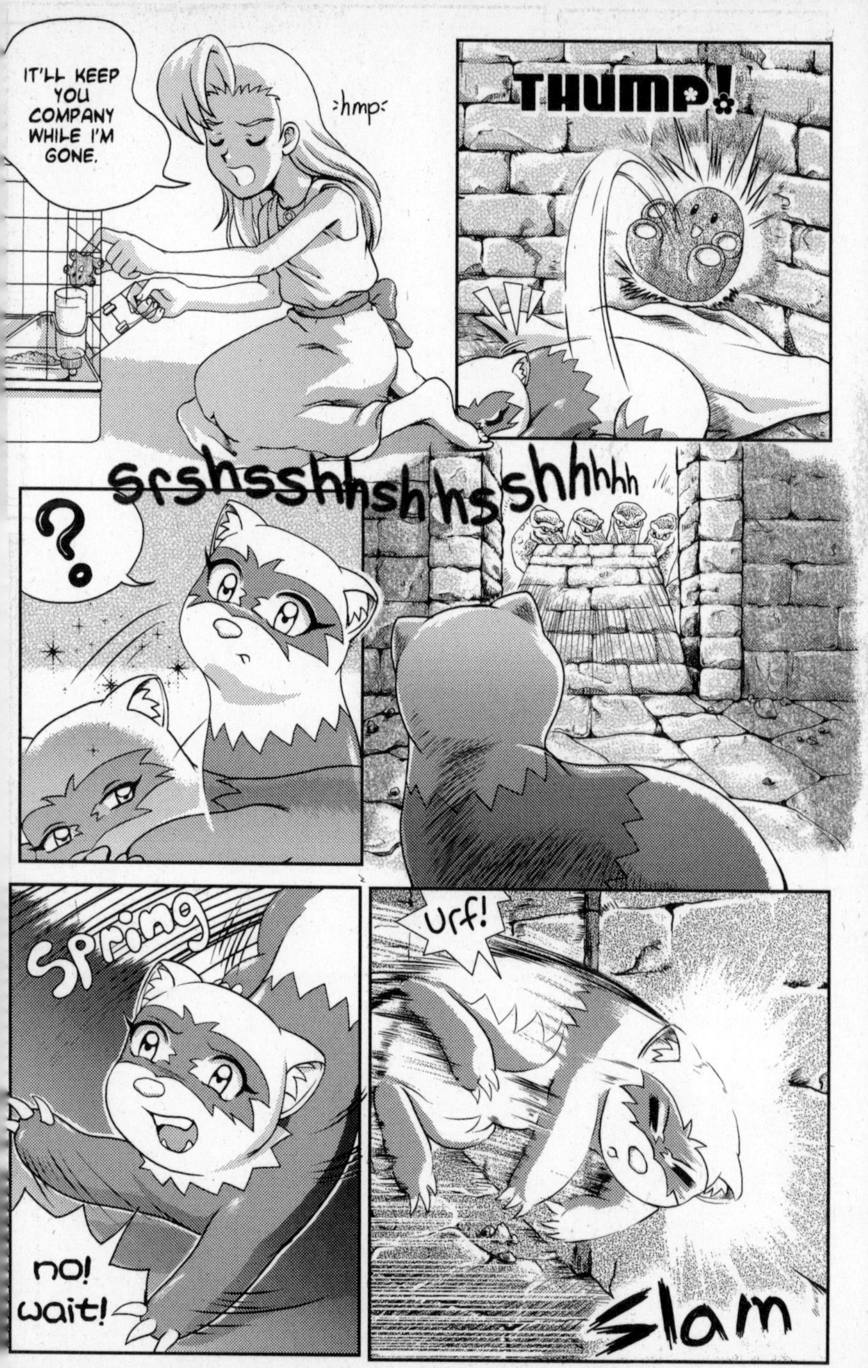
IT'LL KEEP YOU COMPANY WHILE I'M GONE.
:hmp:
THUMP!
srshsshhshhsshhhhh
?
Spring
no! wait!
Urf!
Slam

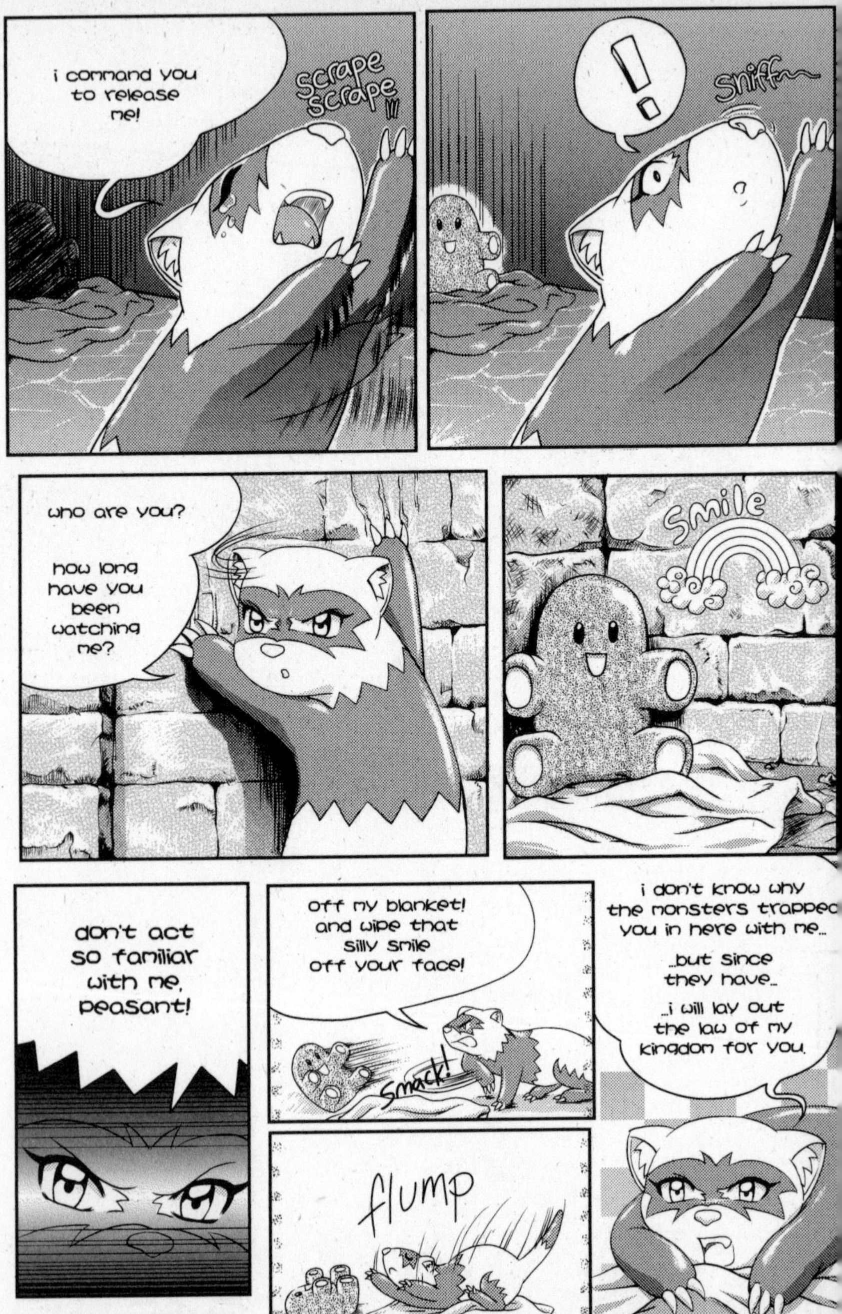

i command you to release me!
scrape scrape
!
Sniff~
who are you?
how long have you been watching me?
Smile
don't act so familiar with me, peasant!
off my blanket! and wipe that silly smile off your face!
Smack!
flump
i don't know why the monsters trapped you in here with me...
...but since they have...
...i will lay out the law of my kingdom for you.

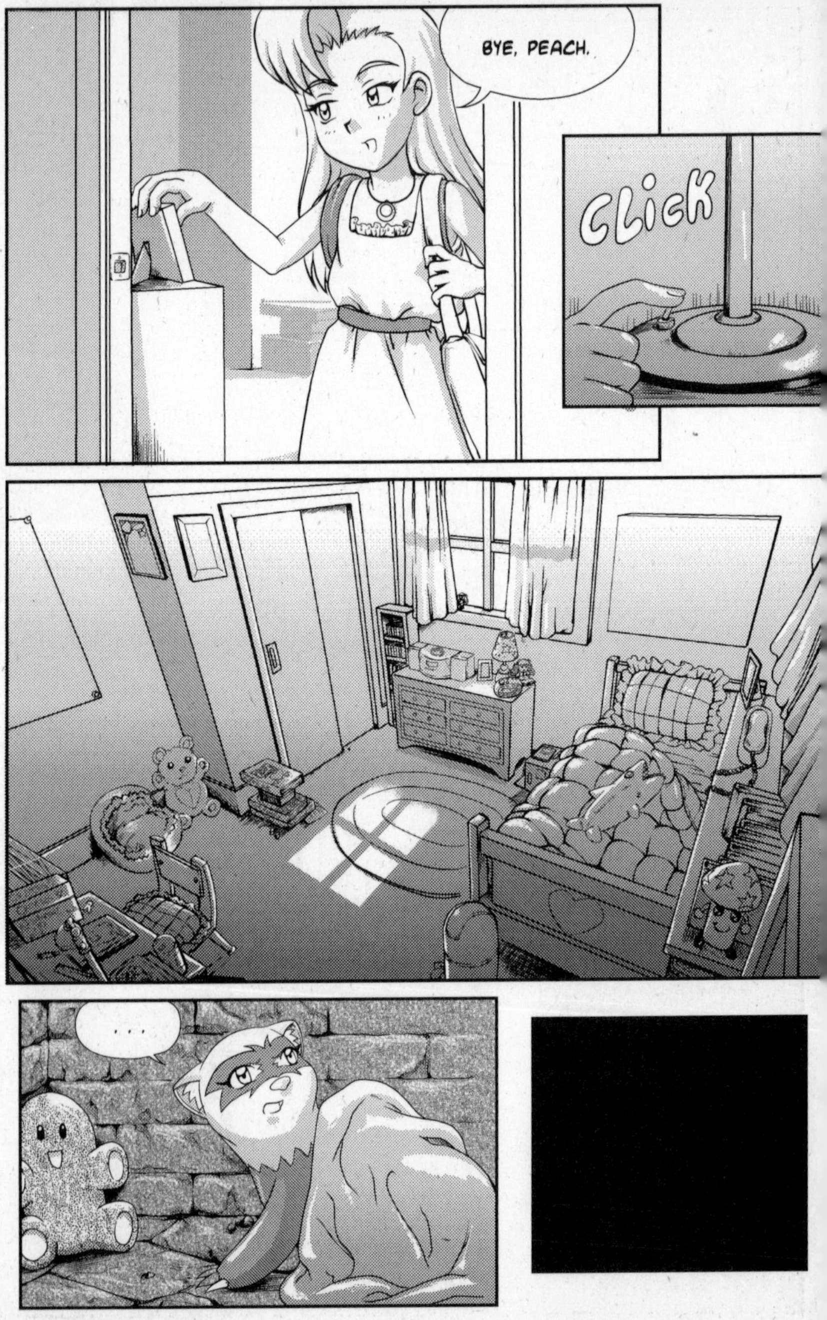
BYE, PEACH.
CLICK
. . .

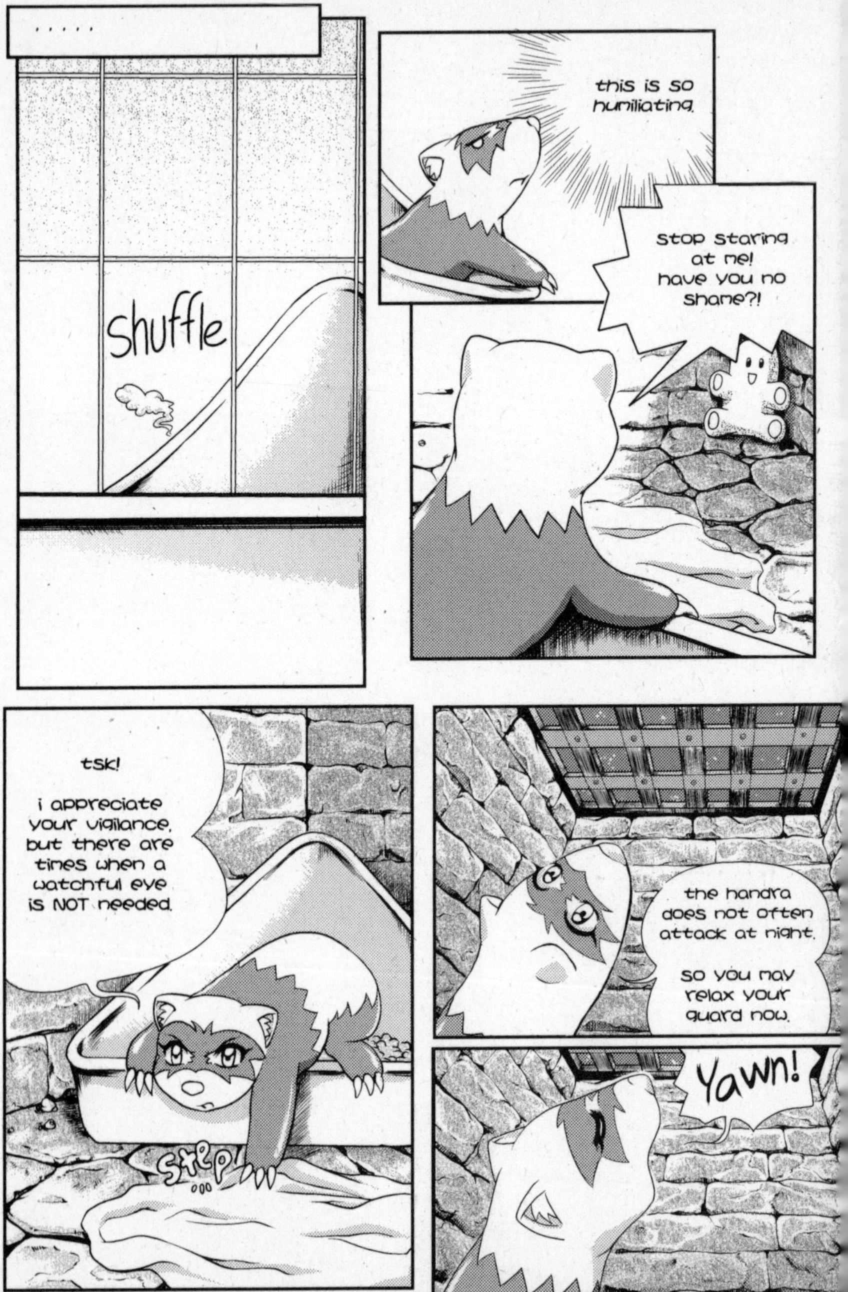
......
shuffle
this is so humiliating.
stop staring at me! have you no shame?!
tsk!
i appreciate your vigilance, but there are times when a watchful eye is NOT needed.
step
the handra does not often attack at night.
so you may relax your guard now.
Yawn!

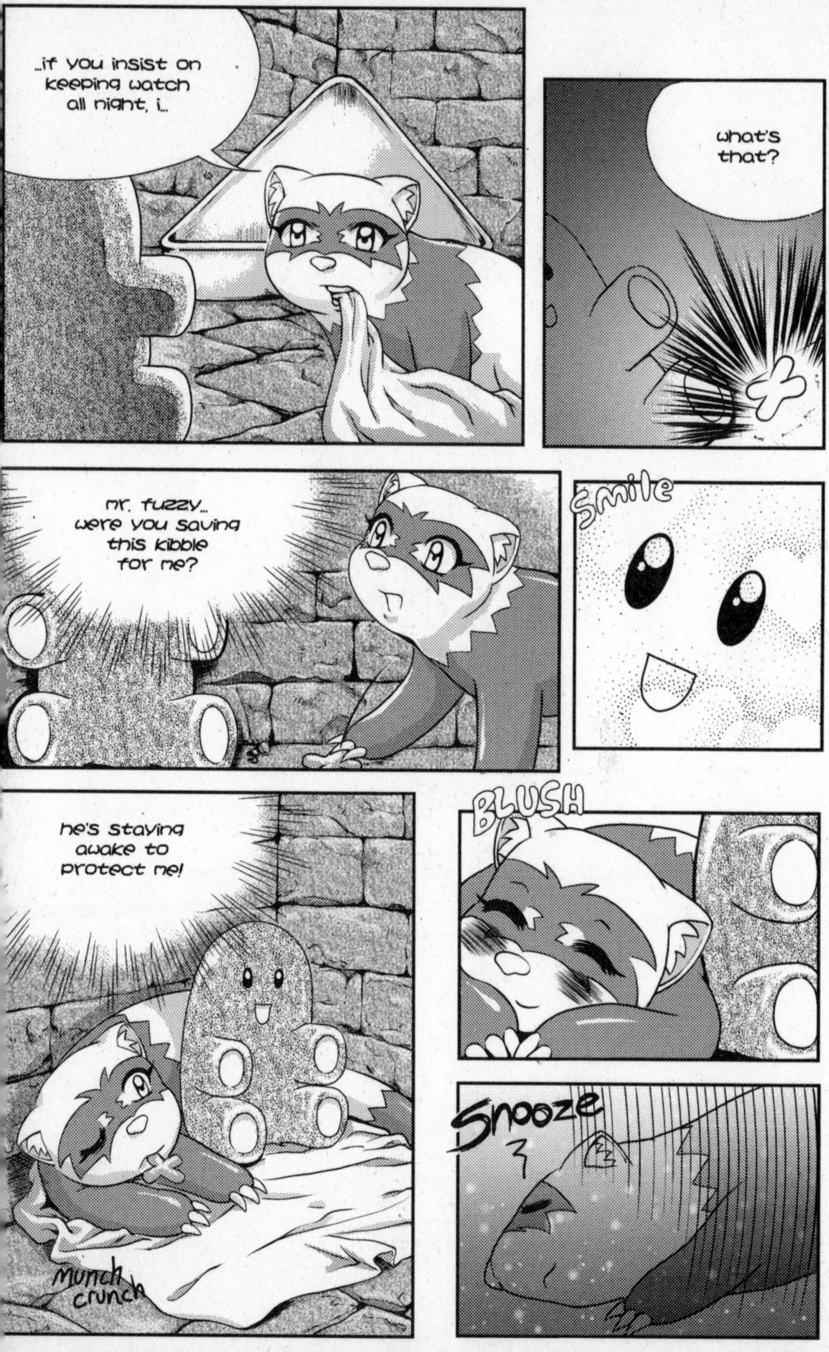
..if you insist on keeping watch all night, i...
what's that?
mr. fuzzy... were you saving this kibble for me?
Smile
he's staying awake to protect me!
munch crunch
BLUSH
Snooze

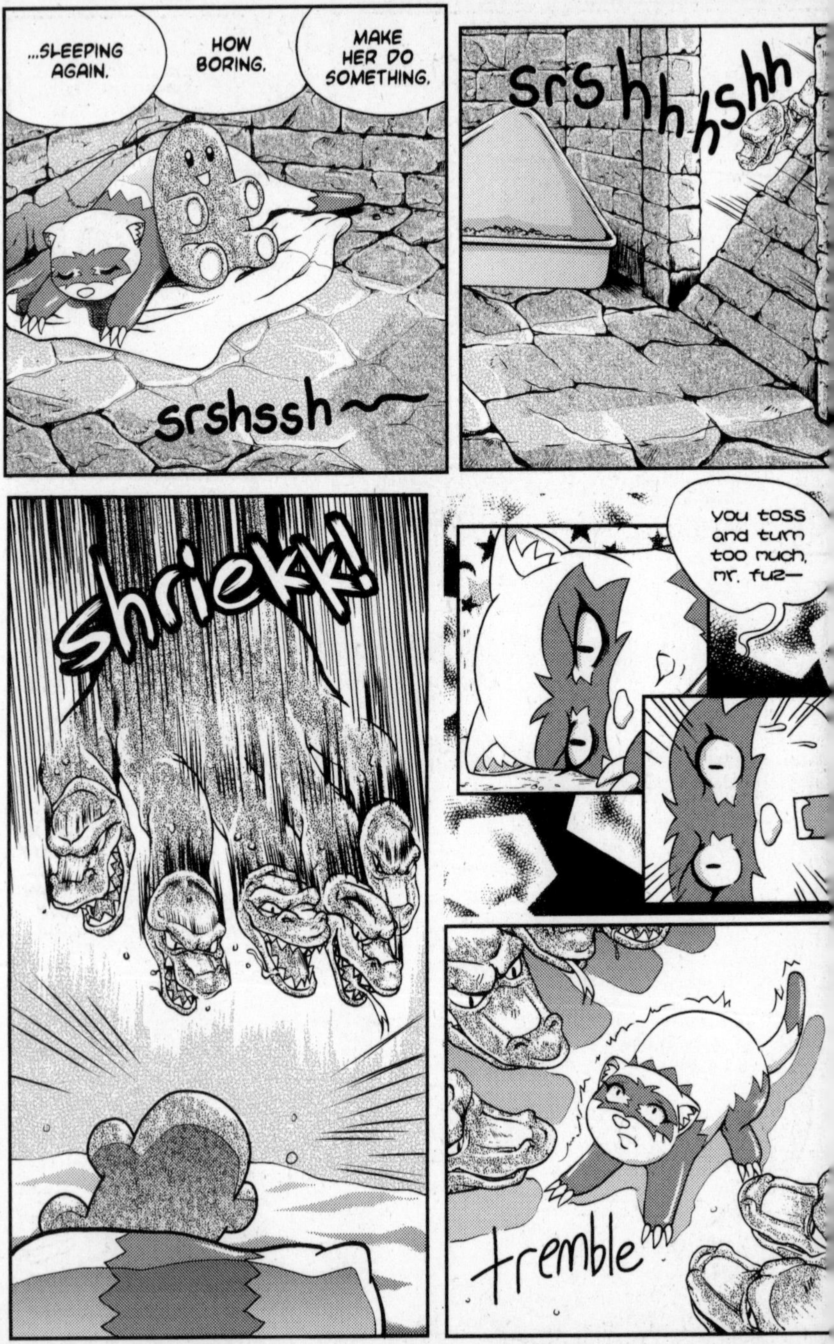
...SLEEPING AGAIN.
HOW BORING.
MAKE HER DO SOMETHING.
srshssh~~
srshhhshh
shriekk!
you toss and turn too much, mr. fuz—
tremble

Squeeze

YOU DON'T HAVE TO PUT UP WITH ANY MEANIE ATTACKS.

EVEN A SEAL-COON KNOWS HOW TO DEFEND ITSELF.

Seal-coon

fling

fwump

The Arena

WATCH THIS! ♡

wick!

tickle ♡ tickle

how dare you, monsters!

AROoo

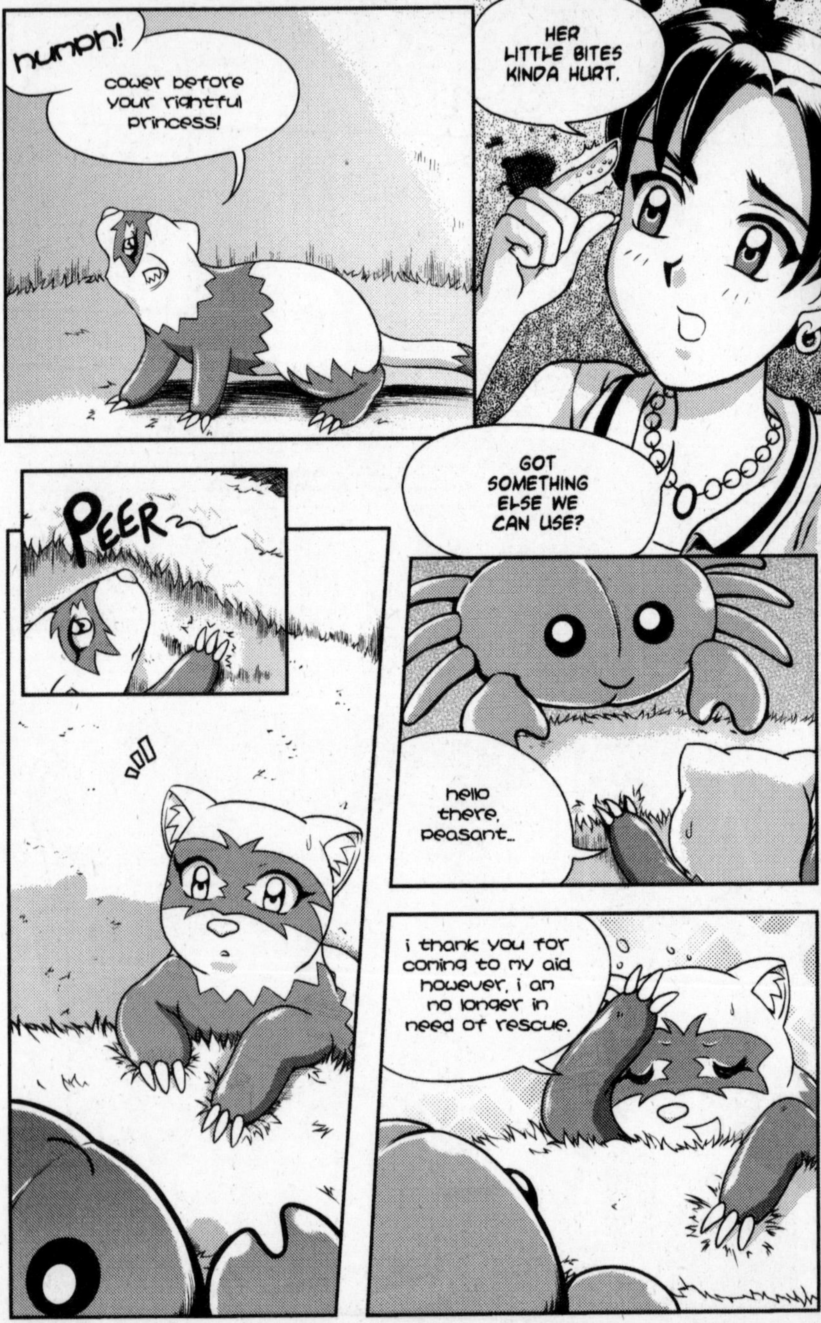
humph!
cower before your rightful princess!
HER LITTLE BITES KINDA HURT.
GOT SOMETHING ELSE WE CAN USE?
PEER
hello there, peasant...
i thank you for coming to my aid. however, i am no longer in need of rescue.

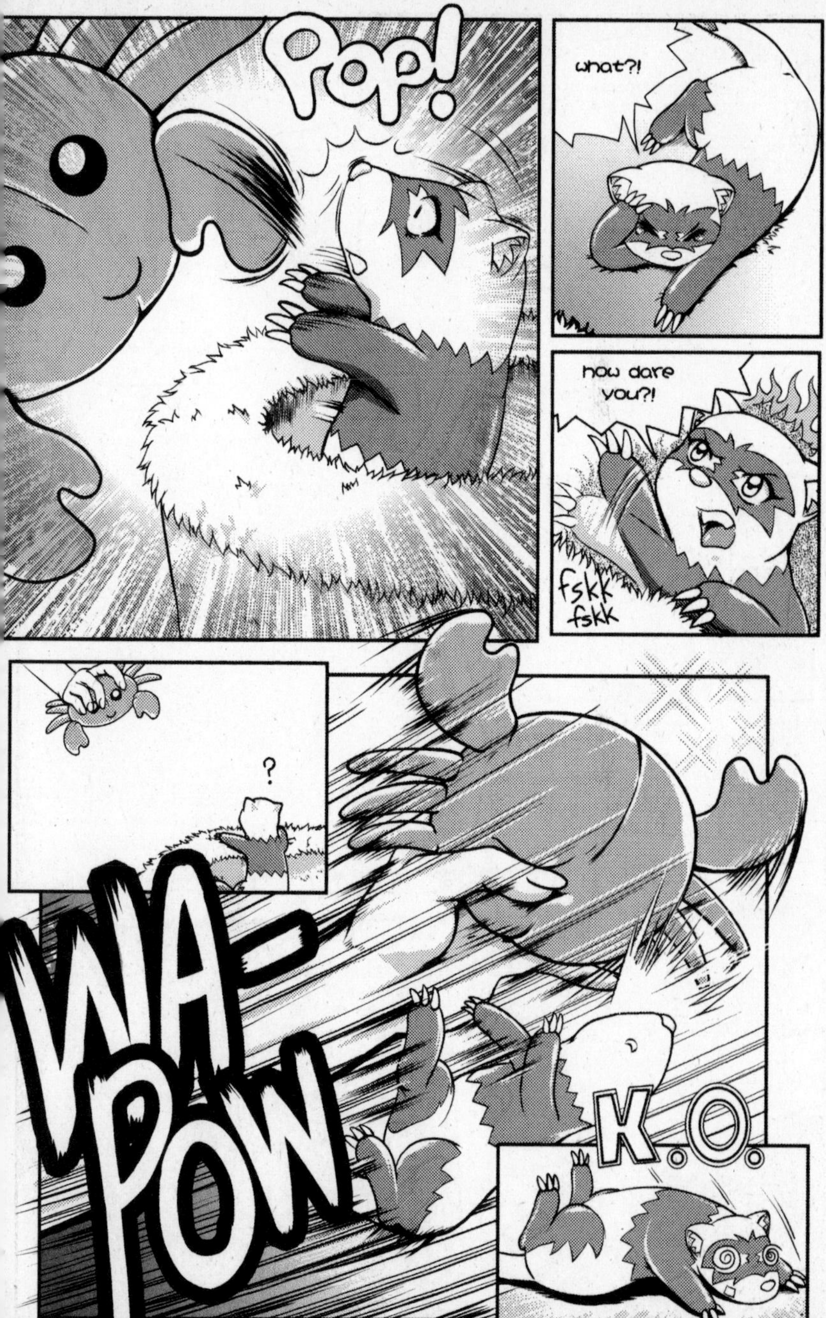
Pop!
what?!
how dare you?!
fskk fskk
?
WA-POW
K.O.

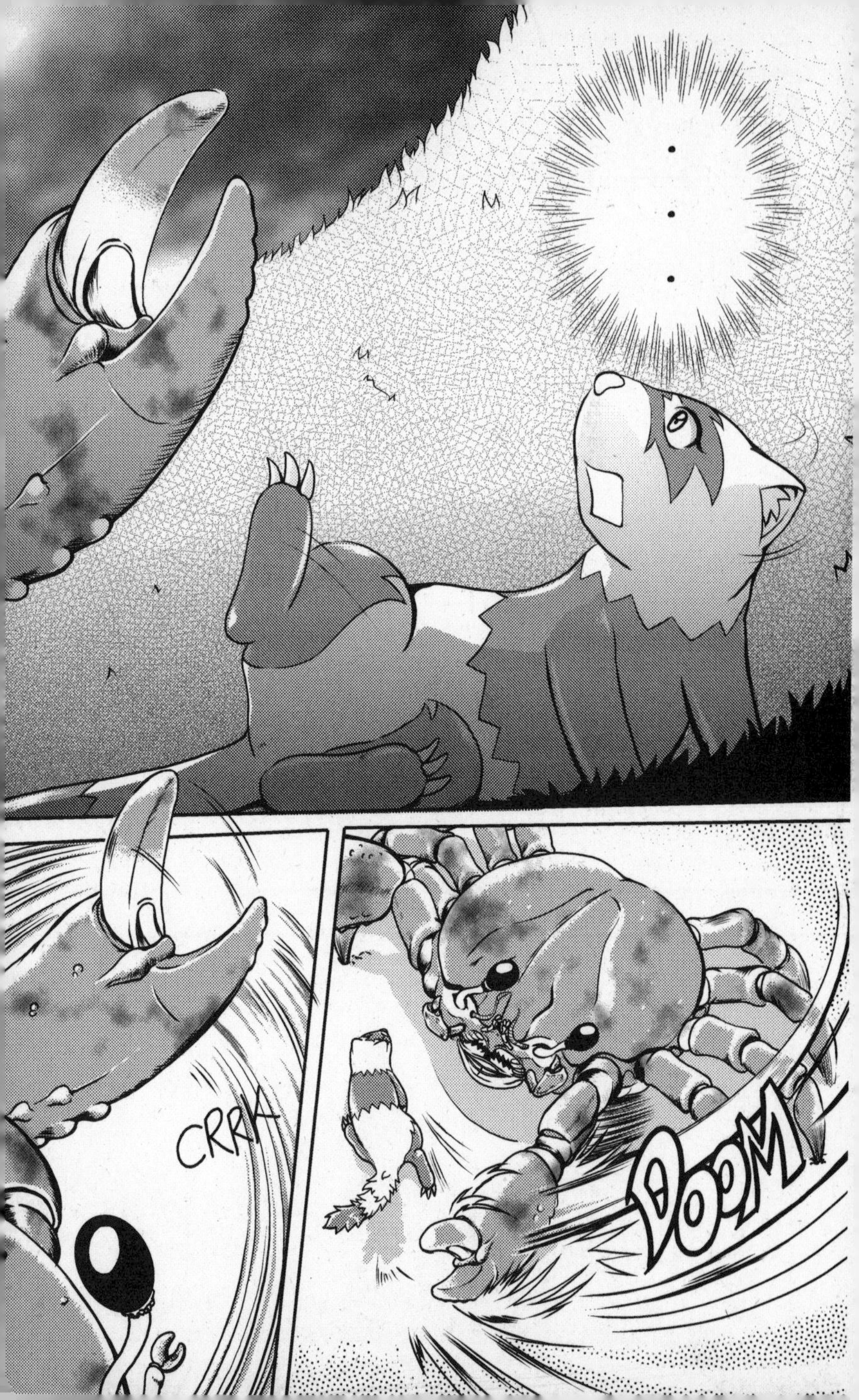
...
CRRK
DOOM

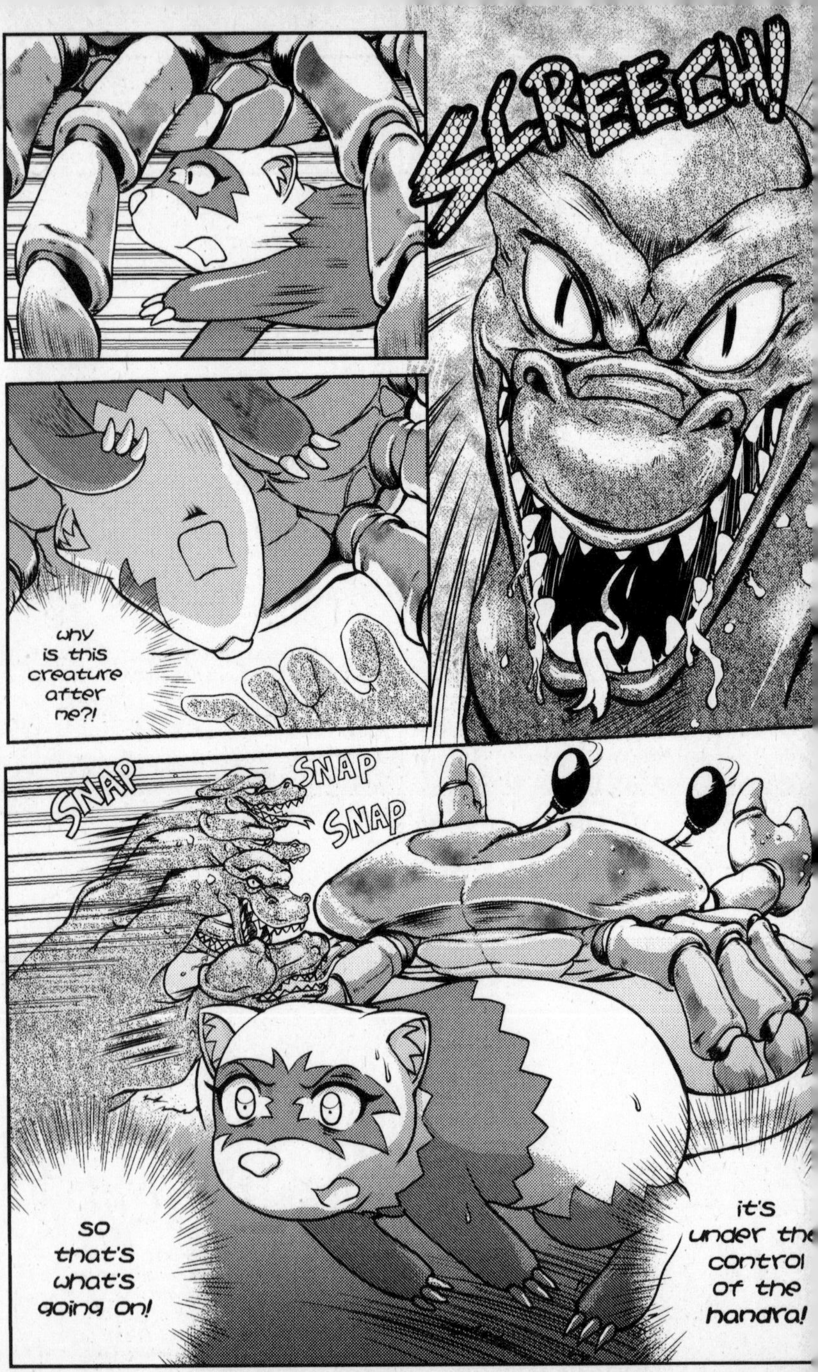
why is this creature after me?!
SCREECH!
SNAP
SNAP
SNAP
so that's what's going on!
it's under the control of the handra!

i'm sorry...

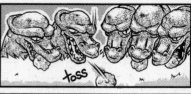

toss

?

THUNK

The Victor

Sniff...

wonderful aroma.

munch munch munch

delicious! amazing! truly gourmet food worthy of a delicate princess' palate.

should i save one for mr. fuzzy?

tch, no.

he failed me like the others.

plus these delectables are too refined for a simple peasant.

toss

was the food a reward for fighting the claw monster...?

. . .

munch chew

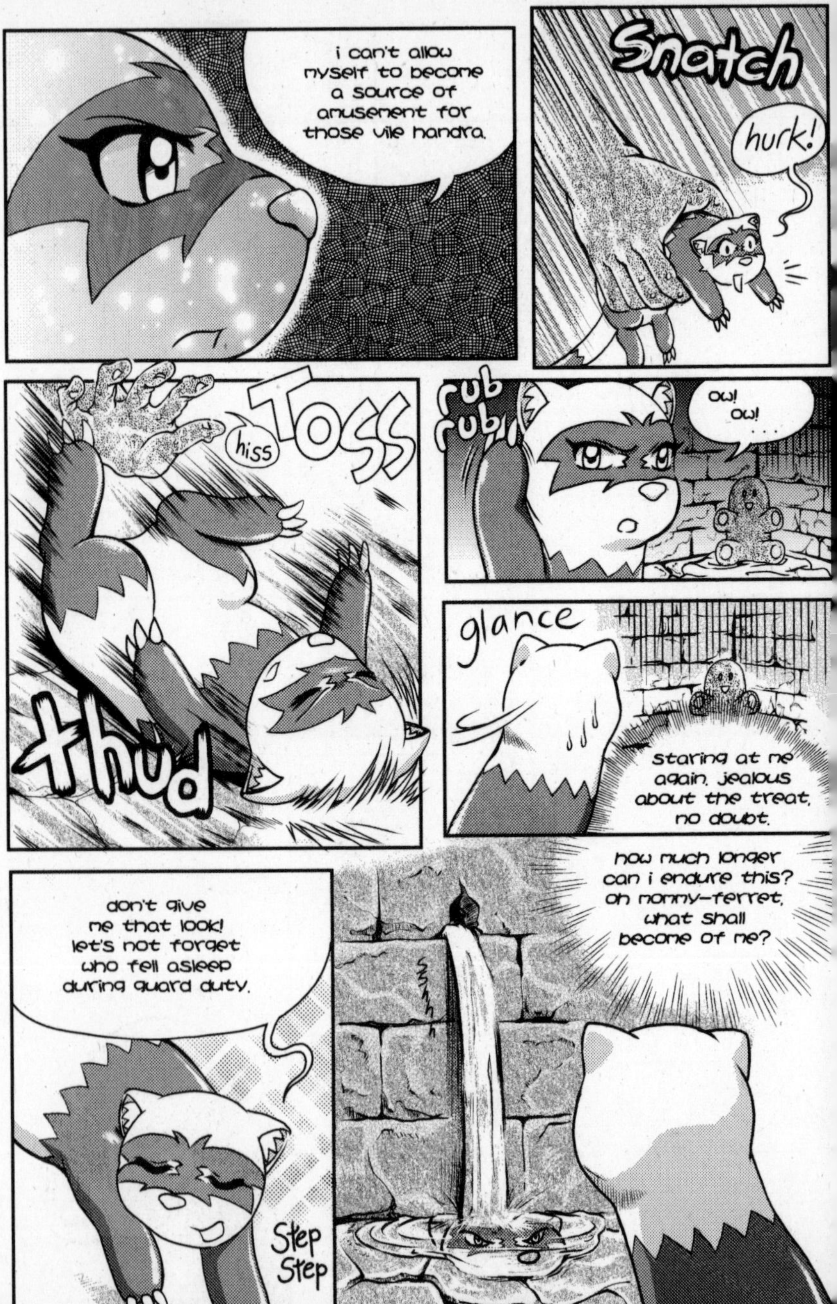
i can't allow myself to become a source of amusement for those vile handra.
Snatch
hurk!
hiss
Toss
Thud
rub rub
ow! ow! . . .
glance
staring at me again, jealous about the treat, no doubt.
don't give me that look! let's not forget who fell asleep during guard duty.
Step Step
how much longer can i endure this? oh mommy-ferret, what shall become of me?

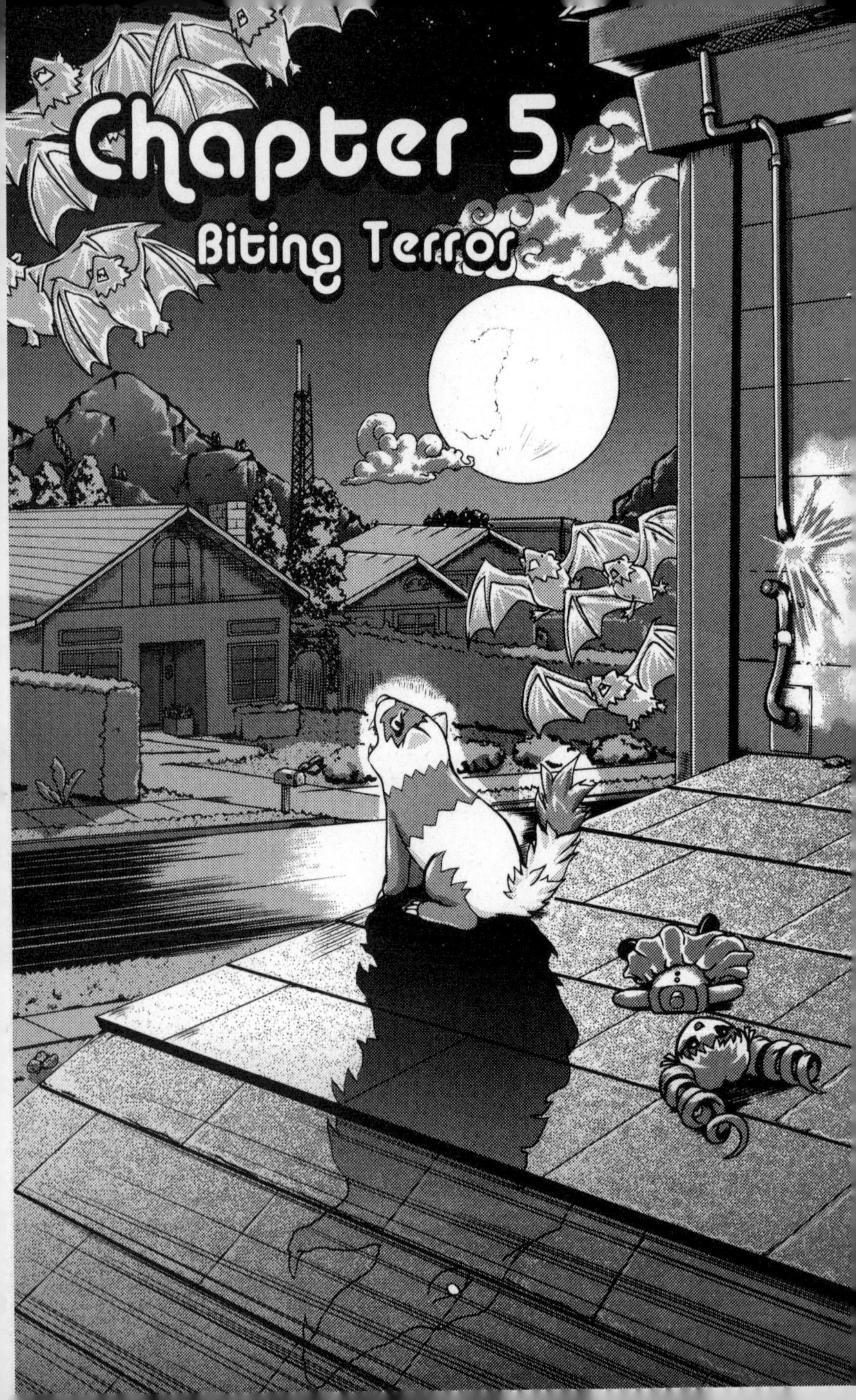
Chapter 5
Biting Terror

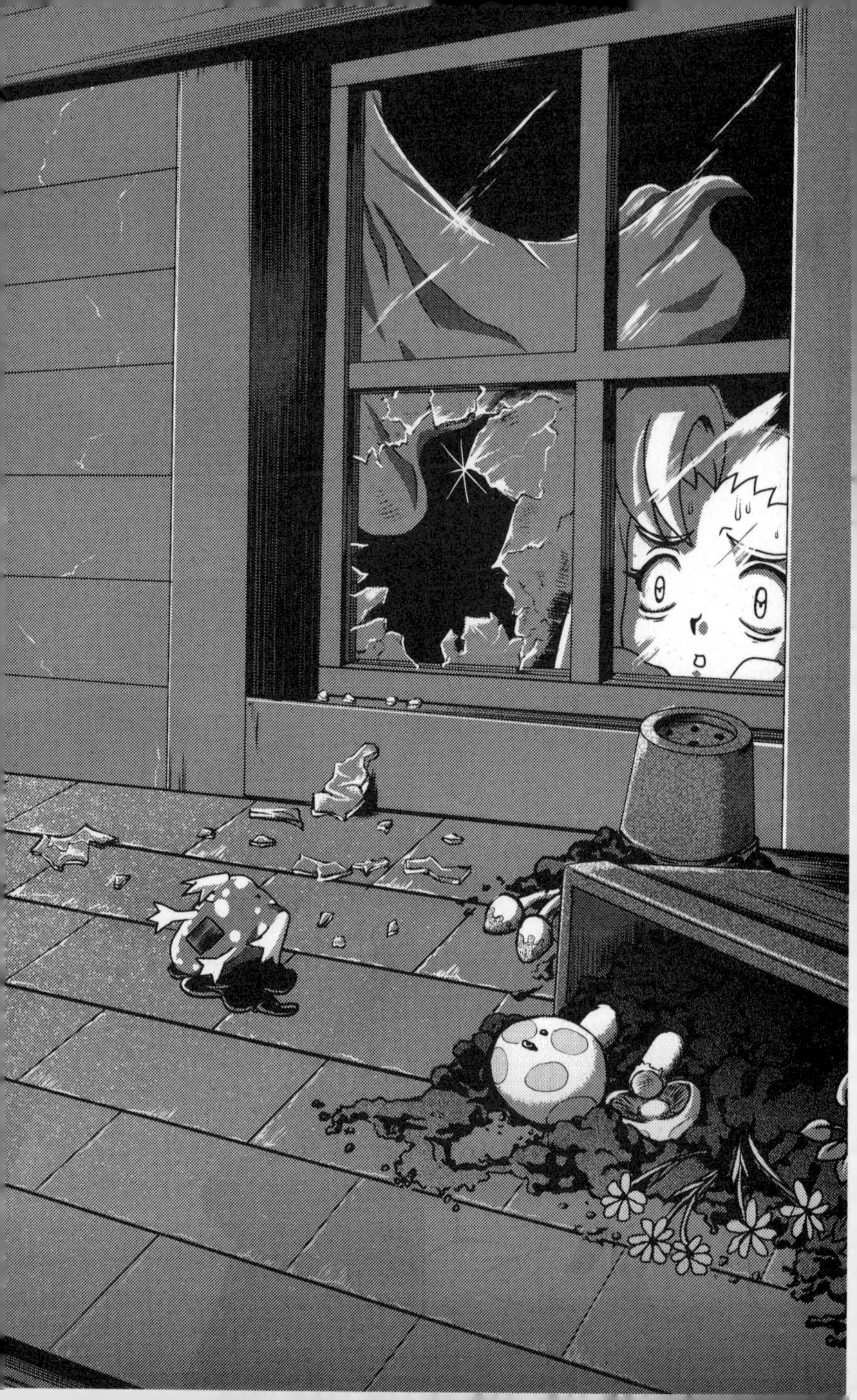

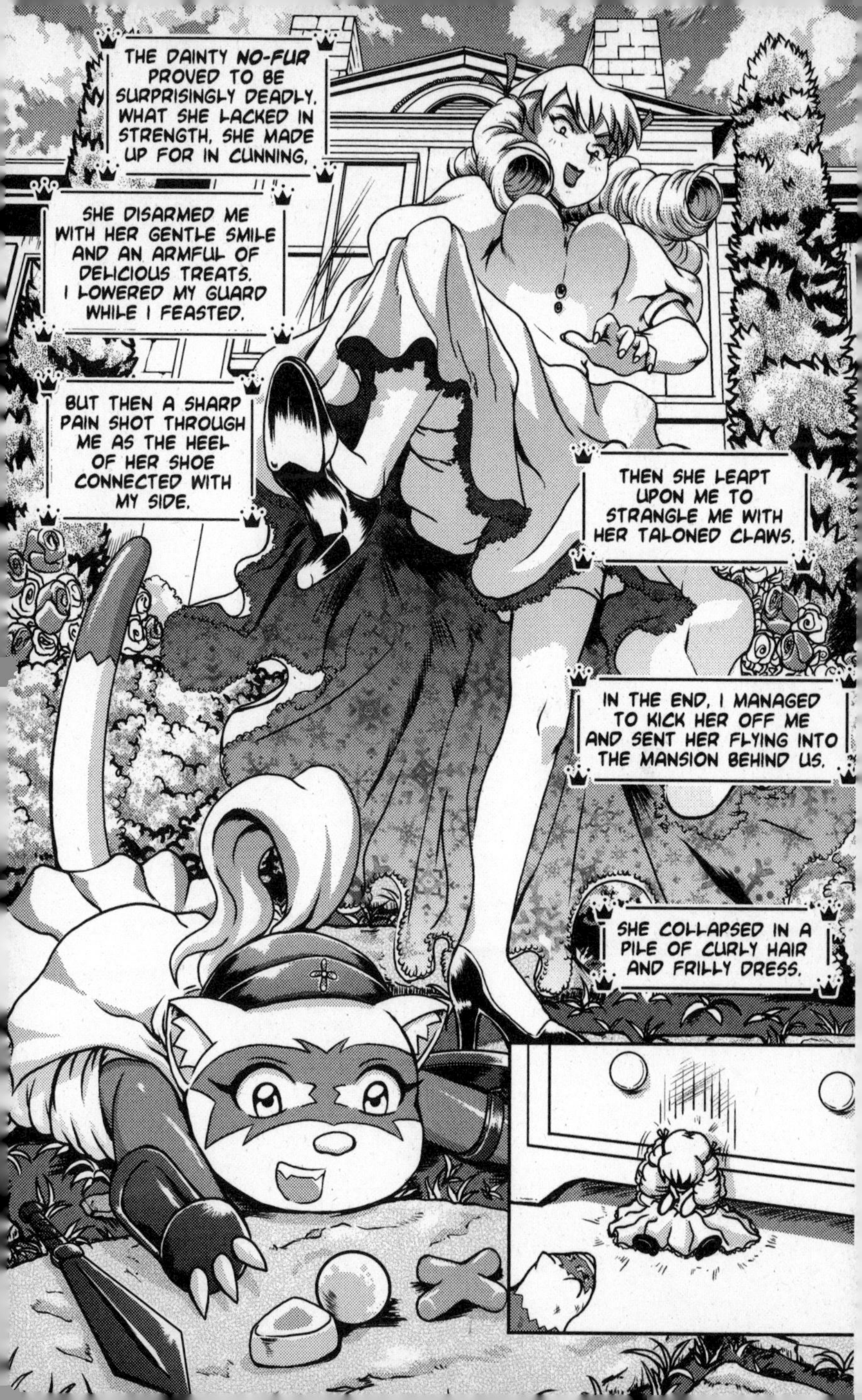
THE DAINTY NO-FUR PROVED TO BE SURPRISINGLY DEADLY. WHAT SHE LACKED IN STRENGTH, SHE MADE UP FOR IN CUNNING.
SHE DISARMED ME WITH HER GENTLE SMILE AND AN ARMFUL OF DELICIOUS TREATS. I LOWERED MY GUARD WHILE I FEASTED.
BUT THEN A SHARP PAIN SHOT THROUGH ME AS THE HEEL OF HER SHOE CONNECTED WITH MY SIDE.
THEN SHE LEAPT UPON ME TO STRANGLE ME WITH HER TALONED CLAWS.
IN THE END, I MANAGED TO KICK HER OFF ME AND SENT HER FLYING INTO THE MANSION BEHIND US.
SHE COLLAPSED IN A PILE OF CURLY HAIR AND FRILLY DRESS.

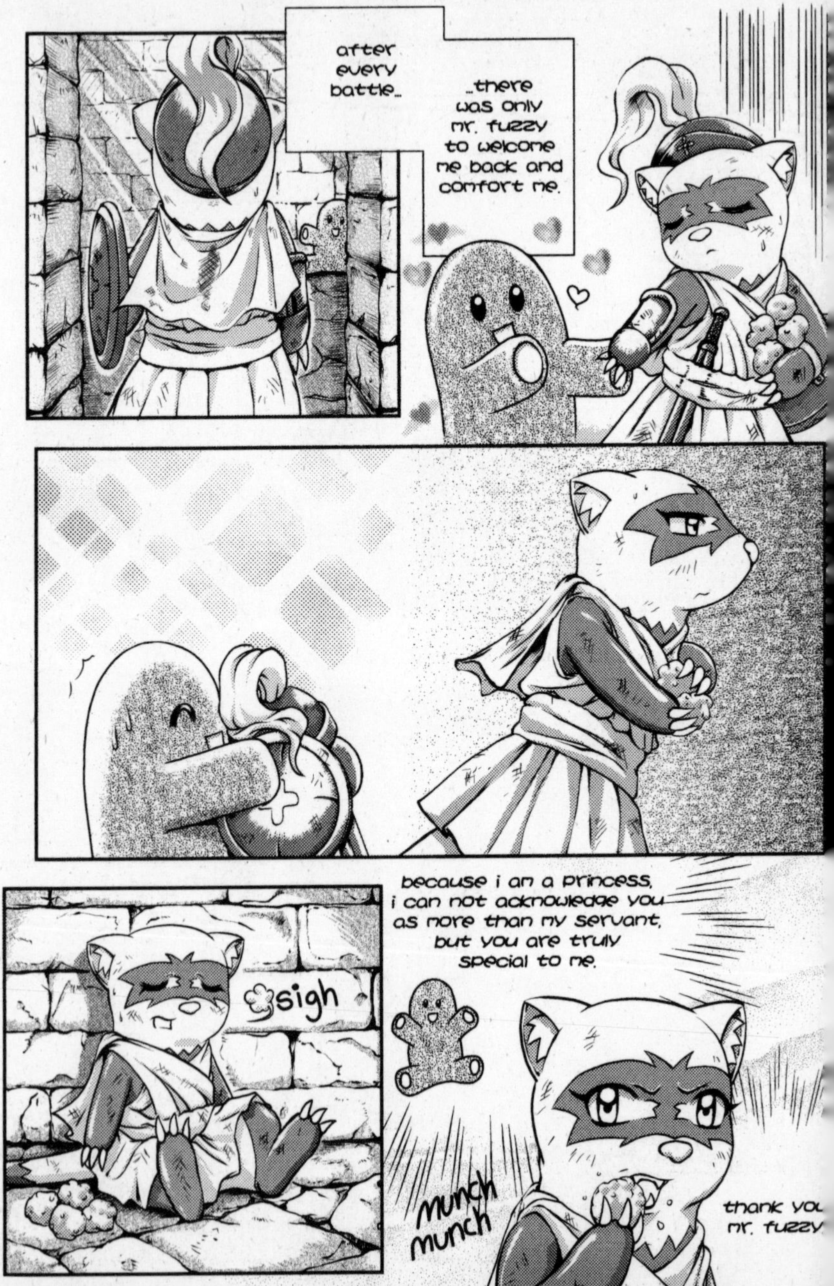
after every battle...
...there was only mr. fuzzy to welcome me back and comfort me.
because i am a princess, i can not acknowledge you as more than my servant, but you are truly special to me.
sigh
munch munch
thank you mr. fuzzy

WHY ARE YOU ATTACKING ME?

THUD

THUD

SWOOO

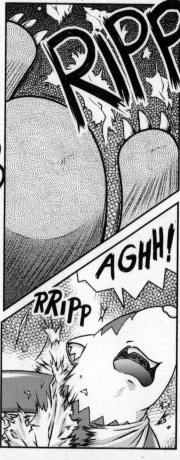

RIPP

RRIPP

AGHH!

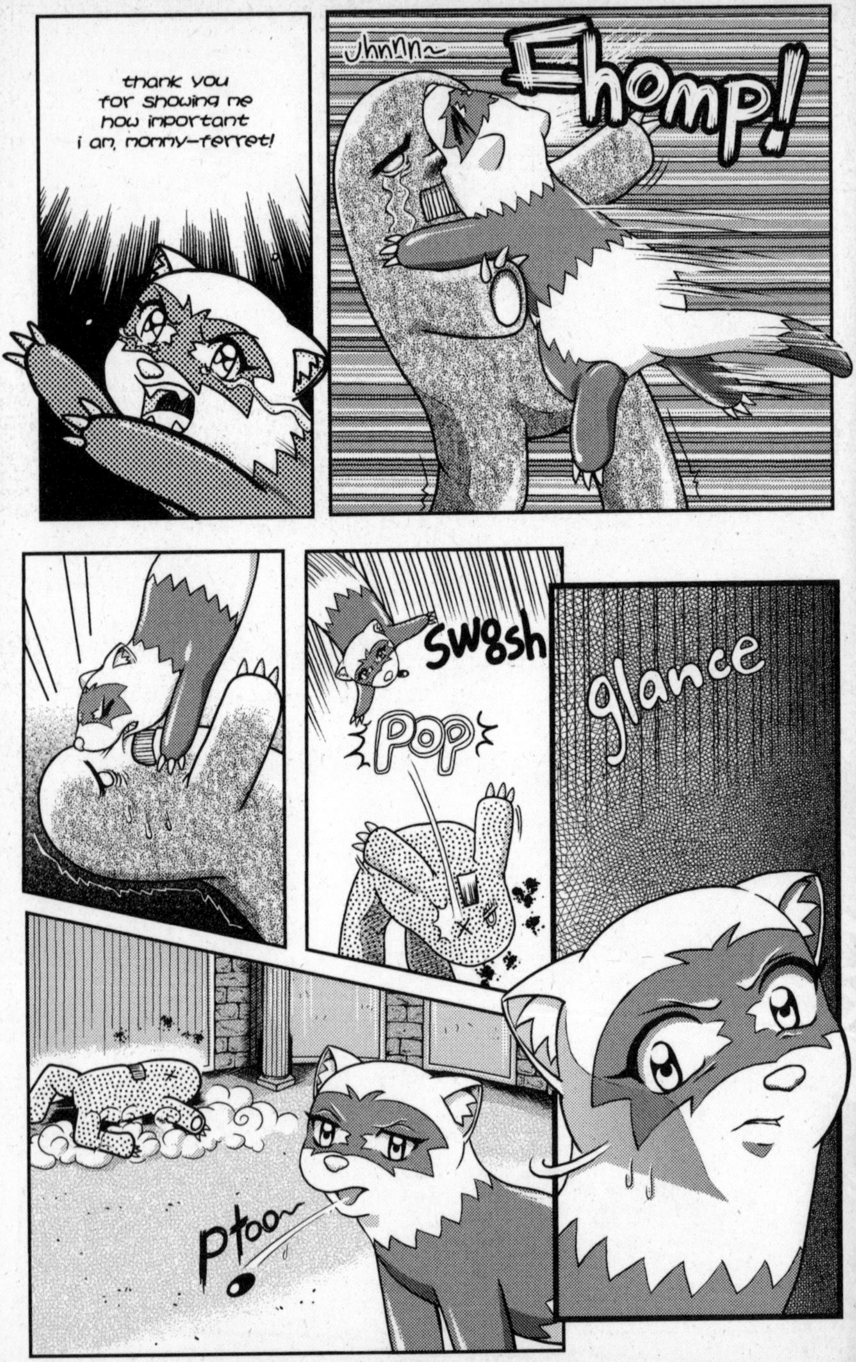
thank you
for showing me
how important
i am, mommy-ferret!
Jhnnn~
Chomp!
Swgsh
POP
glance
ptoo

WHAT'S WRONG? WHAT HAPPENED?

IF IT BITES YOU, WE'RE TAKING IT BACK!

Sniff

N-NOTHING. I UH... SMASHED MY FINGER IN THE CLOSET...

THE CLOSET DOOR!

...

LET ME SEE.

ouch ouch ouch

Yank

Suspiciously angry ferret

Bite Marks!!

WE'RE TAKING HER BACK!

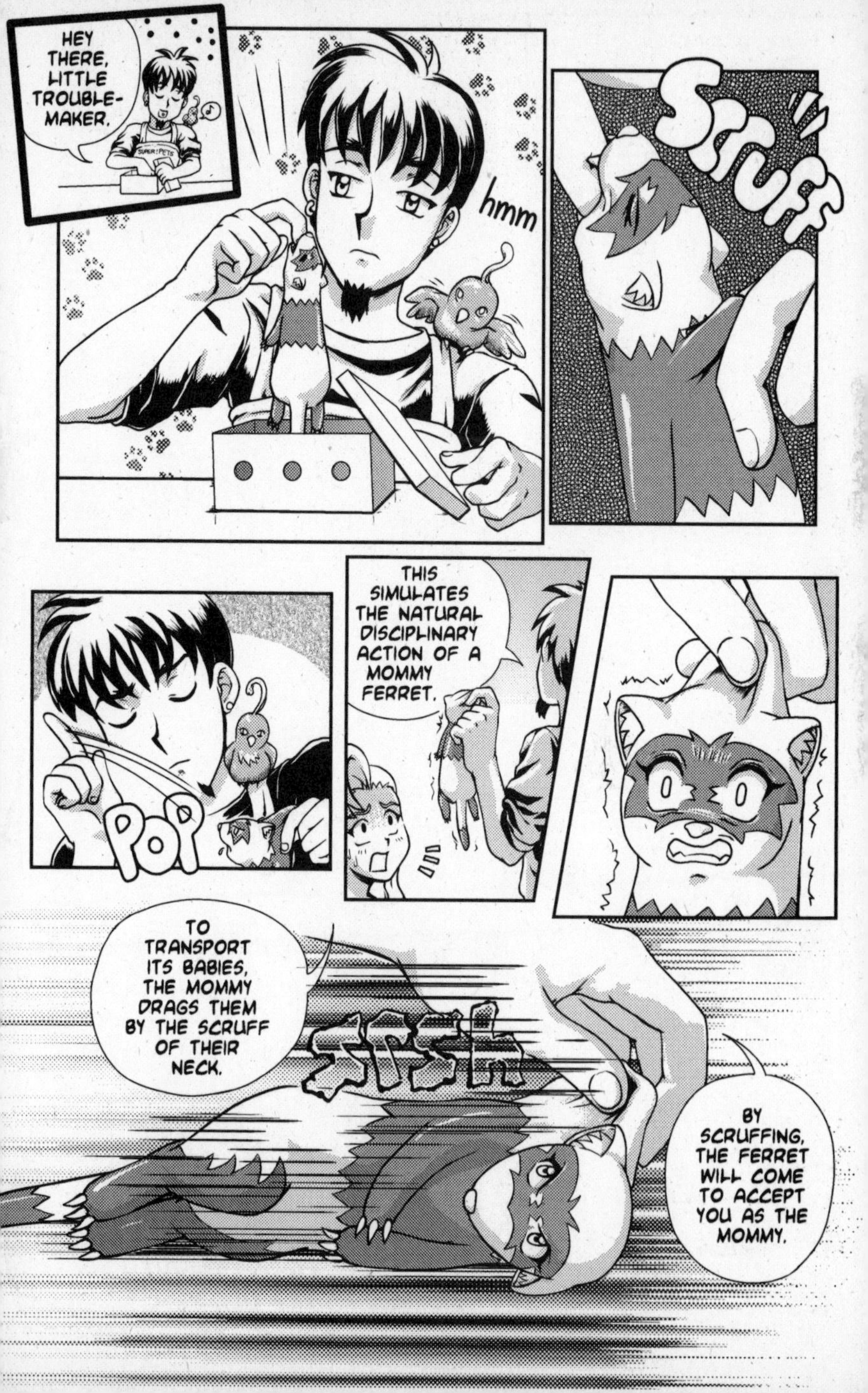
HEY THERE, LITTLE TROUBLE-MAKER.
SUPER! PETS
hmm
SCRUFF
POP
THIS SIMULATES THE NATURAL DISCIPLINARY ACTION OF A MOMMY FERRET.
TO TRANSPORT ITS BABIES, THE MOMMY DRAGS THEM BY THE SCRUFF OF THEIR NECK.
BY SCRUFFING, THE FERRET WILL COME TO ACCEPT YOU AS THE MOMMY.

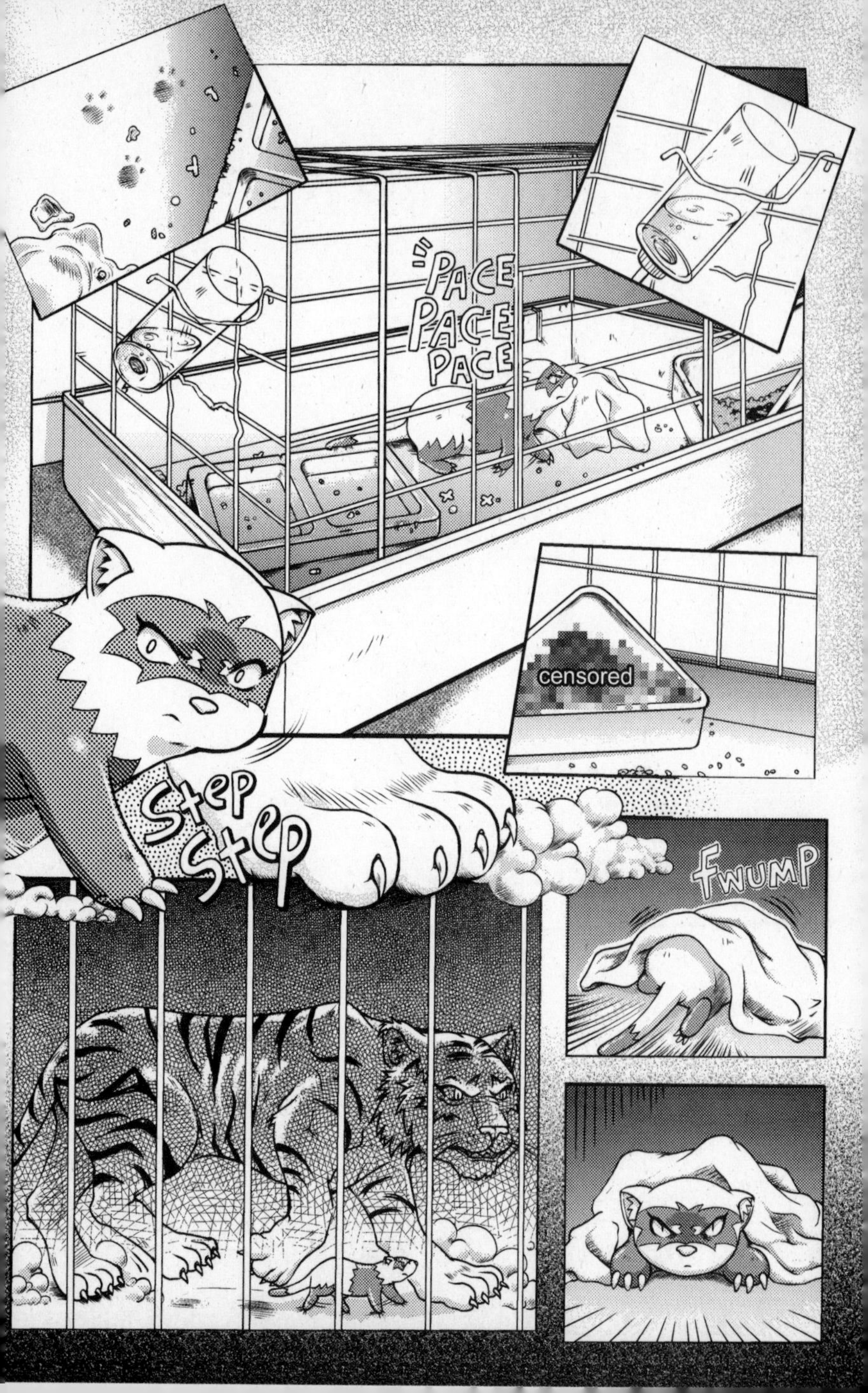
PACE
PACE
PACE
censored
Step
Step
FWUMP

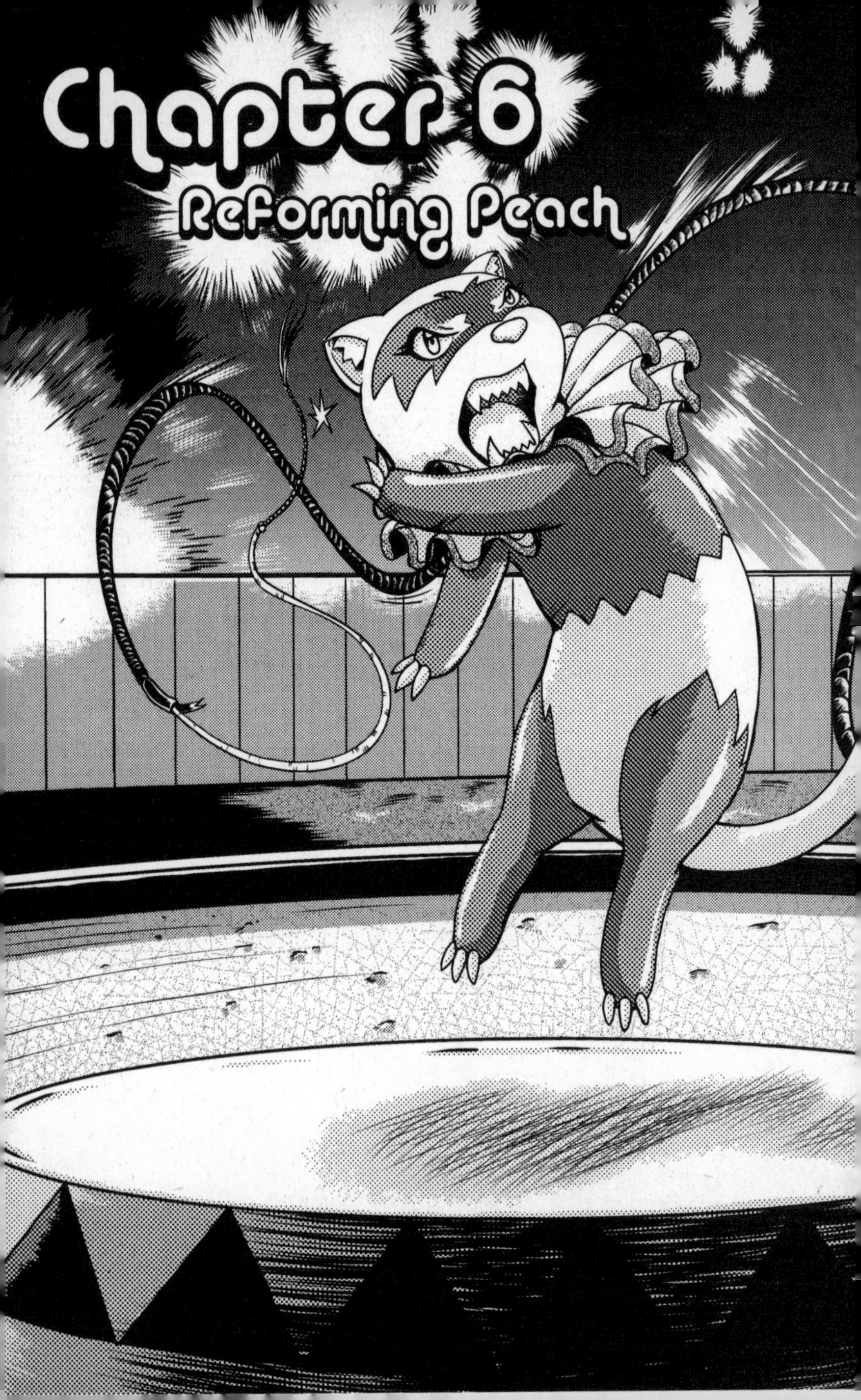
Chapter 6
Reforming Peach

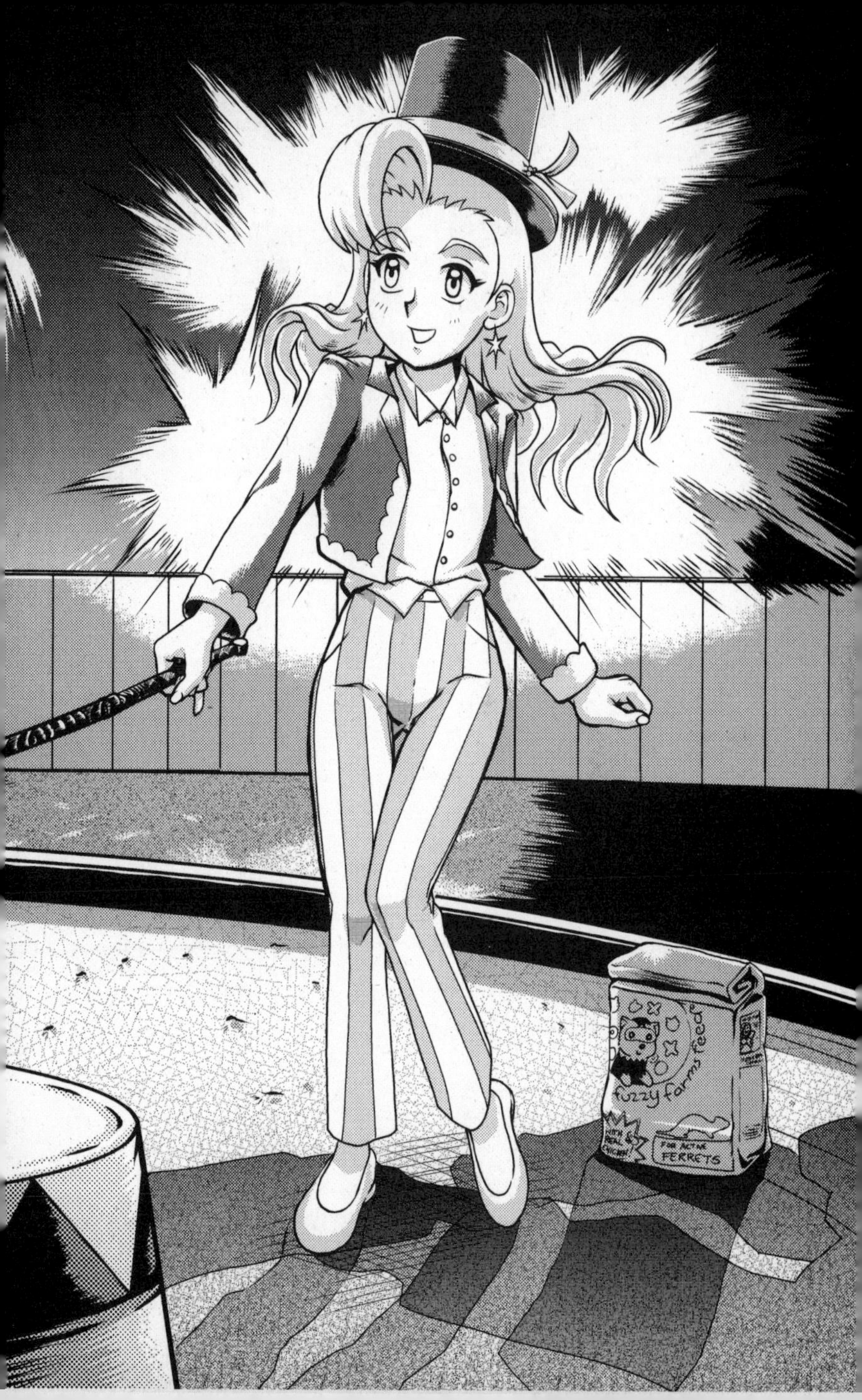
fuzzy farms feed
FOR ACTIVE FERRETS

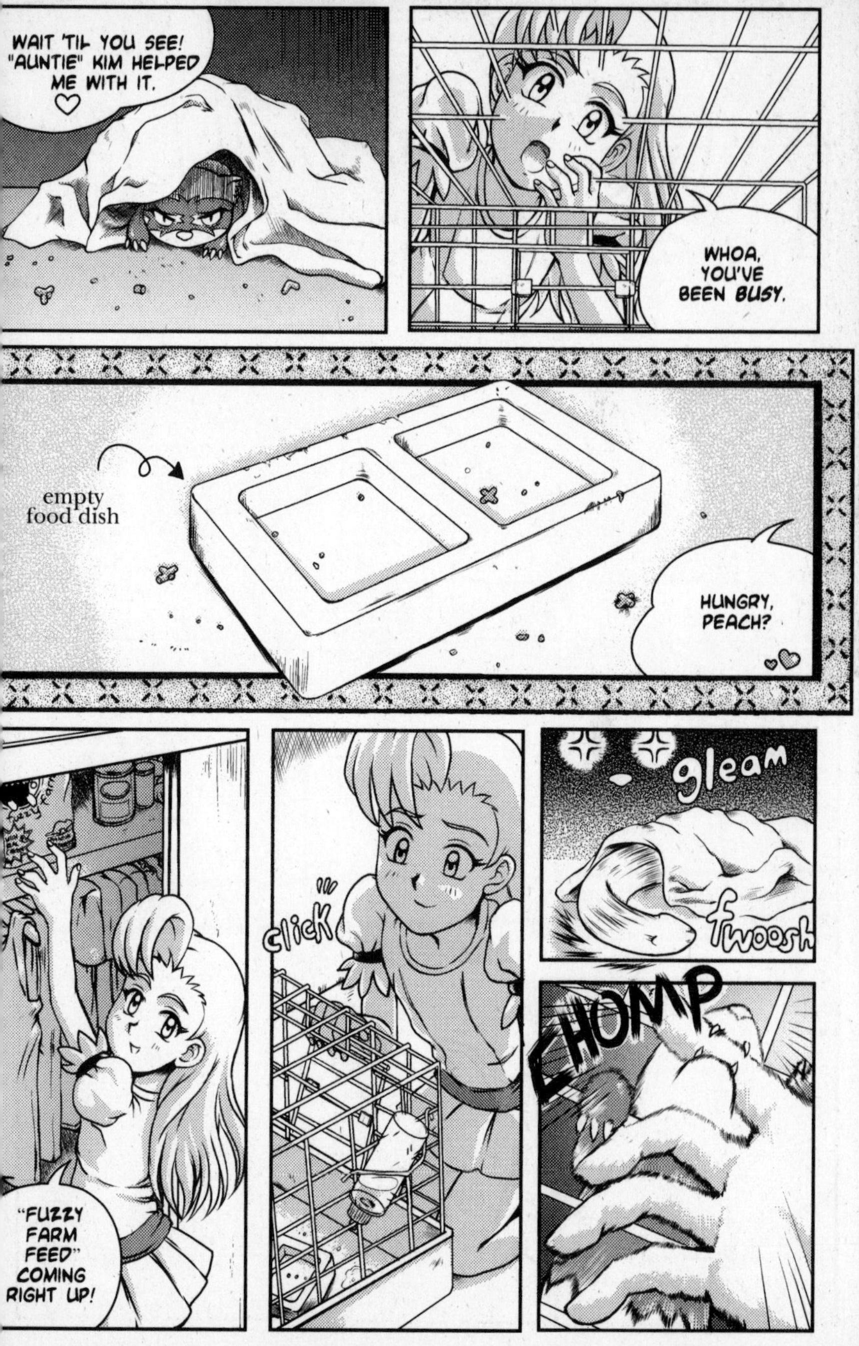
WAIT 'TIL YOU SEE! "AUNTIE" KIM HELPED ME WITH IT. ♡
WHOA, YOU'VE BEEN BUSY.
empty food dish
HUNGRY, PEACH?
"FUZZY FARM FEED" COMING RIGHT UP!
click
gleam
fwoosh
CHOMP

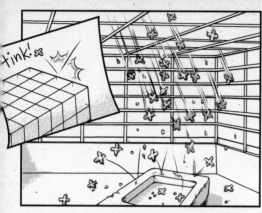

tink!

Doink!

CHOMP

CHOMP

Twoosh

ROAR!

SHE USED TO BE SO GENTLE. WHAT HAPPENED TO HER?

TOK

OH YUUUUUCK! THE LITTER BOX IS FULL.

BUT IF I TRY TO CLEAN IT NOW, PEACH WILL TAKE OFF A FINGER.

MOM'S NOT HOME YET. WHAT AM I GONNA DO?

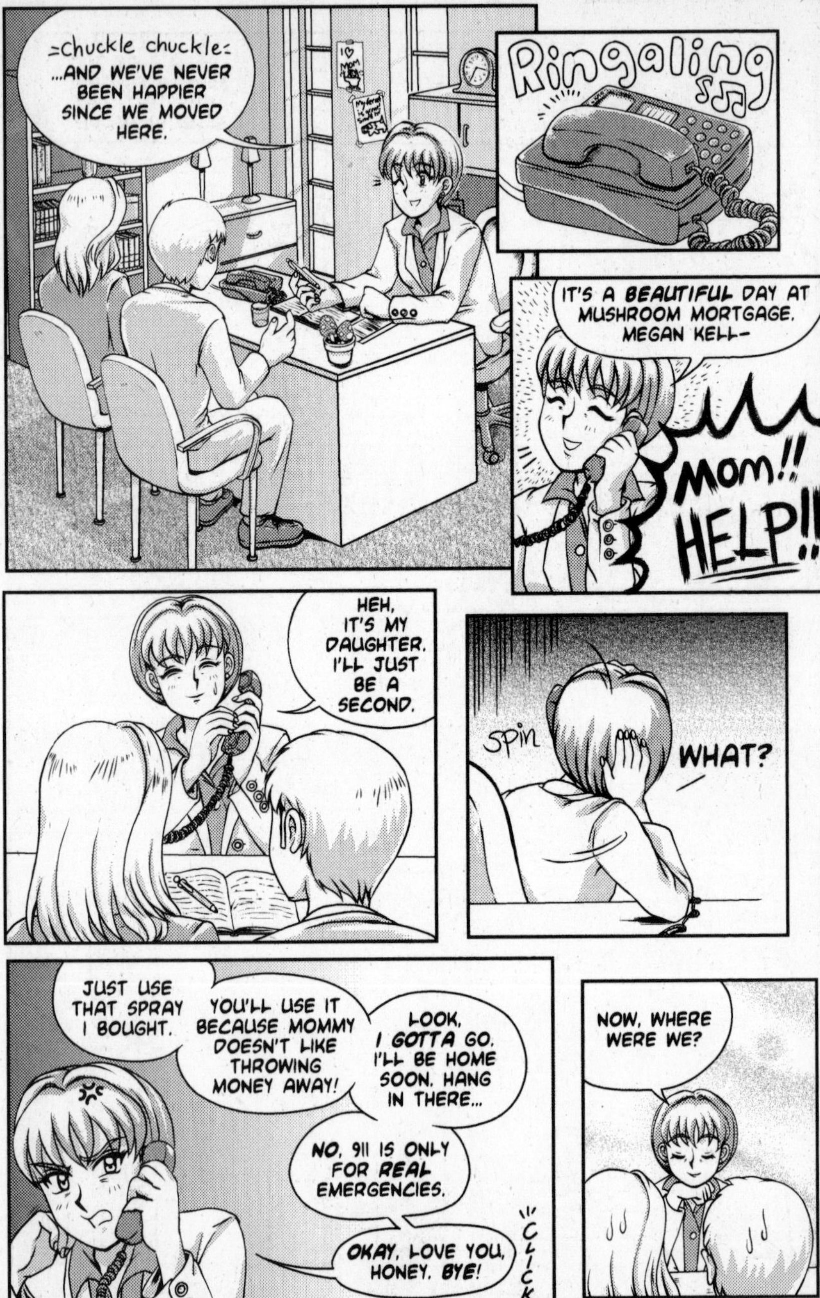
=chuckle chuckle=
...AND WE'VE NEVER BEEN HAPPIER SINCE WE MOVED HERE.
Ringaling
IT'S A BEAUTIFUL DAY AT MUSHROOM MORTGAGE. MEGAN KELL-
MOM!! HELP!!
HEH, IT'S MY DAUGHTER. I'LL JUST BE A SECOND.
spin
WHAT?
JUST USE THAT SPRAY I BOUGHT.
YOU'LL USE IT BECAUSE MOMMY DOESN'T LIKE THROWING MONEY AWAY!
LOOK, I GOTTA GO. I'LL BE HOME SOON. HANG IN THERE...
NO, 911 IS ONLY FOR REAL EMERGENCIES.
OKAY, LOVE YOU, HONEY. BYE!
CLICK
NOW, WHERE WERE WE?

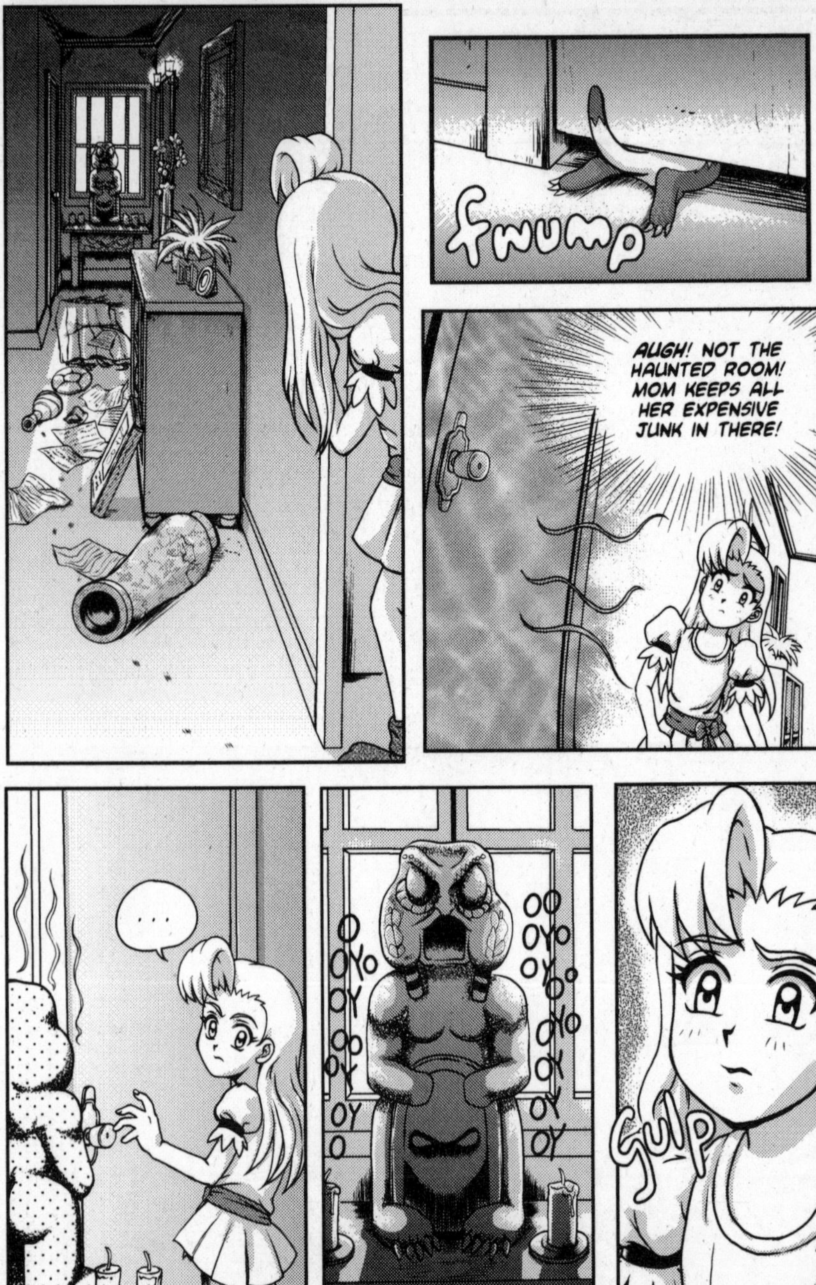
fwump
AUGH! NOT THE HAUNTED ROOM! MOM KEEPS ALL HER EXPENSIVE JUNK IN THERE!
...
OOYO
OOYO
OY
OY
GULP

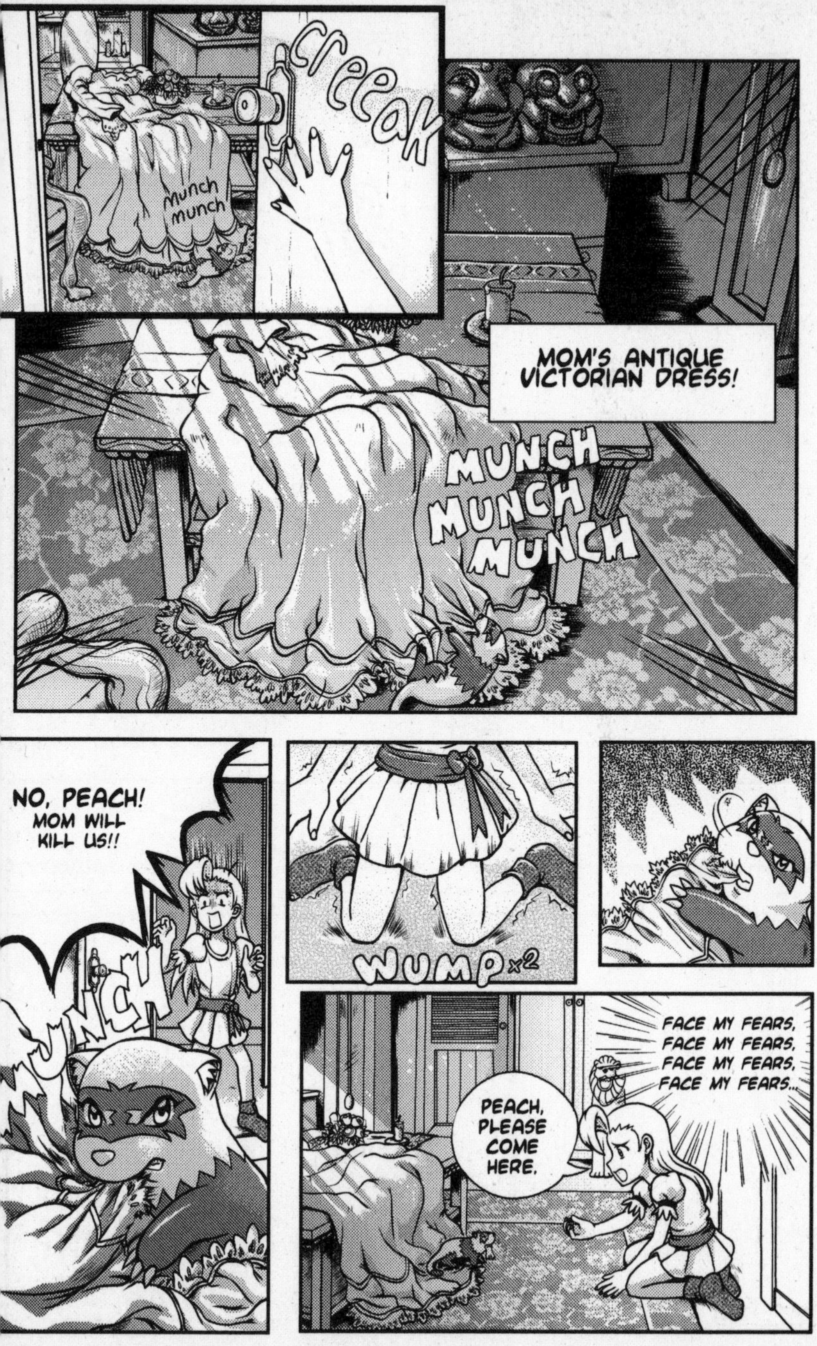
munch munch
creeak
MOM'S ANTIQUE VICTORIAN DRESS!
MUNCH MUNCH MUNCH
NO, PEACH! MOM WILL KILL US!!
UNCH
WUMP x2
PEACH, PLEASE COME HERE.
FACE MY FEARS, FACE MY FEARS, FACE MY FEARS, FACE MY FEARS...

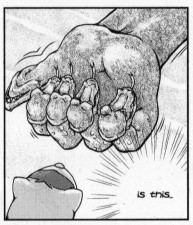

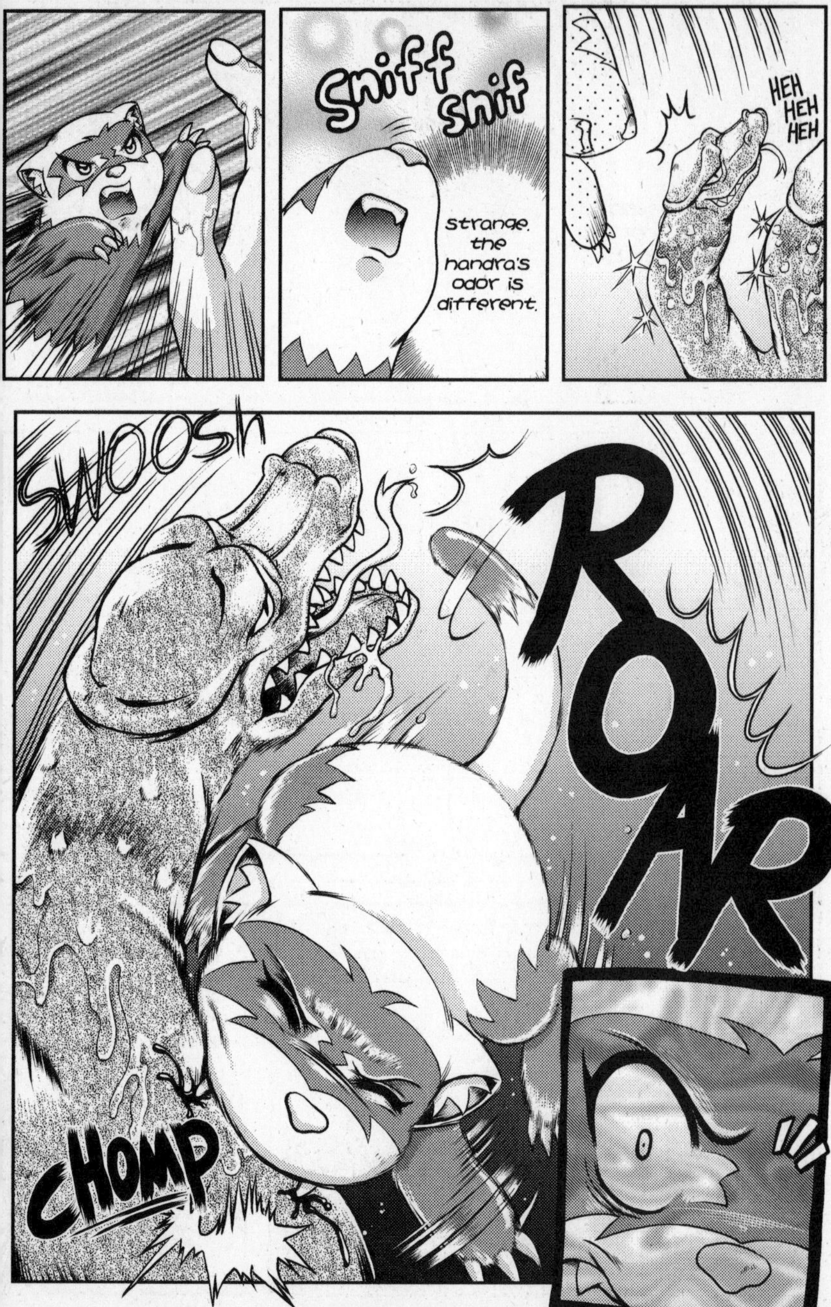
Sniff snif
strange. the handra's odor is different.
HEH HEH HEH
SWOOSH
ROAR
CHOMP

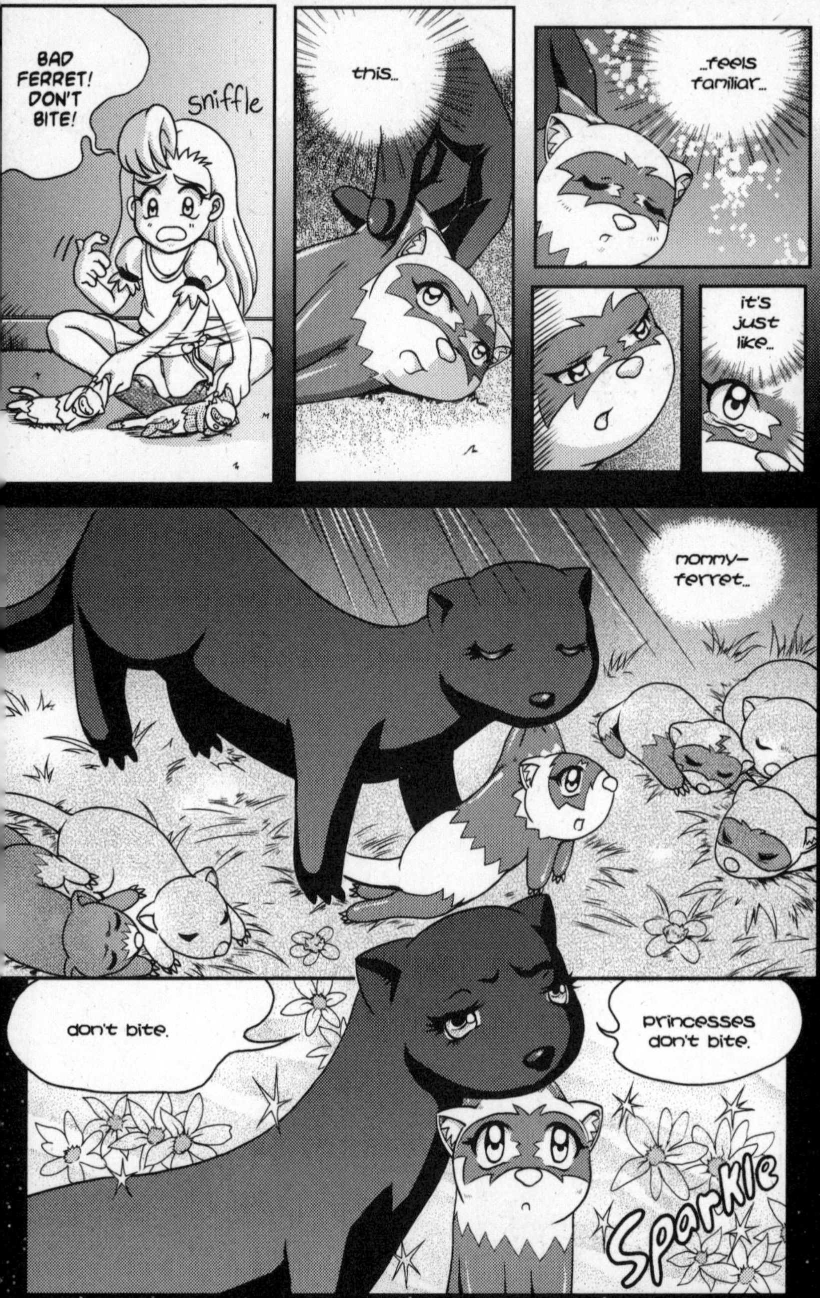

BAD FERRET! DON'T BITE!
sniffle
this...
...feels familiar...
it's just like...
mommy-ferret...
don't bite.
princesses don't bite.
Sparkle

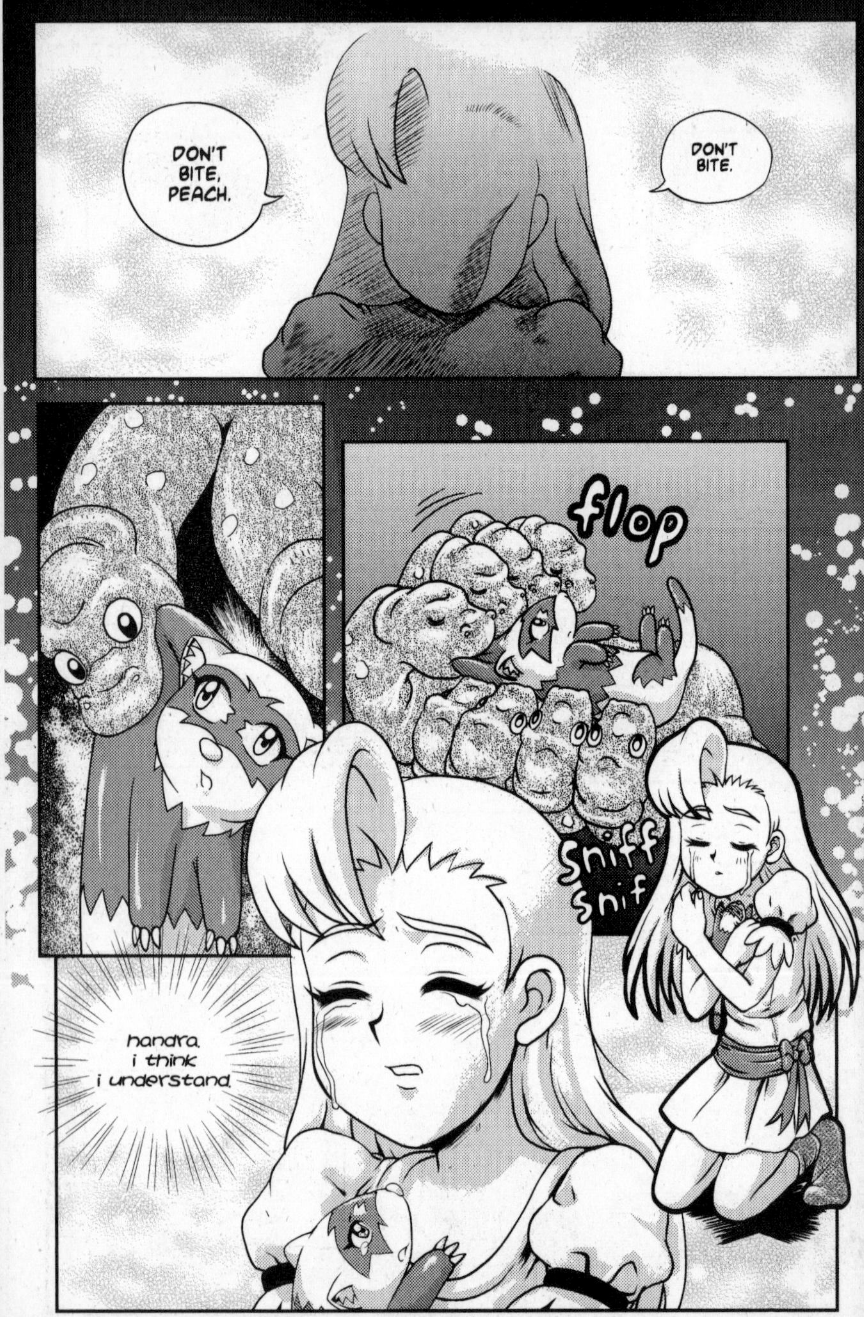
DON'T BITE, PEACH.
DON'T BITE.
flop
sniff
snif
handra. i think i understand.

Smile

ENJOY!

I ALSO HAVE MORE TREATS FOR YOU.

FUZZY FRUITS

Bitter Bite-coated hands

AND SO, THE HANDRA REDEEMED ITSELF.

RAIN OF TREATS

AMANDA AND PEACH HAD FINALLY BEGUN THEIR JOURNEY TOWARDS DEEPER UNDER-STANDING AND FRIENDSHIP...

...THOUGH PEACH STILL NIPS SOMETIMES.

the handra tricked me! these treats were poisoned!

i'll never be able to entirely trust it!

In the next volume of

Peach Fuzz

No way! The exciting day of "Show and Tell" in Amanda's class has arrived! Amanda *finally* has the chance to show off her fuzzy friend Peach to the school. But because some girls have to have anything that's popular, Amanda's classmate Kim gets a ferret of her own. But all ferrets are not created equal and, when personalities totally clash, Peach makes the new ferret her arch enemy! And Amanda, who for once is not feeling invisible to the other kids, takes the school's new obsession with ferrets a step too far and gets the attention of the meanest bullies on campus! Will Peach defeat her new foe? Will Amanda *ever* feel like she fits in at school? Find out in *Peach Fuzz* Volume 2!

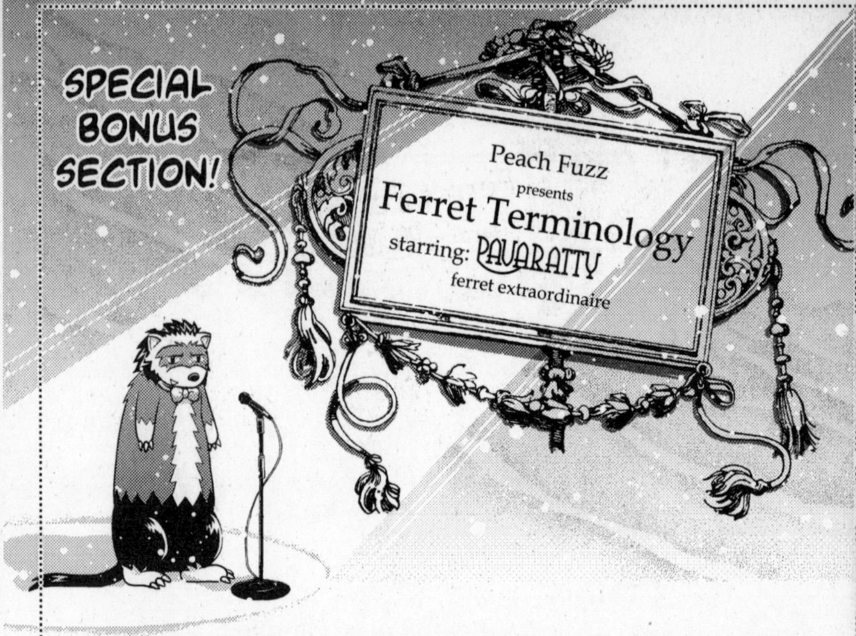
SPECIAL BONUS SECTION!
Peach Fuzz
presents
Ferret Terminology
starring: PAVARATTY
ferret extraordinaire

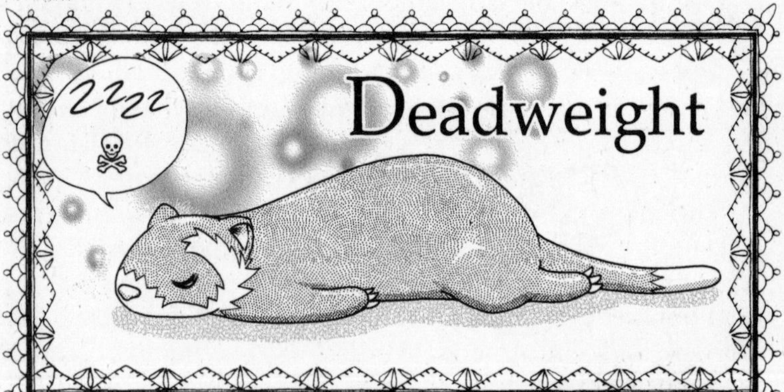
ZZZZ
Deadweight

One of a ferret's favorite activities is sleeping, which they tend to spend about 20 hours a day doing. This is because they require a lot of energy when playing.

As Peach demonstrated in chapter two, ferrets can sometimes sleep so deeply that they can be almost impossible to wake.

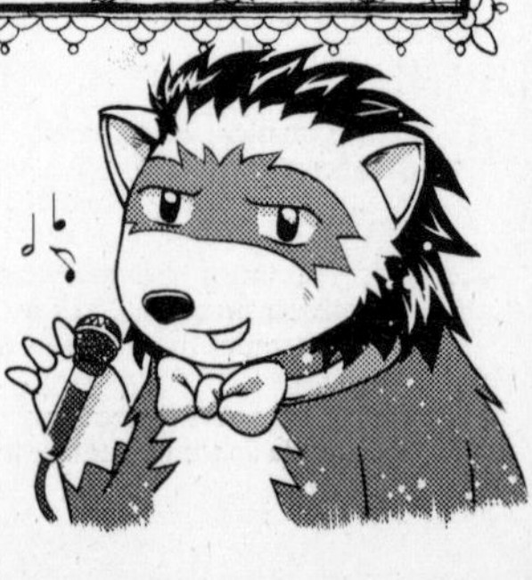

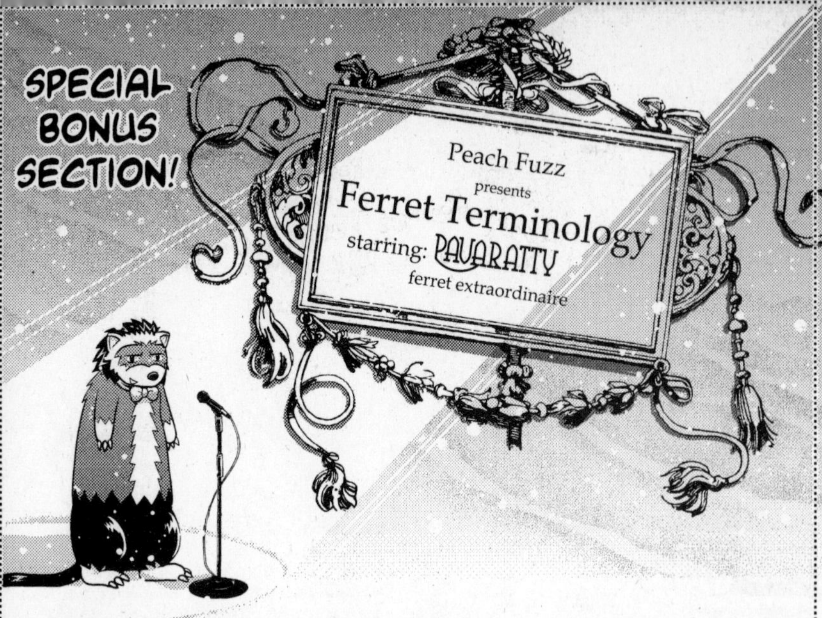
SPECIAL BONUS SECTION!
Peach Fuzz
presents
Ferret Terminology
starring: PAVARATTY
ferret extraordinaire

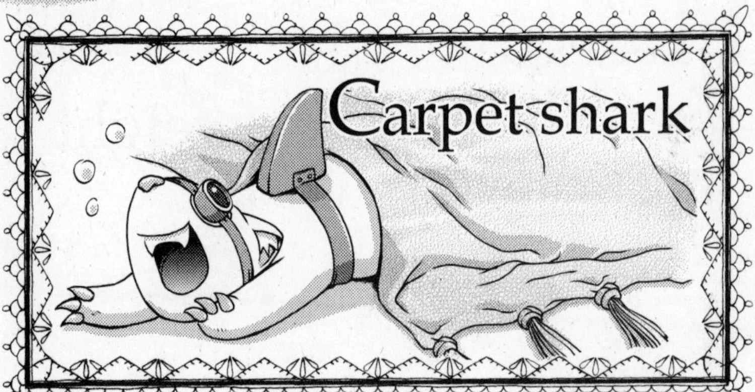
Carpet shark

A common nickname given to ferrets due to their dominance over the carpet...not to mention a mouthful of sharp teeth.

The act of swimming and zigzagging under a throw rug. May involve a surprise attack in which the ferret leaps out from under the rug at its unsuspecting prey.

Please be careful not to step on any suspicious rug bulges! There could be a ferret underneath!

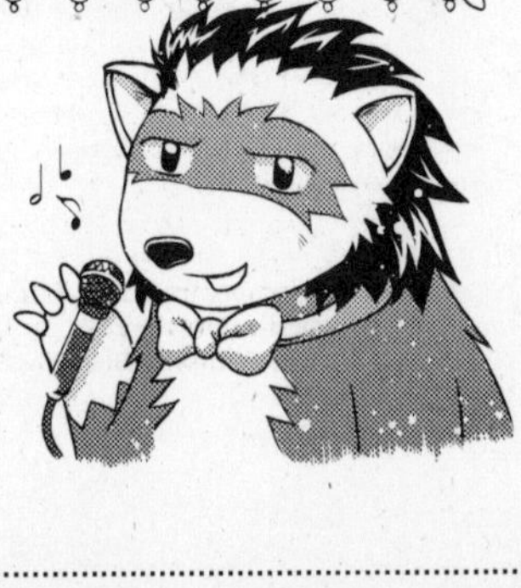

PEACH'S
MONSTER
COMPENDIUM

the enemy!
TAP

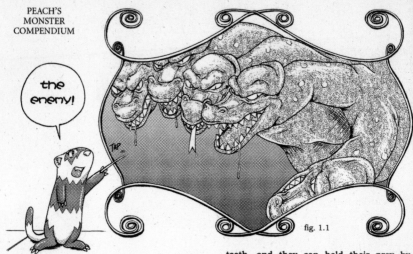

fig. 1.1

Handra

As young kits, we are taught by our mommy-ferrets about the terrifying monster of ferret lore: the Handra! We are warned that this five-headed reptilian beast snatches up bad ferrets and takes them away, never to be seen again. My littermates and I didn't really believe in them, but all the same, we strived to be good little ferrets...just in case. But the truth is the Handra is more than just a mythological beast-it is real! And it snatches up all ferrets, good or bad!

Having been captured by the creature personally, I speak from experience when I say the Handras are cruel, controlling, unfriendly, and selfish! They seem to take great pleasure in keeping a large stable of prisoners under their control, then pitting these captives against each other in battle. They watch from the sidelines and reward the winner with treats.

Handras also seem to enjoy taking on these prisoners in one-on-one combat. I myself have been forced to fight them on numerous occasions. Handras are very strong! They can use their massive frame to push and prod. Worse, they have a powerful bite with sharp teeth, and they can hold their prey by coiling their multiple heads into a constricting grip. Their defense, however, is surprisingly weak. Their thin, furless hide offers little protection from a ferret's bite and they are quick to retreat if attacked head-on.

Handra
No-Fur
Ferret Kit

fig. 1.2

It was originally believed that Handras were an independent and free roaming entity. However, we have recently discovered that the Handras are in fact part of a much larger monster: the No-Fur! To date, very little is known about the No-Fur, but we are undergoing studies to learn more. I personally believe that the key to defending against the Handra will come from a deeper understanding of the No-Fur.

see you next book!